THROUGH THE WOODS

THE FAIREST SERIES BOOK ONE

SHANNON MYERS

Cover Design by: The Final Wrap

Models: Robert Kelly & Deanna Ruge

Photographer: Jeanne Woodfin

Illustration by: Kat Powell

First Printing: 2018

Paperback ISBN- 978-0-9994716-5-4

❀ Created with Vellum

For those who still believe in fairy tales.

And Ali- The Aussie who left an honest Goodreads review three days after my first release and made me feel world famous. I'm so glad we became friends.

ACKNOWLEDGMENTS

As always, I am nothing without the team of people standing beside me, urging me on.

To my Betas- You guys were generous with your time and honest in your feedback. I felt the story was missing something, but couldn't place my finger on it. Your constructive criticism turned this story around and made it so much better.

Neda Amini- Thank you for taking me on as a client and for your willingness to listen to my crazed rantings when I'm standing on the ledge, ready to jump off.

Kat Powell- Thank you for the gorgeous illustration. You completely captured Neve and Charm in a way that I never could. Your talent is evident in every aspect of the picture.

Bex- You are so much more than just my cover designer; you are one of my closest friends. You never cease to amaze me with your kick ass covers and your belief that my writing is not absolute shit, as I so often convince myself.

J. Law- I adore your readiness to drop everything and read my books; usually on a pretty severe time crunch. I also love that you didn't want to hurt my feelings when you beta read this book and instead claimed, "It's good," before clamming up completely. I love the friendship we've built over the last eight years and cannot wait to see where we go next.

Wendi- Thank you for all that you've done to keep me sane. Your ability to find the smallest of plot holes is uncanny, yet ensures that the story always flows. I love that a couple of conversations over books led to such an amazing friendship.

Bloggers- I cannot do any of this without you. Thank you for taking a chance on my books, whether this is your first or your eighth, I truly appreciate your efforts to promote my work out in the Indie community.

Shayla- Thank you for being my best friend and confidante. I know that you were late to the party, but the fact that you read my books has meant more to me than you'll ever know. I love you to the moon and back. PB talks for life!

Forsaken- You guys motivate me every day. I love seeing your excitement over upcoming books and strive to continue to better myself with each book released. Thank you for loving these characters like I do.

Zach- I love you more than anything I could ever write. You keep me sane and fed when I'm in writing mode—sitting un-showered in a bathrobe, mumbling to myself. Thank you for believing in this crazy dream of mine and encouraging our sons to always follow theirs.

He thought, "The wild animals will soon devour you anyway," but still it was as if a stone had fallen from his heart, for he would not have to kill her.

Little Snow-White
-Jacob & Wilhelm Grimm

PROLOGUE

NEVE

One Year Ago...Age 21

*M*y eyes fluttered open to piercing red and blue lights flashing all around me. Men's voices carried from nearby as they yelled to each other, amid sirens screaming in the distance.

I had no idea where I was.

"Miss? Can you hear me?" A yellow man asked, as he knelt next to me, concern marring his features. I was disoriented—exhaustion threatening to pull me back into blissful oblivion. He obviously wasn't yellow, just wearing a suit that color.

Aramid fibers, my brain urged, and I struggled to remember how I knew that.

"Miss?"

I began coughing until my eyes watered, but I couldn't get a full breath. My chest felt as if it would crack open from the strain.

The outer shell usually consisted of a Kevlar type material...what was it called?

Someone else knelt down on the other side of me, shining a small light into my eyes. Mouths moved, but I only heard the rush of blood

1

in my ears. I turned my head ever so slightly to the left and that was when I saw it.

An inferno.

Incidentally, that was when I remembered that the material was NOMEX, but instead of being relieved, I was left with more questions than answers. I felt the moisture on my cheek as a tear escaped, before being lifted onto a stretcher and driven away from the devastation.

I wanted to wail and scream, but I'd caused this.

Not so very long ago, the sirens wailed loudly and the world that I'd known ceased to exist.

I discovered that, sometimes, it's not giants with booming voices or cackling witches who swoop down from the sky—it's not even a curse cast by an enchantress. Sometimes, the foe that steals away everything you held dear is the reflection in the mirror. The villain you never imagined—the evil you never saw coming…*you.*

1

NEVE

Four Years Ago…Age 18

*T*here was a soft knock at my door before Sofia poked her head around the door. "Did you check Blackboard? Because I did and I'm thinking a study break in the form of a campus party is in order." She gyrated her hips, hands swaying above, as she moved to the beat of something only she knew.

I dropped my pen and stretched my arms overhead. I'd been sitting at my desk for who knew how long; my body stiff from hours spent hunched over a textbook, taking notes. I wearily opened a new tab on my laptop and entered my login credentials.

I'd been anxiously awaiting my mid-term grades for the last week. And I'd been regretting my decision to double major in Psychology and Neurosciences for even longer than that.

Things had started out promising enough. I'd scheduled my college classes much like I'd done my high school classes, thinking that I could handle the course load.

My academic advisor had recommended that I not overload myself until I got a feel for the program and the instructors. I didn't want to just take the basics though—I'd wanted to get into the meat of my studies.

So, I ignored his advice and loaded up with a mix of basics and upper level courses that didn't require a prerequisite.

By the end of the first week, I was cursing myself. The classes were unlike anything I'd experienced in high school. It didn't matter how hard I worked, I quickly fell behind. I gave up dinner in the dining hall in favor of ramen noodles in my dorm room, glued to my computer.

When two of my professors threatened to drop me, I gave up my part-time job at the campus bookstore, relying instead on my dad's emergency credit card to keep myself comfortable.

It wasn't like it was going to affect them—I could've maxed the dang thing out every month and I doubt he would've cared as he paid it off.

Spoiled brat?

Maybe.

But I'd worked hard to get where I was and someday—I'd pay them back for everything. I pulled up my grades with bated breath. This was it. This was where I turned it all around.

MCDB 2150 Principles of Genetics...overall grade with the midterm factored in...F.

No.

I'd damn near killed myself studying for that one. I even had the kidney infection to prove it too. *How could I still be failing?*

MATH 2520 Intro to Biometry was just as dismal. In fact, the only classes where my grades didn't make me want to puke were my psych classes. That didn't bode well for me getting accepted into the doctoral program. I couldn't even blame it on the university—the National Academy of Sciences ranked them as one of the best in the country.

Suddenly, the painted cinderblock walls didn't feel like a cozy haven for studying, but more like the walls of a prison. I'd started this semester with a roommate. A roommate who'd cried most every night and ended up moving out three weeks into the semester. I wasn't going to be far behind her if my grades were any indicator.

Sofia cocked her head to the side and fixed me with a curious smile. "Yes? You joining me?"

I opened my mouth to decline when I realized there was really nothing stopping me from going out. So far, my college experience had consisted of me spending every waking moment either in class or chained to my desk. And what did I have to show for it? Nothing. I hadn't pledged a sorority or gone home with a random stranger. I hadn't even gotten drunk. I was nothing like the stereotypical college freshman. In fact, I'd never acted my age and slacked off.

I'd graduated at the top of my class and gotten accepted to every university I'd applied to. My parents wanted me at UCLA, but I'd chosen University of Colorado in Boulder.

While I'd been born in California, I'd never been considered your 'typical California girl.' The girls I grew up with were tall, blonde, and tan. *Me?* I was short, raven-haired, and fair. I'd slather on the SPF 5000 and it never seemed to matter; I'd burn to a crisp just stepping foot outside.

Colorado had been a much better fit. I found that I didn't have to wear a lot of makeup or dress in a certain way to fit in.

Now, it seemed, the closest I was going to get to my dream of becoming a researcher was going to be as a janitor in the science building.

I pushed my chair back from my desk. "I'm in."

It wasn't like my grades were going to improve if I stayed in studying. I deserved a night out—an evening to just be an eighteen year-old. Tomorrow I'd worry about how I was going to pull myself out of this hole.

I stood against the wall, a lukewarm beer in my hand, taking small sips to appease Sofia whenever necessary. It tasted like watered down piss. I was fighting my gag reflex with every swallow. To say that I'd expected more would've been a massive understatement. In all honesty, I wasn't sure how I'd convinced myself that going out was a better alternative to reviewing my mid-term answers and emailing my professors to see if there was anything else I could do to bring my grades up.

I watched as Sofia lost herself to the music, her eyes fluttering closed with every hip thrust from the frat boy behind her. She'd downed several plastic cups of beer upon our arrival and appeared to be feeling no pain.

I choked down another sip, praying that I was close to feeling as free as she appeared to be. It would be nice to just lose control for a while.

"Did you ace your midterms?"

I turned toward the voice. "Do I know you?"

The man laughed and extended his hand, raising his voice to be heard over the music. "I don't think we've formally met, but you were in my stats class. I'm Paul."

I shook his hand. "Neve." I could tell he was waiting for me to elaborate and I gave a small sigh before adding, "I failed my midterms. If I give up sleep, I might have a chance in hell at getting out of my first semester alive."

He regarded me thoughtfully for a moment and I downed more of my beer, trying to fill the awkward silence between us.

"You're only a freshman? You're the one that got special permission from the dean to take a senior level lab, aren't you?"

I bristled at his words. "So? It's not like it matters now. I'm failing almost everything."

He rocked back on his heels. "What if I knew someone who could help you?"

I snorted. "What—like a homework helper? How much is that gonna set me back?"

Paul shook his head and chugged the contents of his cup before latching onto my arm and pulling me toward the stairs. "I know a guy. You see, I was in your shoes my freshman year and I wasn't ready to watch all my hard work turn to shit."

I tried to wrangle myself free, spilling beer onto my hand. "Let me go—"

He stopped walking and turned back to me. "What did you just say? If you didn't need sleep, then you might have a chance at passing. What if I could give you that?"

"What do you mean?" This guy had to be off his meds. Leave it to me to find a lunatic at my first party. I risked a quick glance over the railing and found Sofia and her frat boy wrapped around each other on the makeshift dance floor. Obviously, she wasn't going to notice if I went missing anytime soon.

All the more reason to stay downstairs.

Paul leaned in. "I can get you something to stay awake. It'll keep you focused too."

I should've broken free and run back down to the safety of my wall, but his words had piqued my interest. I'd tried energy drinks... coffee...you name it. Nothing helped keep me awake for longer than a day. "What is it?"

He pointed toward a closed door. "Clint—he—just come meet him and see for yourself."

This was exactly what after-school specials had warned me about. Yet, here I was, following this perfect stranger upstairs to meet 'Clint' and get something to keep myself awake.

"Twenty percent of female college students will report being raped during their time on campus," I muttered to myself as I trudged after him.

Paul gave me a strange look. "What was that?"

I shook my head as he opened the door to reveal a gorgeous man on a leather couch, watching television. His sandy brown hair was spiked up into a fauxhawk and as he turned toward us, I couldn't help but be mesmerized by his piercing green eyes. Eyes that were now narrowing in suspicion.

"What the fuck, Paul?" He complained, while remaining in the same position on the couch, as if his body was unaware of the tension in the room.

Paul pushed me forward, spilling even more beer onto my arm. "My girl needs the goods, man. Get her in the mood." He said the last part with a wink.

"I am absolutely not his girl." This was never about helping me with my grades. The prick just wanted to get into my pants. The bass from the music downstairs vibrated the floor beneath my feet and I wondered if Sofia was still tangled up with her guy or if she was looking for me. It obviously hadn't taken much beer to impair my judgment because I'd now put myself in a very precarious situation.

The man picked up a glass from the side table and took a sip of the amber liquid, suddenly seeming much more distinguished than the punk I'd followed up here. He exuded power and sophistication—heck, even his clothes were designer. He watched me carefully. "You didn't come with him?"

I shook my head. "I told him I was falling behind with my grades and he said Clint could help me. Obviously, that was a lie so, I'll just be on my way."

"Did he try something with you?"

I risked a glance at Paul and noticed the sweat beading along his hairline. He was scared of this man and I knew that if I said yes, Paul was going to be in a world of hurt.

Damn you, Sofia. Damn you for insisting I get out of the dorm for a night.

I shook my head again, while contemplating calling my dad. "No. He just got me up here under false pretenses."

"Out." He gestured toward the door with his head and Paul immediately disappeared, leaving just the two of us. He slid off the couch and slowly walked over to me and I could feel my pulse jumping in my neck as he looked me over.

"I'm Clint," he said by way of greeting, as he patted me down and checked me for a wire. His touch conjured up all sorts of conflicting feelings inside of me, even as I began to suspect that he'd obtained his lifestyle through highly illegal means.

"Neve," I whispered through quivering lips, effectively killing the smallest hint of a buzz from the beer.

He ran a soft hand lightly down my arm. "Hey, don't be afraid. Unlike the fuckboy who brought you, I won't take anything you don't willingly give me."

I exhaled and nodded, debating whether to run or press myself up against his muscular body. This was nothing more than his pheromones acting as a catalyst for the sexual attraction I was feeling. I just had to hold it together a little bit longer and then I could go back to my dorm and forget this ever happened.

When he placed the bag of white powder on his coffee table, all of my previous suspicions were confirmed.

He caught my stare and explained. "Blow. Snow. Coke. It'll help you stay awake and keep you focused."

Oh, hell no.

I took a step back. "Um, well..."

I envisioned telling him that Paul had been mistaken. That I hadn't known what he was dragging me up here to do. I ran through several different scenarios that would get me the hell out of there—

"I forgot I had an eight o'clock lab..."

"I left my flatiron on in my dorm room..."

"I just remembered I'm supposed to say no to drugs..."

Every scenario ended with me getting shot in the back as I tried to escape. I paused to fathom how I'd ended up in this predicament, but came up short.

I wet my lips with my tongue and settled for, "Um, Clint, I'm not sure—I mean, I've never done anything—"

He cut me off. "You've never used before, have you?"

I shook my head and laughed nervously. "I've never even been to a party until tonight. Paul just said if I wanted to get my grades up that you might have something to help me. I guess I thought that maybe it was caffeine pills or something like that."

I was rambling, but couldn't seem to stop vomiting up words. I could've told myself that it was just the one time. Bought the damn drugs, used them once, and then gone back to my dorm—forgetting that I ever came here. But, that wasn't me.

He easily swiped the bag from the coffee table and returned it to his pocket before smiling. "How about we get to know each other over something a little more refined than that cow piss they call beer?"

I set my still mostly full cup down on the table as Clint walked over to a sideboard and grabbed a decanter. "So, first time to a party, but surely not your first time drinking?"

I winced. "Actually... yes."

He paused before pouring. "Well then, at least you're with someone who can steer you in the right direction." He handed me the glass and raised his in a toast. "To first times. Just knock it back like a shot. It'll go down easier that way."

Clint wasn't what I expected in a drug dealer—well, my only experience up until this point was based upon the aforementioned afterschool specials with bad music. I'd expected some greasy drifter with bad hygiene, but he was none of those things.

He was someone who would fit in seamlessly in my world. The thought sent a flutter of excitement through my body, but I shook it off, trying to stay focused on the task at hand. Nothing like transitioning from attending my first party to taking shots with the resident drug-dealer. The incredibly sexy drug-dealer.

I downed the contents of my glass before my mind had a chance to continue. It was only going to lead somewhere dangerous. The liquid burned as it hit my throat, warming my chest on the way down.

He immediately poured us another. The second one went down even smoother than the first. When we began, we were on opposite ends of the couch, but each shot moved me closer to him. He asked me about my classes while his hand rested lightly against my thigh and instead of shifting away, I leaned into him, while explaining how I'd ended up in Colorado.

Clint took a sip of his drink. "So, now what?"

I shifted the empty glass in my hand, watching amusedly as it distorted the shape of the coffee table underneath. "I don't know," I admitted. "I guess if things keep going like this, I'll be back in Cali by Christmas."

He leaned in until his lips hovered less than an inch from mine. "I'd like it if you stayed."

I nodded and swallowed. "I—"

Clint's mouth latched onto mine with a focused possessiveness and my sentence cut off in a moan. Every flicker of his tongue weakened my resolve to walk out of here unchanged, while the scrape of his teeth against my mouth left me with an unfamiliar ache for more.

He pulled back and panted, "I knew the minute you walked in here that you didn't belong with someone like Paul. You need more than he could ever give."

My body shuddered at his words and I knew that I wasn't capable of walking away anymore.

I wanted more.

I wanted it all—recklessness and bad decisions be damned.

He ran the pad of his thumb across my lower lip with a grin. "Goddamn am I glad that you showed up tonight. Any other firsts you want to try tonight?"

I glanced at his pocket and then back up at him. "Would the coke really help me stay awake?"

He pulled the bag from his pocket and held it up. "You snort some of this and you can go without sleep for days—I hear it's perfect for students with full course loads."

I blurted out, "Cocaine is the second most popular illicit recreational drug in the United States."

He smiled amusedly. "Oh yeah? And what's the most popular?"

I tried to match his smile, even as anxiety mixed with liquor, churning my stomach into a rough sea. "Marijuana—um, weed. Sorry, I tend to ramble off random facts when I'm nervous or uncomfortable."

He cupped my face in his hand. "I think it's pretty fucking adorable, if we're being honest. I don't want you to be nervous around me though. I'm not going to push you."

I pressed my cheek into his palm. "If I'm going to do it, I want you to be the one to show me."

I tried to push my desire down as Clint showed me exactly what to do, his knee brushing against mine in the process. "It's gonna burn like a bitch, but if you can make it through that, you're gonna feel amazing."

I followed his instructions exactly—suddenly hyperaware of everything around me. Even the hairs on my arms seemed to be standing at attention, searching the air around me for new sensations. I felt more awake than I had in years and all the stress regarding my classes seemed to fade away until I was suspended in a euphoric state. This was a memory that was going to stay with me forever.

"Cocaine raises the level of the neurotransmitter Dopamine. Did you know that?"

Clint's mouth dropped to my ear and I shivered as he pressed a soft kiss against my jaw. "No. What else?"

I moaned softly, while marveling at how vibrant everything seemed. Clint's hair wasn't just a sandy brown—there were strands of gold mixed in. I'd missed it before, but now I could see everything.

It was as if my eyes had finally been opened.

"Um, thirty-eight million people have reported using cocaine at some point in their lives."

He pulled back and smiled again, soft dimples appearing in both cheeks. "You can thank Paul for that first bump. I can get you more…" His voice trailed off as he gazed at my body.

I stood up unsteadily. "Dance with me."

I was going to experience what Sofia had before I left here. It was only right. I'd never wanted to dance as much as I did in this moment. Clint reached for a small remote and a stereo kicked on in the corner, playing some pop ballad. I was dreaming, I knew that, but I wasn't going to let my fantasy go to waste. We moved together in time to the music and just like everything else between us, it was perfect.

"We should be on *Dancing with the Stars*," I mumbled, mesmerized by how small my hips looked in his hands.

He let out a low chuckle and squeezed me tighter.

Suddenly uninhibited, I stumbled back and stripped off my tank, tossing it onto the carpet. He undid the buttons on his Polo and pulled it off, before joining me. His hands gripped my hips again as we moved to the beat of the music. If I thought Clint was attractive before, the cocaine pushed those feelings into overdrive. I felt like a supermodel and, based on what I was feeling through his jeans, he shared similar feelings.

I wanted him. Badly.

I lost all interest in dancing about a minute into it and began working to get his pants off instead. He backed me up against a wall and kissed my throat while fighting to get the zipper on my jeans down, as his teeth nipped at my breasts through the lace of my bra, forcing another moan from my lips.

I felt like I was floating somewhere high above my body as he slid into me. Sex with him while high was incredible—it was deeply spiritual; the way our bodies connected. He was tender...loving, you might say. It made the handful of times with my boyfriend in high school seem like a joke. This wasn't some fumbled attempt in the backseat of his dad's sedan. This was a man, taking what was his.

This was why people made such a big deal about sex.

I peaked in his arms, but didn't once come down from my high. It was wrong, but everything about it felt right. As I steadied myself against his shoulder, I knew that I could never do it again.

"How are you feeling?" He murmured into my hair, before pulling out, leaving me empty. Hollow.

"I—I can't do this," I confessed.

He chuckled and pressed a kiss to my forehead, still holding me upright. "I'm assuming you mean the blow. It's not for everyone. If you're referring to me, I hope you'll reconsider. That was the best sex I've ever had."

My heart fluttered again at his words, but I frowned. A drug dealer wanted to be with me. This hadn't been part of my plans.

He tilted my face up to his. "Look at me, Neve. Do I look messed up to you?" I shook my head and he continued, "Exactly. I sell it, but I don't use. Ever. It's a business, baby. Plain and simple."

I chewed on the corner of my lip while mulling over his words. He was right—the sex had been amazing. If he kept his business away from me, maybe we could make it work.

The coke had me feeling invincible; like I could take on the world.

Maybe instead of locking myself away in the castle that was Hallett Hall, I should take a chance and let myself fall for someone.

It was time for me to live a little.

"Okay," I agreed. "Let's see where this goes."

He flashed his white teeth as he grinned. "I'm going to take such good care of you, Neve. Just you wait and see."

2

NEVE

July…Age 22

"Will Clint be in a good mood when he comes home tonight?" I whispered the words as I shook the black orb in my hand.

'Don't count on it' appeared within the blue triangle and I let out a small sigh of disappointment.

So much for a peaceful evening.

Maybe relying on a Magic 8 ball to solve my problems wasn't the best use of my time, but I had nowhere else to be. I'd become what my parents had feared most—an unemployed nobody, shacked up with her loser boyfriend.

I certainly never saw it working out like that.

"You either need to buy something or leave." The store owner glared at me from the other side of the counter and I immediately felt guilty—as if I'd been doing something wrong.

"I was just browsing—" I said calmly before he interrupted.

"I know what you're doing—you're either casing the place or looking to shoplift. I don't tolerate either; so get out."

I opened my mouth to protest when he pointed to the sign hanging on the door.

'We reserve the right to refuse service to anyone.'

I tossed my purse over my shoulder and held my head high as I walked out. I guess novelty stores were cracking down on the types of customers they allowed.

The bell chimed over the door as it swung shut behind me and I turned around with a smirk, middle finger in the air. That smirk faded the minute I caught my reflection in the glass.

Is that what I looked like?

No wonder he threw me out.

My hair hung in unwashed clumps around my shoulders. My eyes were sunken in, cheeks concave. A fading yellow bruise was the only color on my ghost white skin.

I lowered my hand and turned away. I couldn't bear to stare at myself any longer. It was like staring at a stranger. The shopping center was almost empty, save for a handful of cars. Everyone was off enjoying their fourth of July weekend. I bet the Res was packed.

The Boulder Reservoir was a popular hangout spot and this weekend would be no different. In another life, I would've been out there with friends.

A lone desk chair rolled aimlessly across the parking lot as the breeze caught it and I found myself mesmerized by the sight of it.

How had something like that ended up here?

It was a great metaphor for my life. That chair and I had a lot in common. I should've graduated a couple of months ago. Instead, I was here, watching my life roll past. Looking back on it, I should've never allowed Paul to drag me upstairs. I should've thrown my beer in his face and run as far away as possible.

I'd snorted another line before I left Clint that night, with promises to meet up the next day. As I'd taken the bus back to my dorm, I'd decided that I would continue seeing him, but only use if I had a lot of studying to get done.

Unfortunately, I found that after a couple of lines, I could stay up all night. I wasn't hungry when I was using either, so my fears of gaining the 'freshman fifteen' were alleviated as well. My grades improved a lot—since I didn't require sleep, nothing could stop me.

What goes up must come down though.

I'd convinced myself that because Clint had personal feelings for me, he'd never let me get addicted. I had this crazy idea that he somehow had my best interests at heart.

I was wrong.

The man who started out being perfect, slowly became something else. In the beginning, he took me to the nicest restaurants in Denver and bought me gifts just because. By the time I realized that things weren't as they seemed, I was caught in a downward spiral. I began skipping classes in favor of getting high and having sex with him. I craved the pleasure I got from it—coke alone wasn't enough. I needed Clint just as badly.

I was beyond addicted to cocaine and him, while he'd broken his own rule and gotten hooked on cocaine and H.

Clint was no longer Clint.

In his place was a temperamental monster. The insidiousness was subtle and his skill at hiding it was better than the mob. Once I'd sobered up enough to see how bad things had gotten, it was too late. The man I loved had been taken over by addiction.

I'd known that cocaine use was highest among college-aged young adults and had always made the conscious decision to stay away from it and weed, hadn't I? I learned much later that marijuana might've been the best choice for me back then. At least it would've diminished the stress over my grades.

So, I made excuses for him—I said I'd never put up with abuse; then again, I also said I'd never do drugs. It was a bit like a lobster in a pot of water that was slowly getting hotter. By the time the lobster realized that something was wrong, it was too late—the damn thing had been boiled alive.

There weren't any shades of gray when it came to my relationship with Clint either. I'd seen enough over the years to know that I was firmly ensconced in 'accomplice territory.'

If the cops ever caught on to his illegal activities, I was going down as well.

I noticed the owner of the shop watching me suspiciously, so I moved over a few buildings before sinking down onto the sidewalk.

The breeze picked up again and the chair rolled a few feet to the left before coming to a stop. I'd never wanted to be an inanimate object more than I did in that exact moment.

A drop of crimson hit the sidewalk between my legs, quickly followed by another. I stared at it in confusion until I realized it was coming from my nose. Again. I wiped at it with the back of my hand. Instead of being concerned, it just made me crave another hit.

This had to be rock bottom. My life had become a vicious circle of white snow and blood red reminders that I needed a fix. I was headed nowhere—scratch that. I was headed toward my imminent death, yet I was too far gone to stop now.

My mind no longer raced with thoughts of *coulda, woulda, shoulda.* It was wholly occupied only with thoughts of the next bump.

The most pathetic part was that I was friggin' content to continue living like this. At some point over the last few weeks, I'd reached acceptance. I was just like that chair, letting outside circumstances move me any which way they pleased.

It'd been so long since I'd made up my own mind on anything—so long since I wasn't under the influence of either cocaine or Clint.

I told myself I was smarter than the drug; convinced myself that I could handle it. Instead, I was completely powerless against it all.

I stood up and pinched my nostrils closed in a poor attempt to stop the bleeding. I inhaled through my mouth and immediately began coughing as the blood ran down the back of my throat.

The chair continued its path across the parking lot, not even stopping to say goodbye.

Lucky chair.

It probably didn't have a significant other, prone to murderous rages, waiting on it at home.

The first thing I noticed when I turned the corner onto our street was that the house was dark. I took a hesitant step closer before I noticed the second thing—Clint's truck wasn't parked in the driveway.

It didn't matter what time of day it was; the house was always lit up like a runway. A beacon on the hill in Boulder, shining its light to lost junkies in need of a fix. I looked up and down the street, waiting to hear the deep rumble of his truck, but it remained empty.

Quiet.

Too quiet.

I debated my options. I could either wait on the front porch for my boyfriend to show up, or I could put on my big girl panties and go inside to wait.

I swallowed hard, the copper taste still heavy on my tongue, and pulled the house key from my purse. The lock stuck as I turned it and I had to throw my shoulder into the door as I forced it open.

I almost fell headfirst into the living room floor, barely managing to catch myself at the last possible second. I shakily stood up and closed the door behind me; making sure it was locked in the process.

The house was silent and I laughed to myself. "Stupid, Neve. Getting scared over not—"

A hand clamped down over my mouth and spun me around, shoving my face up against the wall. A scream ripped from my throat as the hand tightened around my jaw, squeezing it until I felt like it would shatter.

"Shut the fuck up, bitch. Where is it?"

The voice was deep, but muffled, and I wondered if the person was wearing a ski mask like they did in the movies.

He slammed my head roughly against the wall. "I'm giving you one more chance. Where is it?"

Cold metal pressed into my lower spine and I fought the urge to scream again, knowing it was the quickest way to end up dead. I didn't have the slightest clue what 'it' was, but I wasn't about to let the guy holding a weapon on me know that.

"I—I don't know. Clint will be here any second and he can help you..." My voice was foreign to my ears. It spoke with a calmness I most certainly did not feel.

There'd been threats against Clint before, but no one had ever gone this far. No one was that stupid.

"Okay, bitch. You're going to pass along a message—you think you can do that?"

I nodded quickly as the metal dug into my spine.

"Good girl. Clint has twenty-four hours to get me the money. If he doesn't, what happened to you will be just the beginning. Got it?"

As my brain fought against the fear to determine what he meant, something sharp sank into my side. He quickly pulled the blade out and ran the edge of it down my throat, leaving a wet trail.

"Try to stay conscious long enough to deliver the message." The man let go of me and my knees immediately buckled.

My side burned as if it was on fire and my vision blurred from the pain. I waited until I heard him leave before crawling toward the kitchen. My tank top grew wetter with each movement and I began to feel lightheaded.

Just a few more feet and I'd be close enough to grab the phone.

I came to right outside the kitchen. The only difference was that every light in the house was now blazing around me, but I had no idea how long I'd been lying like this.

"Clint?" I whispered.

I heard his footsteps draw closer and I instinctively wanted to curl myself into a ball.

"Neve?" He gave me a puzzled look. "What the fuck are you doing on the floor?"

I pointed to my side and the carpet drenched in my blood. "There was a m-m-man—said you had twenty-four hours—stabbed me." My words were nothing more than jumbled nonsense, thanks to my tears.

He stared down at me, his eyes filled with concern and fear. "Jesus, Nevvie, you're bleeding all over the fucking place. Hold onto me."

I gave a silent prayer of thanks that Addict Clint hadn't shown up tonight. He pulled me to my feet and I swayed unsteadily against him, my grip on his shirt loosening. "Clint..."

His grip tightened on my arms as he pulled me over toward the sofa. "Sit down, baby."

I dropped back against the cushions with a loud groan of pain as Clint sat down beside me. His hands felt along my side before he gently lifted the material away from my skin. "Tell me what happened," he commanded.

I closed my eyes as exhaustion clouded my thoughts, struggling to remember even the smallest of details. "I didn't see his face. Is there—" I paused as a wave of pain washed over me. "Is there someone you owe money to?"

Clint stared through the front window, refusing to look at me. I thought that he'd check me over again; at the very least, tell me what the hell was going on. He did none of those things. He focused on the coffee table in front of him, straightening three lines of coke with a razor blade on a large mirror lying on the surface.

"You know what we're gonna do, baby? We're gonna ask the mirror to give us the answer. You get a little snow in you and the bleeding'll stop. 'Kay?"

I nodded. Maybe he was right. I just needed a little bump to take the edge off.

Clint took the shell of a broken pen and snorted a line. Then he stared expectantly at his reflection in the mirror. He was doing that a lot more lately; staring into the damn thing as if it held the secrets of the universe.

He passed the pen over to me and held my hair back as I forced my body to bend down and slowly inhale the middle line. I pushed off the coffee table and fell back against the cushions with my eyes closed. "The trunk is most frequently stabbed in cases of penetrating trauma. However, only subcutaneous tissue is affected eighty-five percent of the time. Did you know that?" I panted through each breath, fear wrapping its tendrils around my chest.

Clint patted my head before snorting the last line and continuing his staring contest with his reflection.

Within a few minutes, my heart rate increased and I knew that he was right. The coke was healing my body—it was probably coagulating all the blood at this very moment. I didn't even hurt as badly. Maybe I wouldn't need to go to the hospital after all.

"Let's go!" Clint leapt up off the couch, startling me with the volume of his voice. He grabbed my hand and yanked me to my feet. "We're going to pick up Trev. He'll know what to do."

3

NEVE

*W*e picked up Trever and continued driving until we were out of the city and on a winding mountain road. The two men carried on a terse discussion from the front seat, while I lay in the backseat with my head against the glass.

Coke used to give me such a high, but now the euphoria only seemed to last for a few minutes. Once those few minutes were up, I was overwhelmed with sadness again.

It made me want my mom.

You know how, as a kid, moms could fix anything? That was how I felt—completely despondent and in need of my mom to step in and make everything right again.

I just needed to lay my head against her chest while she stroked my hair—well, it was definitely not going to happen in this lifetime, but I yearned for it nonetheless. Thinking of her caused my throat to tighten. I wasn't going to cry over it. Not now.

I reached down and felt my side. Blood was still trickling out, but it seemed as if it had slowed some. I was still struggling to stay awake though. Maybe Clint was taking me to a doctor.

Yeah, that was it.

He was going to find me a mountain doctor that worked with outlaws all the time. He'd know just what to do to fix a stab wound.

I closed my eyes and dozed until the truck stopped suddenly and my head hit the seat in front of me.

"Neve, wake up. We're here." Clint had the back door open before I was even fully conscious. I was completely disoriented as he pulled me from the warmth of the truck and out into the cool mountain air. It didn't matter that it was July—Colorado was always chilly at night; even more so up here in the mountains.

I wrapped my arms around myself and stumbled on the uneven ground as I fought to remain upright. We were in the middle of the woods. Maybe the doctor's place was hidden back in the trees?

Trev's face made me pause. He looked scared. I held a hand up and waved at him weakly. "I'm fine. It's just a scratch, really."

Clint wrapped his arms around my body and I leaned into him, as crickets chirped around us. "Baby, the man who came to the house— did he give you a name?"

I shook my head and snuggled closer into him. The light breeze made the hair on the back of my arms stand up and I wanted nothing more than to climb back into his truck and fall asleep again.

"What exactly did he say?" His tone was different, but in my weakened state, I was unable to determine if he was angry or not.

I held on tightly to him as I repeated the same thing I'd told him back at the house. "Well, he said you had twenty-four hours to get him the money or what he did to me would seem like nothing once he got ahold of you."

His fingers dug into my shoulder blades painfully. "He said all that, did he? Was this before or after you fucked him?"

The addict was back.

I stiffened as my brain sent out a warning, seconds too late. He shoved me and I fell back against the soft earth, cracking my elbow on a large stone as I landed. Pain shot down into my fingers and I clutched at my arm in agony.

"Clint! I didn't even know the man—I'd just gotten home—"

He was on top of me before I could finish my sentence. "Tell me the truth!" His eyes were wild and unfocused, indicating that he'd done a lot more than just coke tonight.

I shook my head and tried to pat his chest with my good arm. If I could just calm him down, he'd see how crazy this was. Trever made no move to interrupt, choosing to turn the music up in the truck to drown out our voices instead.

Clint's hand cupped my face before moving down my body. Before I could breathe a sigh of relief, his fingers dug into my side, reopening the wound again. The breeze hit the wetness on my shirt, only making me feel colder.

"You lied, Neve. I saw it in the mirror. You were with him. How long have you been sleeping with him behind my back? Did you tell him where it was?"

Gone was my high and just like every time before, my heart broke as the madness overtook him. Why couldn't he see what he was doing to me? It hadn't mattered that I'd never once cheated on him, the Addict was convinced that I was on a mission to destroy him.

I'd just opened my mouth to reply when his hand shot up and wrapped around my throat. I brought both arms up and attempted to break his contact, but he easily blocked me.

"I don't know who all you've been talking to, but I'm not going down because some cokehead bitch can't keep her mouth or her legs shut." He squeezed harder as tears rolled down his cheeks and fell onto my face. The cracks in my heart spread as his words pierced me until only caverns remained.

This wasn't him.

I struggled in his grip, but he didn't let up. Being choked was just one more thing that wasn't at all how it was portrayed in the movies. According to Hollywood, the person being choked would make all sorts of loud gurgling and coughing noises. That wasn't even close to real life though.

As Clint's hands squeezed, the only noises that escaped my lips were little puffs of air as it was forced from my body. I clawed at his arms and face, but still the only real sound was coming from the stereo in the truck.

Clint made small grunts as he put all of his strength into his hands. "I want to rip you apart until you hurt as badly as I do. Why'd you talk to him? I trusted you!" He roared as more tears fell from his eyes.

My vision began to blur and my bladder released. I was going to die listening to Clint sobbing above me and Eddie Vedder wailing from the truck about the lost love of his life shining like a bright star in someone else's sky.

My eyes rolled back into my head just as there was a loud metallic sound.

Heaven's made of metal and the moon's made of cheese.

"Neve, get up!" The voice sounded close by.

God?

Only good girls made it to heaven...

Yeah, I was definitely in Hell. God would've let me rest.

"Neve, wake up." The voice was insistent, even going as far as hitting my cheek.

My eyes fluttered open to Trever's face mere inches from mine. "Get up. You have to get up."

I coughed until I thought a lung would come up, my eyes streaming.

He pulled me to my feet, but my limbs didn't feel like my own. Nothing about my body seemed familiar. He shook my shoulders roughly.

"You have to run. Run, Neve! Don't stop!"

I looked down and saw Clint sprawled out on his stomach, a shovel lying nearby. Trever hooked a finger under my chin and brought my eyes up to meet his. "He brought you here to kill you. He thinks you're a nark. If he comes to and sees you here, he'll finish it. Nod if you understand."

I nodded and took a deep breath. Clint groaned from nearby and Trever shoved me toward the tree line. "Go!"

I'd thought that failing every class my first semester and losing my scholarship was the scariest thing I'd ever been through. I now realized how incredibly naïve that had been. I forced my body to move as fast as it could. Luckily, there was still enough coke and adrenaline in my system to push me along. I knew that if he caught up to me, I wouldn't get another chance.

He was probably killing Trever at this very moment.

I didn't want to die.

That thought propelled me forward and I jogged faster, low-lying tree branches and limbs scraping along my face and arms. Blood poured steadily from the wound in my side, but I refused to stop, even as my lungs felt ready to explode.

I had to keep going.

An object in motion tends to stay in motion...

Fine time for my brain to make a reappearance.

"Aghhh!"

An object in motion tends to stay in motion with the same speed and in the same direction, unless acted upon by an unbalanced force.

My ankle caught on a tree root and I cried out in a harsh whisper before slamming to the ground. My brain urged me to get up and keep running, but my body was done. I'd twisted my ankle; with my luck, it was probably broken. I was also losing a lot of blood from where Clint reopened my stab wound. On top of all of that, the bastard had just tried to choke me to death and it felt like I'd swallowed a million razor blades. My limbs were so heavy—there was no way I could move them.

What was I even running toward anyway?

I had to be a hundred miles away from Boulder and at least twenty from the nearest town.

I was done.

Just then, I heard a loud crashing sound coming from the direction I'd just run from, so I forced myself up onto my forearms and army crawled over near a fallen log. He was going to find me, but I wasn't going to lie still and wait for death. Dirt and forest debris clung to my side. If only it were fall; I could've used a pile of leaves to hide in right about now.

The crashing got louder and then stopped. I held my breath and closed my eyes, as if doing so would make me invisible. Clint had to be within five feet of me.

Right then and there, I sobered up long enough to pray that he suffered from night blindness.

Anything that would keep him from seeing me lying on the forest floor.

I continued holding my breath, even as my body pleaded for air. There was a loud retreat back into the trees and then the sounds of the forest were the only thing surrounding me again.

The air turned colder and I shivered involuntarily as I inhaled a grateful breath, my tank top and Bermuda shorts doing nothing to keep me warm. I pressed my body up against the log, seeking warmth from any source I could find.

The trees above me looked like a giant blanket, just begging to be pulled down over my body. I couldn't have chosen a more perfect place to die.

Apathy? Wasn't that a sign of hypothermia?

I fought to stay conscious, but with that thought, my vision swam and everything went dark.

"Fuck if I know how she got here, but we can't leave her."

"Charm's gonna flip his shit over this. We can't just bring random women back to the club—"

"Well, what do you suggest we do with her? Leave her here to die?"

The male voices continued arguing nearby as I struggled to open my eyes. My body, on the other hand, disagreed with even the mere thought of consciousness so my eyes remained closed.

I listened to the men, but their voices were unfamiliar to me. It didn't sound like Clint or Trev. In fact, I was certain I'd never heard them before in my life. He hadn't found me. That was really the only thing I had going for me at the moment.

Hands touched my throat and I stiffened in response. "She's got a pulse." From there, they moved down my side, stopping at the wound that was making me feverish and delusional. "But, she's in pretty bad shape."

Maybe I was hallucinating this entire thing. I'd fallen in the middle of nowhere. There was no way that someone had found me so soon. I'd simply conjured up a mountain doctor in my mind, a man ready to piece a cokehead like me back together. He'd probably discovered me as he'd taken his evening constitutional. I pictured him having a cane that he'd carved himself and cheeks that were permanently rosy.

I was losing it. The reality of my situation was that I'd stranded myself in the middle of the wilderness. There were no hiking trails that I'd passed as I ran for my life and it was even more impossible to assume that someone had just miraculously stumbled upon me.

"She's been stabbed. It needs to be treated." If I was going to keep with the narrative in my mind, I'd call that voice Doc. He seemed to know what he was talking about.

The faint scent of cigarette smoke and cologne hit my nostrils and for whatever reason, it reminded me of my dad, even though he'd never smoked a day in his life. This was the best hallucination I'd ever experienced—my whole body was participating. Maybe I was still high.

"Fuck, do whatever you want. It's your funeral." That was obviously Grumpy.

There was a loud sneeze followed by a curse. "Did she have to end up in a pile of flowers? Shit, my eyes are watering like a motherfucker." That one would be Sneezy.

"I think we should keep her," a chipper voice added. I'd call him Happy.

I mentally ticked off the list of my imagined rescuers. Obviously, I was still missing a few. Strong arms lifted me up off the ground and an involuntary groan of pain escaped past my lips. I felt as if I'd been forced through a meat grinder. My elbow gave a sharp protest at the movement, another reminder that last night had not been some drugged-up dream. Fingers dug into my ankle and I damn near cried out again.

An object at rest will remain at rest, unless acted on by an unbalanced force.

Hello, unbalanced force.

"Careful with her. We don't need to add to her injuries." Maybe Grumpy had a heart after all. "I, for one, don't want her staying any longer than she has to."

Maybe not.

I was jostled along uneven terrain before being placed gently in the backseat of a vehicle. I needed to sit up and take in my surroundings.

I could get a grasp of where exactly I was—maybe find a landmark. Just in case I had to run again.

The vehicle hit a bump and all plans of moving went out the window. Pain barreled through me like a locomotive and I couldn't think of anything but how badly I hurt. Beads of sweat ran down my face and I couldn't distinguish whether it was from the fever or the movement.

I flirted briefly with the idea of sitting up again before fully committing to unconsciousness.

4

NEVE

"Miss? Can you hear me?"

I groaned and kept my eyes squeezed shut. My alarm hadn't even gone off yet. Surely it was too early for class to start.

"Miss, you need to open your eyes."

Events came rushing back to me and my eyes flew open in shock.

Clint. The woods. The men I'd heard while lying on the forest floor.

It had all been real.

I recognized the man's voice. It was Doc. I was slightly disappointed to see that he wasn't three feet tall with a long white beard and kindly face. He'd sounded older, but couldn't have been a day over thirty. His light brown hair looked as if it'd been windswept into the perfect position—something that no doubt had taken the right hair products along with a lot of time and patience. Dark scruff covered his face, making it hard to determine his exact age. I would've guessed his height as close to six feet, with muscles in all the right places. If his body was any indicator, he was no stranger to hard work.

Like a young Clint Eastwood.

Clint.

31

Ugh.

I couldn't think about him.

I shook my head to clear my thoughts. "W-where am I?" My voice was nothing more than a raspy whisper. I knew it was a side effect of being choked, but briefly considered the possibility that it could be permanent, sending a jolt of fear through me.

The man gave me a sympathetic smile. "You're safe now. Let's leave the rest for later. Want to tell me—"

"What? You're shitting me, right?!" A loud voice roared from the hallway and I shrank back as the door was thrown open.

"What the fuck is going on here, Doc?" The man was gorgeous; his dark hair fell right below his jawline, slightly curling at the ends. If Joe Manganiello and Jason Momoa had a love child, this man was definitely it. He was tall, but muscular—like he spent hours in the gym and his eyes—they were such a dark shade of brown that it was almost impossible to see his pupils.

Those same eyes narrowed when he looked at me as if I were something he'd found stuck to the bottom of his boot.

The man he and I referred to as Doc stepped in. "Charm, we found her out in the woods, all alone. She was unconscious...she'd been stabbed—"

Charm held a hand up. "Enough." Then he turned those dark eyes on me again. "What's your name?"

I tried to swallow, but my throat was completely dry. "It's N-Neve." I'd wanted to sound brave, but that went out the window the minute my voice cracked.

Charm, whose personality was in direct opposition to his name, crossed his arms over his chest. "Neve. How the hell did you end up in these woods?"

I was still lying down, looking up at him. It was a submissive position, so I propped myself up on my elbows, ignoring the stab of pain in my side and arm. "Pass."

"Oh, fuck no!" He exploded with anger, just like he'd done out in the hall. "You do not get to waltz into my fucking clubhouse and demand a pass when I ask you a direct question!" With each word, he moved lower and lower until he was shouting directly into my face, his spittle hitting my cheeks.

Doc stepped in and wrapped an arm around Charm's shoulders. "Okay, let's have you stand over here for a bit, yeah?"

Thinking about the events that led to me being here only made me feel like crying, and I refused to shed a tear in front of these strangers.

"You a cop?" Charm bit out from across the room, scowling at me as if I'd been caught trying to torch the place.

I laughed at the absurdity of it, pushing myself right into another coughing fit. With streaming eyes, I managed to rasp out, "Not even close. I'm a nobody. Can I leave now?"

His eyes narrowed and he looked ready to agree when another man entered the room. His wavy blond hair was unruly, covering one eye in its quest to escape his head, but the big grin on his face commanded all of my attention. His beard would've covered it up had he not styled the ends of his mustache to curl upward. He was one pirate hat and some eyeliner away from joining Captain Jack Sparrow and his merry buccaneers. "Hey Beautiful. Have a nice nap?"

It was Happy.

The more I stared at him, the more I realized he was built like a pirate as well—tall and lanky.

His personality was infectious and I found myself smiling back. "Hey, yourself."

"Rooster, get the fuck out."

Rooster?

I'd really hoped his name was Happy. It suited him.

Charm began hustling him toward the door when Rooster spoke again. "Wait—Charm, it's a sign. Don't you see? I was just wishing that we had a club whore and then we find her."

His smile was so earnest that I almost forgave him for referring to me as a whore.

Almost.

Instead, the implication of his words sank in. I was at the mercy of a group of men—men wearing leather vests. Friggin' hell—I'd been rescued by bikers.

Way to go, Neve. Out of the frying pan and into the fire.

Given that we were in the middle of the wilderness, I was going to go out on a limb by assuming that they weren't exactly on the right side of the law either. Doc ignored the confrontation and strapped a blood pressure cuff around my arm.

Charm roughly grabbed the front of Rooster's shirt. "We're not that kind of club, asshole."

Wait—so they didn't have any women here?

Happy/Rooster took a step back, straightening his shirt in the process. "Yep, got it. Just thought it might be a nice change. See ya later, Beautiful."

I tipped my chin up in reply as Charm turned back to me. "So, my men find you unconscious in the forest less than twenty-four hours ago and now you think you're well enough to leave?"

I nodded just as the first trickle of blood ran from my nose. I tried to quickly brush it away, but both men's faces changed. The scowl disappeared from Charm's face, seemingly replaced by several different emotions all at once. It was the same look I'd gotten from my parents when they realized what I'd gotten myself into—disappointment...anger...sadness. It was all there on his face. I turned away, feeling even more uncomfortable.

"Well, that explains a lot," Charm began. "When's the last time you had a fix?"

I looked at Doc. "What day is it?"

He glanced down at his watch. "July fifth for the next thirty minutes."

I sighed. I could lie and say I'd never used, but what was the point? I was in the middle of a biker's den; if anyone had coke, it'd be them. I knew I might have to cozy up to one of them to get it, but that was a small price to pay. Doc would be my first choice, since he rescued me and all.

"I had a line last night. So, I guess it's been about twenty-four hours."

Charm sank down onto a chair, giving nothing away with his facial expression. "Let me guess, you want more."

I nodded, a little too eagerly. "Yeah, if you've got it—"

He rubbed at the stubble on his face while Doc continued getting my vitals. "And you plan on paying for it...how?"

Damn.

I was definitely going to have to sleep with one of them. I was wrong yesterday—this was rock bottom. I looked between the two men. I would've preferred Doc, but I needed someone with the power to get me coke.

C'mon, Neve. Seductive.

I licked my lower lip, my tongue slipping into each crack. So, I didn't have soft lips anymore, but I still had a nice body. "I could..." I trailed off as Charm laughed bitterly, a look of utter disgust on his face.

"You're shitting me, right? You're not about to offer up yourself as payment are you, little girl? That's sure as hell not an even trade, in even the loosest sense of the words."

Even Doc was trying to mask a smile and in that moment, I hated both men in front of me. I hated them more than I hated Clint, if that was possible.

"You'd be lucky to have me—" I started, only to be cut off again.

"Sweetheart, you look like a mangy dog that needs to be put out of its misery," He pointed at my side. "Obviously, someone already tried and failed. My men? They want a woman—not a skeleton." He chuckled to himself again before getting up and walking to the door.

"I think I can get her patched up. What do you want me to do with her after, Charm?" Doc asked.

He never even turned around as the door swung open. "Put it back where you found it, Doc."

I couldn't go back out there. All my bravery was gone—I would die in the wilderness. What if Clint was still hanging around, hoping to finish the job?

I pushed myself into a sitting position, my head spinning from the effort. "Wait—I could help you—"

He paused, halfway out the door, and turned around to face me. "How do you figure?"

35

I struggled to think of something…anything. My eyes landed on a broom in the corner. "I could cook and clean for you and your men. I'm good at it."

I didn't know if I was good at it or not, but I was desperate.

Charm nodded to himself. "Fine. Detox her, Doc. Then we'll see where we stand. I ain't agreeing to anything more tonight."

The door slammed shut behind him and I breathed a sigh of relief. Doc didn't seem as happy with the decision.

"Neve."

I plastered a smile on my face. "This is good; I won't let you down."

He pinched his brow. "When's the last time you ate anything?" My face fell when I couldn't remember and he continued, "You and I both know that you're lying. I get it; I do. But, Charm? Fuck, you better miraculously learn how to be Martha Stewart in the next few days."

I tried to swallow again, but my mouth was like cotton. Doc started pulling various sized straps from a drawer and I watched him curiously.

"What's all that for?"

His teeth gnawed at the corner of his mouth as he worked. "Detox, Neve. Trust me, it's easier this way."

My heart began to beat a little faster. I'd just traded the Colorado wilderness for sobriety. I'd told myself that I'd quit before, but my willpower was nonexistent when it came to a line of snow.

Doc's plan?

To strap me to this bed until I sobered up.

On one hand, it was a hell of a lot better than any of the ideas that I'd had before. On the other, I doubted I'd survive long enough to celebrate.

5

CHARM

I walked into the basement today and left feeling as if I'd seen a ghost.

I knew it was impossible, but I could've sworn she'd come back to me.

When the girl looked up at me with those eyes, I was drawn to her immediately; stupid enough to think it was a sign from above or some shit. Then her goddamn nose started bleeding, and I knew that I would never be that lucky.

If the girl had been sent here, it was as a cruel joke. She was skeletal, yet offered up her body for drugs as if she was some prize.

How many times had I seen club whores do the exact same? Letting bikers lead them around naked with the chain of addiction wrapped tightly around their throats. They'd degrade themselves happily for their next fix.

They were all the same and trying to fix them was nothing more than a lesson in insanity. I wasn't willing to watch another person piss their life away, even if Doc seemed to think that this girl could be different.

*R*ooster barged in, waving a hand in front of my face. "Are you okay?" He might've pulled me away from the past temporarily, but this girl had unearthed something that couldn't be reburied.

Of all the things I expected my men to drag back to the clubhouse, she wouldn't have made the top one hundred. They knew better.

I slammed my fist down onto my desk with a growl. "What the fuck did I say about bringing strays into my club?"

I said the words and then froze at the look on Rooster's face. I sounded just like Luck. The thought only served to piss me off even more. I hated this girl. The men and I had a past that was best left forgotten and then she showed up, bringing it all back into the light.

He took a step back and raised his arms. "Look, Prez. If you'd seen her, you would've made the same decision. She—"

I yelled over him. "I would have? Are you sure about that? Did you know that she's a cokehead?"

I knew what they'd thought. Hell, I'd wanted to believe that she was just some hiker that had wandered off the trails and ended up in our territory. However, the stab wound and flip flops were big indicators that someone had intentionally left her here to die and the last thing I needed was for the cops to start poking around my clubhouse.

Rooster fell silent and leaned against the wall. "She was unconscious when we found her so Doc didn't manage to get her full medical history before bringing her back here."

I narrowed my eyes. "You tryin' to be funny?"

He sighed. "Not with you. I forgot you had your sense of humor surgically removed when they named you Prez. I'll let Twitch know so he can keep an eye on her."

Yeah, involving Twitch was a surefire way to ensure that everyone stayed sober around here. Maybe he'd actually succeed in killing himself this time around.

"She's not staying," I yelled as he slipped out of the office.

I had rules for this club and I wasn't about to break them for some junkie, even if she did have the bluest eyes I'd ever seen.

6

NEVE

*D*ay three...*I wanted to die.*

The cravings were unlike anything I'd ever experienced. If it were up to me, I would've given in by now. I wanted to shed my skin and these restraints and run until I found what I needed. It felt as if there were millions of insects roaming over every part of my body. I needed to scratch and claw at my skin until I got relief, yet my captors kept me bound.

"Formication...that's all this is." I mumbled quietly to myself, feeling each word as it rolled around in my mouth.

Funny how, in the midst of withdrawals, I was able to retain access to the useless information in my head. Useless, because it didn't change a thing about the predicament I found myself in. Here I was, chained to a table like a rabid animal—but at least I knew the medical term for the sensation of insects crawling on my skin.

I think I'd called poor Doc every name in the book. The friggin' idiot still refused to release me though. Sure, he'd loosen the bindings long enough to help me to the bathroom, but there always seemed to be someone else nearby, so all plans of escape were just out of reach.

I was exhausted, but couldn't sleep.

When I did manage to doze off, my dreams were nothing short of nightmares. Most of them involved me falling into large piles of snow where I'd snort line after line until everything else faded away.

Then I'd wake up, expecting to feel relaxed, only to remember that it was a dream and I was still strapped down to a damn table. To say I was irritated would've been the understatement of the century.

For every action, there is an equal and opposite reaction.

"You need to try and eat something. You're starting to ramble to yourself like a crazy person." Doc held up a bowl of what might've been oatmeal and my stomach turned.

The first twenty-four hours I'd been starving and had eaten everything they put in front of me. It had been so long since I'd ingested real food, so my body had rejected it almost instantly.

I'd ignored the pangs of hunger after that; refusing anything that Doc or Rooster brought me. Everyone else seemed to stay away—I guess my screaming to be let go got to them.

I shook my head as he held the spoon toward my face. That was the problem with being strapped down in here. It was obvious that this room was used as a makeshift clinic for the bikers when needed, so everything smelled medicinal.

Sterile.

Not at all what you'd want to smell while trying to eat.

There were no windows, so I was treated to the sight of Doc's face and bare walls day in and day out. A girl needed sunshine. I'd tried and failed to convince Doc that he should move my bed outside.

"Charm wouldn't like it."

That seemed to be the end to every argument. *Charm this. Charm that.*

And where was the man himself?

Damn if I had a clue—it wasn't like he'd given me his itinerary before leaving me in here. Hell, he'd been ready to send me back into the forest to die.

Jerk.

Doc sighed and placed the bowl on a small table before lifting my shirt to change the bandages around my wound again. Trace amounts of blood had seeped onto the sterile white pad, but it was so much better than what it was when they brought me here. He'd done the best he could, stitching me back up, but I was going to have a gnarly scar. He was a biker, not a plastic surgeon—he was also the man who saved my life, so I couldn't exactly complain.

And I didn't—mostly. I kept my mouth shut when they brought me gently used clothing that had obviously belonged to a female. I'd had a lot of questions, but chose to keep them to myself. I didn't need Charm changing his mind about letting me stay, especially since I didn't know if Clint was still combing the woods looking for me.

I had to wait it out. Maybe I'd win the trust of these bikers and then make a break for it—Clint would eventually lose interest in hunting me and I'd be free.

For the first time in four years, I'd be on my own.

The thought was equally exhilarating and terrifying.

Doc finished placing the new bandages before resuming his quest to get me to eat. I shook my head and he sighed. "You need to eat. Don't make me resort to Plan B."

I laughed weakly. "What are you gonna do—force it down my throat?"

He didn't even crack a smile. "Alright, Princess. You wanna do things the hard way? I'll be right back."

I wasn't worried—perhaps I should've been, but from what I'd seen over the last few days, these bikers were nothing like their TV counterparts.

They didn't even have club whores—I thought that was a prerequisite for all motorcycle gangs.

My nose itched and I stared angrily at the restraints around my arms.

Great.

It began running and I knew that it was probably another nosebleed. I'd had them daily for as long as I'd been using.

The cravings hit me hard, threatening the resolve I'd built up over the last three days. I forced my eyes closed and concentrated on my breathing.

When I was stressed out as a kid, I could always count on my mom to talk me off the ledge. She'd sit with me in the floor, my hands clasped tightly in hers, urging me to *"just get through the next breath."*

It wasn't always a quick fix, but eventually my breathing would even out and the weight on my chest would disappear.

A lone tear slipped down my cheek.

God, I'd messed up everything.

"Little Girl."

The sound of his voice startled me awake. I couldn't even remember falling asleep.

My eyes flew open and there he was, the man who thought I resembled a mangy dog in need of putting down.

"It's Neve." I forced out through gritted teeth.

"Don't care. Why are you refusing to eat?" His hand brushed across the scruff on his face just as he'd done a few days ago—as if it was a nervous tic.

I shook my head and his eyebrows raised in surprise. He obviously wasn't used to someone openly refusing him. "I'm not hungry."

The chair creaked as he shifted his weight, his eyes never leaving mine. His tongue clicked against his teeth. "Here's what's gonna happen—you're gonna eat something. It might come as a shock to you, but Doc ain't in the habit of babysitting little bitches with attitudes the size of Texas."

I expected him to say more, but he shifted back in his seat and cracked his neck, obviously turning the conversation over to me. My eyes burned with unshed tears at being referred to as a bitch. "I'm. Not. Hungry."

His jaw tightened as I enunciated each word and I knew that I'd effectively pushed his buttons. "Ain't nothing I'd love more than to throw your sorry ass back out into the woods, but Doc vouched for you. So, do the man a solid and eat some goddamn food."

Charm stood up and walked out, slamming the door behind him, and I breathed a small sigh of relief. That relief was short-lived when he burst through the door a few minutes later.

He began pacing the room, his fingers tirelessly stroking at his chin. "Okay, here's how this is going to go. You're going to make good on that little promise of yours, starting today."

My eyes widened in shock. *I'd just been stabbed a few days ago and he wanted me cooking and cleaning?* I pointed to my side. "But I'm still recovering—"

"You're going through withdrawals. The way I see it, you're well enough to deny food, so you're well enough to cook and clean. You can start by getting dinner for tonight. If that doesn't work for you, then I suggest you get the hell out before sundown. The forest is hard enough to navigate during the day. At night, it'll be damn near impossible."

He turned to leave again and it took every ounce of strength to swallow my pride. Keeping my eyes focused near the floor, I admitted my fears. "I'm just scared I'll throw it all up again—the food, I mean." Under my breath, I added, "And I'm as good as dead out there."

Charm kept his back to me, but I watched the way his shoulders seemed to tighten. Filled with worry that he may have overheard the end of my sentence, I began stumbling over my words. He left the room mid-sentence, shutting the door quietly behind him.

He was going to find Doc and tell him to gas up the truck so they could take me back; I just knew it. I was busy formulating a plan that didn't involve me being mauled to death by bears when the door opened and Charm reappeared, carrying a mug of steaming liquid.

He set it down on one of the counters before coming over and untying my bindings. "I think we can let you out of these for the time being, yeah?"

I nodded and slowly pushed myself up into a sitting position, but my muscles protested the movement, having gotten quite comfortable with being strapped down.

We eyed each other warily as he sat back down in the chair and took the mug in his hands. He dipped a small spoon into the liquid and blew gently on it before offering it to me. "Broth—it'll be easier for your stomach to manage."

I opened my mouth and took a sip. My stomach rumbled and growled in appreciation and his mouth twisted up, as though he was trying not to gloat.

"Thank you." We appeared to have called a truce for the time being. Charm patiently fed me broth by the spoonful as though I were a small child, and instead of being bothered by it, I was filled with something unfamiliar.

Comfort.

I couldn't tell you the last time I'd experienced that feeling.

The mug was soon empty, yet here we were. Sitting and studying each other.

Charm looked to be a million miles away and I tried to sound lighthearted as I broke the silence. "Tell me, do you always make a habit of feeding the prisoners? I kind of thought a job like that would be beneath a club 'Prez.'"

His face darkened. "Just when I think that maybe you ain't fit to be up and moving around, that smart mouth of yours proves me wrong."

I shouldn't have said anything. He was much better when he was silent. "I didn't mean—"

"I'll let Doc know that you're ready to be put to work. Stick with the broth for a couple days, your stomach will be workin' just fine again." He rolled the stool backward before jumping to his feet and I fought against my baser instincts to keep my eyes on his face and not linger on the way his denim jeans hugged his thighs.

Obviously, my libido was still in working order. I pushed those thoughts aside. The man saw me as no better than an animal, after all. "Charm, I'm sorry. I didn't mean to upset you—It just struck me as odd, you helping me like you knew exactly what you were doing." A strange expression crossed his face, but it was gone before I could decipher it.

"Like I said, I'll get Doc in here. If you can't fulfill your end of the deal, you're out. Got it?"

I nodded and he left again, slamming the door shut behind him. It appeared our thirty-minute ceasefire had ended.

7

CHARM

I fed the girl…just like before with her.

She'd been oblivious to the pain it caused and had rambled off insults, but when she looked up at me, it was impossible not to see another face. One that was so familiar to me that I'd caught myself reaching out to cup her face; I probably would've begged her to get better too.

I was letting some addict dredge up shit that I hadn't thought about in years.

*D*oc followed me outside and waved off the two prospects on guard duty—my only prospects. Their eyes had gone wide when I'd thundered through the door—hands resting on their guns as if expecting to be thrown into battle.

Maybe we were.

She'd shown up and suddenly, I didn't know which way was up. I'd needed to get out—breathing the same air as her only left me feeling impaired.

"Hey, I'm gonna get her up and moving around. You really want her cooking tonight?"

"Did I stutter, Doc? Did it not seem like I made myself perfectly clear? She's your houseguest and it's time she earned her keep."

He nodded and grumbled, "No, I'm just trying to get a handle on what the fuck is going on around here."

That made two of us.

I never should've accepted her offer to cook and clean. Why hadn't they just dropped her off in town? Made her someone else's problem.

I rubbed at my chin absently before turning back to him. "I said she could cook one meal and we'd go from there. I ain't agreeing to anything else until I've seen how this goes."

Doc nodded again before disappearing and I called the prospects over the minute they came back outside. "Here's a fifty. Go into town and get our usual from Gio. Be back by six."

They nodded and took off and I felt the weight on my chest lessen. I was going to handle this situation so that we could get back to business as usual. She was going to fail and our deal would be off.

8

NEVE

*O*nce I'd been issued my marching orders, Doc had come to my rescue once again. He led me into the industrial style kitchen and pulled a big red book out from one of the lower cabinets. It was the *Betty Crocker Cookbook;* my mother had an earlier edition when I was growing up. This one only looked to be a few years old.

I blinked away the sudden tears that formed as I flipped through the binder of recipes. It was always the little things that got to me; things that reminded me of her.

"I found it a few years back; thought it might come in handy one of these days."

I eyed Doc skeptically. "And you had it hidden because..." My voice still sounded as if I'd gargled with broken glass.

He looked completely sheepish as he answered, "Thought if Charm knew we had something like this in here, he'd expect one of us to cook. I got enough on my plate without playing housewife to a bunch of bikers—no offense."

I laughed and continued turning pages when Doc stopped me, pointing at a recipe for chicken pot pie. "What about this? Seems easy enough—the recipe serves six. If we triple that, we should have enough food for nine people." Seeing my confused expression, he continued. "We're growing men; gotta keep our strength up."

Once dinner was decided, Doc sent two of the guys out for supplies and showed me around while they were gone. The building was laid out like a hunting lodge—with wood paneled walls as far as the eye could see. The main living areas were situated in the middle of the lodge, on the lower level, with apartments upstairs. A large stone fireplace separated the living room from the dining room. It probably kept the entire place warm during the winter. As we walked, I found myself wondering if the building had been a hotel at one point. It was certainly large enough to have been.

We continued up the wooden stairs toward the apartments and I noted that each piece of wood appeared to have been hand carved. The upper level was open to below, which probably came in handy if anyone ever decided to break in. The men could probably just pick them off one by one without having to go downstairs. Judging by the rack of guns lining the wall, that was their exact plan.

Doc continued in his role as official tour guide and I pushed through the pain in my side in favor of learning more about the men who held me captive. Or rescued me. I guess it depended on who you asked. We came to a closed door at the end of the hall and Doc swiftly turned around, heading back to where we'd come from.

"Wait—what's that room?" I stopped and pointed.

"Charm's room—we're not going in there, unless you've got a death wish I don't know about."

I simply shook my head and followed him dutifully back downstairs. Our tour ended just as the men got back. I recognized Sneezy almost immediately.

Just like Rooster, Sneezy went by another name—PD. And he was identifiable from almost anywhere in the lodge; you just had to listen for the constant sniffling. It was a good thing he kept his wavy hair close-cropped or else it would've been covered in mucus. I cringed at the thought and looked away.

The other man had been a little more difficult. He came in and dumped several plastic bags onto the kitchen counter before digging through one and pulling out a small brown paper bag.

After a long drink from the bottle, he smiled over at me. "You had a hell of a lot of stuff on that list." He tilted the bottle back again before continuing, "I'm just gonna go lay down for a bit—I'm not as young as I once was." He'd only taken a couple of steps before he turned back and thrust out his hand. "Guardrail."

I took it and amusedly replied, "Neve."

In keeping with the distorted fantasy in my head, I decided to call him Sleepy—only because *Drunky* hadn't been a character in the Disney movie.

I wanted nothing more than to lay down and surrender to oblivion for a few hours too as I unpacked groceries, but this meal would either earn me a safe-haven or send me back into the depths of Hell. It was do or die time.

I placed the bags of frozen vegetables into the sink to thaw, deciding at the last minute to run hot water over them as I still wasn't entirely sure what I was doing.

Feeling as though I was being watched, I turned around to find a biker sitting on a stool, studying me as if I was hosting a show on *Food Network*. I would learn later that this was the indelible Joker, but for the time being, he was my silent sous chef.

His hair was shaved on the sides, much different from the other men, leaving only an inch or two of light brown hair on top. He had a small freckle below his right eye—eyes that could only be described as Caribbean blue. Not that I would know personally, but his eyes looked like the resort advertisements I'd seen in magazines.

The stubble that lined his face was a mixture of blond and light brown, giving it an almost silver appearance in the afternoon sunlight streaming in through the upper windows.

I grabbed the plastic packages of chicken and a cutting board while the biker watched me intently. I was just coming to the conclusion that he'd been sent to babysit me when he tapped four fingers against his chin twice. It took a minute for my brain to catch up and determine that it was sign language for 'talk.'

Every year, my mother signed me up for summer camp. A list was posted in the mess hall with various activities and, for whatever reason, I always chose sign language as one of mine. I guess I thought it'd come in handy in the future—at that point in my life, I'd still planned on becoming a doctor.

Instead, here I was, using my skill to communicate with a silent biker while playing cook to a bunch of outlaws.

Oh, how the mighty had fallen.

Thinking of camp dredged up thoughts of my mother, so I did the only thing I could; I talked about her with my quiet companion.

"My mom would make chicken pot pie a lot growing up. I would watch her, but I never really got the hang of cooking, you know?" He nodded, never breaking eye contact with me and I realized that I'd just admitted I had no idea what I was doing. "It took me a lot longer to get it down."

I looked down to make a few more cuts to the chicken and when I lifted my head up again, I noticed his head was cocked to the side, watching me curiously. His expression was one of open interest, but he was so quiet that I decided to call him Bashful.

I finished chopping up the chicken and placed it into a large bowl before reading over the recipe again. When I chuckled, Bashful held his hands out while shrugging his shoulders, as if asking what I found funny.

I pointed at the recipe. "My dad loved it when my mom made this, but every time he'd apologize to her for all the time and effort that went into making it. She'd brush it off, but tell him he could make it up to her by rubbing her feet once he was done with the dishes."

The memory caused my throat to tighten up, and I was forced to pause as I regained control over my emotions. "It was Bisquick—she cheated and made the crust from a baking mix. We never caught on."

I didn't talk after that.

Cooking was no different than chemistry—I was simply taking a set list of ingredients in specific doses and recreating the experiment in a different lab. At least, that was what I told myself.

Once the chicken was cooked, I added everything to two large casserole dishes and popped them into the large oven before setting the timer.

"Well, well, well—you must be feeling better." Rooster poked his head around the corner.

I shrugged. "I guess as good as I'm going to get."

Not like your boss cares...

He looked me over, and I realized that Bashful had disappeared on me at some point. "You get a room yet?"

I shook my head and continued wiping down the countertops, trying not to give anything away. A room meant permanence, right?

Rooster excused himself and came back a few minutes later with a bag under his arm. "Come with me. One of the guys can take the shit out when the timer goes off."

"It's not shit—it's good food," I protested.

"My apologies. One of the other dickheads around here can take the deliciousness out for you," he joked as he led me upstairs and towards one of the apartments. His earlier comments about me being a club whore came back full force and I stopped walking, my body stiffening in response. It had been one thing to offer my body when I was still high, but now that I was sober, I didn't want to be anyone's plaything.

He put a key in the door and then looked back over his shoulder. "You comin'?"

I shook my head and took a step back. "I'm not—I can't do that—"

He laughed. "Darlin', I don't want a thing from you—but the truth is, you need a shower. Badly." He held the bag up. "I found some girly shit you might like too. You're safe with me, Scout's Honor."

I took a tentative step forward. "You were a Boy Scout?"

He pushed the door open and walked in. "Me? Oh, fuck no." Seeing my eyes widen, he amended. "I won't lay a hand on you, Biker's honor."

I took the bag from his hand. "Didn't think bikers had any honor."

He laughed again, as if my words were of no consequence. "You got a point there, Darlin'. How about this? I like my partners willing and able-bodied. And you're neither. No offense."

53

"None taken." I studied the words on the back of his leather vest as he moved through the small apartment, gathering up armfuls of clothes.

Scarred Savages MC.

A skull with flames exploding from the eye sockets grinned back at me and I winced before looking away. Biker gangs were meant to be feared, so it's not like there would've been a kitten riding a Harley on the back—although that would've been adorable.

The one percent emblem was proudly displayed to the right of the skull, opposite the MC logo. As if there was any mistaking what these men were.

At the bottom of his vest was the word *Kasselhessen*. I was even further from Boulder than I'd previously thought if I'd ended up in the mountain town of Kasselhessen. I didn't know much about the town, other than it was founded by German immigrants in the late 1800s—well, that, and it was obviously home to these outlaw bikers.

"Bathroom's that way. Clean towels are in the cabinet. I'm going to try and scrounge up some more clothes for you." Rooster gestured toward a closed door, dismissing me.

I was pleasantly surprised to find that the bathroom was relatively clean. He had an extensive array of shampoos and soaps and I took my time sampling a little from each one. I doubted that he'd even notice and, judging by the river of red coming off of me, I needed it. I managed to avoid my bandages, washing around them as best I could.

I let the hot water run over my body until I began to worry that Rooster was going to break the door down to ensure that I was still breathing.

As I used my towel to wipe the steam from the mirror, I tried to avoid looking at the bones protruding from my chest as I carefully dried myself off. I failed and actually jumped back in fright, certain that a ghost was in the room with me. I looked like a dead girl—my eyes were sunken in, a necklace of bruising visible around my neck. I had bruises almost everywhere I looked.

Charm had been right—I did look like an animal that needed to be put down.

There was a light knock at the door and I rewrapped the towel tightly around my body before opening the door about an inch.

"Found you some clothes." Rooster's face peered at me through the crack. I pulled the door open just enough for him to pass me the clothes before shutting and locking it again. The clothes were extra small, but still hung off of my frame. I cinched the cotton pants as tight as they would go before pulling my damp hair up into a ponytail.

The bag he'd given me contained lip balm, deodorant, lotion, a tube of toothpaste, and a toothbrush. After using them, I felt almost human again.

Almost.

I pulled on the oven mitts and carefully removed the casserole dishes from the oven. It looked even better than the picture in the cookbook.

"Damn, Neve. Why didn't you get lost in the woods sooner?" Rooster grinned over my shoulder before stabbing a bite of steaming chicken pot pie with his fork.

The silent biker nodded earnestly, as if he was seconding Rooster's comments.

"It must be somethin' if it's got Joker piping up." The man I recognized as the voice of Grumpy said, rolling his eyes on his way out of the kitchen.

I tried to determine if he was teasing or not—I hadn't heard 'Joker' say a single word since I met him a few hours ago. He'd shaken my hand and bobbed his head before sitting down to watch me cook. That had been the extent of it.

"Gunner, it's the shit!" Rooster talked through a mouthful of food, exhaling in an attempt to cool his mouth and I hid a small smile, staring down at the saucepan of broth in front of me.

Take that, Grumpy Gunner.

I didn't think I'd seen the man do anything but scowl since I'd arrived; which was a real shame, because he had a beautiful face. He was a little taller than Doc and though no one had said it, it was apparent that he'd served in the military.

You know how some men just carry themselves a certain way? Well, that was Gunner. And his way screamed, *"Back the eff off."* He wore his dark hair slicked back and his facial hair was trimmed so perfectly, that I'd bet my next meal he didn't leave the bathroom until every hair on his head obeyed him.

I mostly just tried to stay out of his way.

Rooster abandoned his post at the oven when I told him he couldn't have another bite. I'd been hidden away in the basement, but I didn't remember the guys making so much noise. They must've just been looking forward to a home-cooked meal.

I tested the side of the casserole dish with the back of my hand and decided that it probably wasn't too hot to carry before making my way into the dining area.

My mouth dropped open at the sight of cardboard boxes and the men shoveling slices of pizza into their mouths like savages.

My face burned with embarrassment as I stood frozen next to the table. "What is this?"

Charm looked over his shoulder at me as he grabbed himself a slice. "I gave you an opportunity to cook dinner. You took too long, so I improvised. You're out." He stalked down the hallway and I hurriedly set the dish down on the edge of the table before jogging after him, managing to corner him at the end of the hall.

"You didn't even give me a fair chance! You set me up to fail!"

He shrugged and tried to push the door closed, but I stuck my foot out and caught it before it slammed in my face. To say I was taken aback by the contents of the room would've been the understatement of the millennium. I wasn't sure what I expected—perhaps a dungeon of some sort. "You have a desk!" It wasn't a question, but an accusation. Bikers didn't have offices. They had rape rooms and torture chambers, sure, but nothing that would lump them in with regular folks.

He sat down in a large brown leather chair and kicked his feet up onto it. "And?"

Why did he hate me?

It wasn't as if I'd planned on getting stabbed and choked before being left for dead in the woods.

My chest tightened when I realized that it wasn't hatred reflected on his face. It was indifference, which was so much worse. I took a deep breath, hoping the pain would subside. "I made a meal. That was the agreement."

He took a bite of pizza, taking forever to chew. "What do you want —a trophy for making one lousing fucking meal? Sorry, Sweetheart, this ain't youth soccer. We had a deal, it didn't work out, and now I want you gone. Is that clear enough for ya?"

I rubbed at the base of my throat. "I—I'd like another chance. Please." I was pleading, but I couldn't let him kick me out. Thoughts of being alone in the wilderness again had me rubbing my throat furiously as the pain intensified.

Charm crossed one foot over the other and pointed behind me. "Door's that way."

I could've stayed and argued, but what was the point? He wanted me gone and nothing I said was going to change his mind. I ignored the stab of pain in my side and slammed the door shut behind me before marching upstairs to find my room. I'd barely made it to the top when a hand closed over my wrist, yanking me back down a step.

"You wanna slam doors like a fucking toddler? You can do it up here where no one can hear you, Sweetheart. I ain't runnin' a daycare." Charm dragged me into a room that I assumed was going to be mine, but I wrenched myself from his grasp and stumbled back into the hallway.

"You just want to lock me up like some prisoner...holding me against my will."

His eyes widened in shock. "Against your will? Let's go." He latched onto my bicep and pulled me back down the stairs.

"Go to hell!" I forced through gritted teeth.

His jaw worked angrily as he replied, "Oh Sweetheart, look around you. I'm already there."

It didn't matter how hard I dug the rubber soles of my flip flops into the wooden stairs, Charm was a lot stronger. With hardly any effort on his part, he forced me through the living area and out the door. Several of the bikers raised their heads, but when they saw it was him, they immediately looked away.

"Here you are. Free as a fucking bird. Go. Run. Get high. Whatever the fuck you want to do. I ain't stoppin' you." He deposited me onto the gravel and turned to go back into the lodge, but I snagged the edge of his leather vest, stopping him.

"Please, Charm. I'm—I'm—I'm sorry. Please don't leave me here." I kept a death grip on him and watched as his chest heaved up and down with each angry breath as he looked down at me.

He was going to beat the shit out of me and for the first time in my life, I wasn't so sure that I didn't deserve it. With that thought, I reluctantly let go and took a step back.

The intensity of his stare seared me, so I focused on the ground in front of me, expecting his fists.

After what felt like an eternity, he spoke. "I'll give you tomorrow. That's it. Think you can handle that?"

I nodded earnestly. "I can do it. I swear to you."

His gaze softened for a fraction of a second before the glare fell back into place. "I won't tolerate any more of the shit. We clear?"

I shakily nodded again before he walked back inside, closing the door quietly behind him and leaving me with the stars.

9

CHARM

She touched me.

I can't recall the last time anyone made contact with me and lived to tell about it, but it was as if she feared the monsters in the wilderness more than she did the one standing right in front of her.

Just one more indicator that this girl isn't firing on all cylinders. If she were, she'd have run for her life when I gave her the opportunity.

She was fiery though; I'd give her that.

I'd grown up, surrounded by women who did as they were told, when they were told to do it. This girl's defied me every chance she's gotten and by all rights, her ass should be wandering the woods for help now.

But her small hands on my kutte jolted me back to another time and place...

I don't know what to think now.

*G*unner slid onto the bar stool next to mine and signaled the bartender for a beer before turning his attention back to me. "Well, that was an interesting way of handling things back there."

I'd fled the clubhouse after our encounter outside, needing a clear head and a change of scenery. I should've known that he wouldn't have been far behind. He seemed to be the only one, besides me, who hadn't immediately fallen under the junkie's spell.

So, maybe I didn't exactly know how to decode my feelings. It didn't mean shit. She was just another junkie and she'd show her true colors to everyone else soon enough.

I downed the shot of bourbon in front of me, irritation creeping up my neck. "You have a better plan? I'm all ears."

"Look, I knew she was trouble the minute we found her. Way I see it, Doc fixed her up and now her ass can be on its merry way out of our fucking territory. Someone's gonna start looking for her—you and I both know it."

He was right. Underneath the cokehead, there was something there. It was obvious that she was an intelligent girl, even if she'd made some piss poor decisions—it was there in her eyes. She was sharp and girls like that had families who reported them missing. Last thing I needed was for the law to think that my club was into kidnapping.

I frowned at Gunner. "Did you just come down here to tell me how to run my club?"

He shook his head. "Been looking at our numbers. If something doesn't change soon, the entire house of cards is gonna come crashing down on all of our heads. We went from running the entire state and now we're lucky if we can bribe a gang into doing business with us. We need to go back to what we were doing before."

I propped my arm up on the bar and rested my forehead against it. Before was when Luck ran things and, while he'd been wildly successful, the club and families had suffered at his hands. I'd sworn that I wouldn't run shit like that because, if we failed, the entire town was going to go down with us.

This was what Luck would call being in between a rock and a hard place. The bastard would've made the decision easily though—there'd always been a line of hang-arounds, just waiting to prospect for the Scarred Savages. To Luck, his men had always been replaceable.

He'd chased after anything that lined his pockets and made the club more powerful. It had been his undoing in the end. The same men who'd been willing to stick out their necks for him no longer saw the benefits. I think they'd probably known it all along—they'd just needed someone to point them in the right direction.

That was where I'd come in.

Now, I woke up every morning, wondering when they'd come for me. I wasn't going to be able to retain my hold on the club if I didn't start making some tough decisions soon. I couldn't let a pair of blue eyes distract me from my goal. I was going to have to find men to join us—I faulted Luck for a lot of things, but his ability to amass an army was not one of them. And I'd use just about any means necessary to keep Kasselhessen running.

10

NEVE

"*N*eve."

I pushed my face deeper into the warmth of my pillow.

"Neve, get up."

The deep timbre of the voice reluctantly pulled me back to consciousness and I blearily blinked a few times before rolling over. It was still dark.

"Neve."

I snapped, "I'm up. You expect me to start cleaning when it's still dark out?"

I shouldn't have complained. He'd given me my own room last night even though I deserved to sleep outside after my outburst. I'd left them downstairs talking afterward while I fell into bed, exhausted, but I distinctly remembered locking the door behind me when I came in. I should've known he would've had a key.

"Get up."

I sat up and rubbed my eyes. There was just enough light coming in from the hall for me to make out his silhouette crouched on the side of the bed. "Can I at least pee first? Or is that not allowed?"

Charm chuckled quietly. "I think I can make an exception."

When I came out of the bathroom, he was still crouched in the same position.

I yawned before asking, "Where should I start? Is there a cleaning cart somewhere downstairs that I could use?"

He stood up slowly and handed me a sweatshirt. "Put this on. You'll need it. Got you some shoes as well. Size six, right?"

My heart started beating a little faster. "Um, yes. Where are we going?"

He walked past me and stood near the door. "Get your shoes on. We'll talk outside."

My heart was hammering wildly in my chest at this point and my eyes were on the verge of welling up with tears. He was going to take me back out into the woods.

After he told me that he'd give me another chance.

That lying sack of—

"Sometime today would be nice, Neve."

I hurriedly forced my feet into the tennis shoes he'd left and pulled the sweatshirt over my head before following him downstairs. The lodge was deathly quiet.

He was getting rid of me while the other men slept. He'd probably tell them I ran away too.

I forced a sob back and instead continued walking to my imminent death. Charm slowed down enough for me to catch up to him outside, but instead of heading toward the vehicles, he led me down a small path that ran near the back of the lodge, using a small flashlight.

Maybe this was where he took all the mangy dogs to be put down. The thought forced a bubble of hysterical laughter out and Charm turned back to me, swinging the flashlight up toward my face.

"You okay?" I couldn't see the expression on his face, but I imagined it was one of confusion.

I nodded, blinking through the brightness, and he took a few more steps before stopping near a ledge made of stone.

"What is this?" I'd thought he was taking me back into the woods; not throwing me off of a cliff.

Charm pointed to the stone. "You'll see. Come here."

I shook my head and took a step backward. "I—I'm sorry if I came across as rude last night. I can be better...I swear." My throat tightened and I rubbed at it, unable to hold back the tears. It was a great time to realize just how much I wanted to live.

"Please don't hurt me." I managed to force out and Charm reared back as if I'd slapped him.

"You think I brought you out here to hurt you? Jesus." He ran a hand roughly over his face. "I just wanted to show you something. Come. Sit."

He extended his arm and I reluctantly placed my hand in his as he pulled me up onto the ledge. We sat on the cold stones overlooking the darkness. When he wasn't looking, I dried my tears on the sleeve of the sweatshirt he'd loaned me.

"Do you drink coffee?"

Caught off guard, I stuttered, "I-I-I used to...before—"

He interrupted, saving me from having to explain that once I'd found cocaine, I'd forgotten about my other vices. "I'll be right back. Stay there."

I nodded and picked at my fingernails. I still didn't know why we were sitting outside in the dark, but if he wanted me to stay on this rock, I'd do it.

He came back a few minutes later, carrying an armful of things and had me stand up while he spread a blanket down, before handing me a travel mug of hot coffee. The steam wafted up, hitting my nostrils, and I groaned in pleasure.

The sky had lightened just enough for me to see the strange look he was giving me. "You alright?"

God, he must've thought I was a complete basket case. "Yeah, it's just been so long since I had coffee. I forgot how much I loved even just the smell of it."

He took a sip from his own mug and looked out over the ledge, before pointing off in the distance. "Watch. Just keep your eyes focused back in this direction."

As if he planned it, the sky began to turn different shades of purple and pink. He'd woken me up to watch the sunrise. I couldn't remember the last time I'd taken the time to watch a sunrise or sunset.

The sky gradually lightened with orange streaks and then there it was. A burst of light broke through the darkness, illuminating the beauty surrounding us. I closed my eyes and let it warm my face, tears sliding silently down my cheeks. It was stunning. When I opened them again, Charm was watching me.

"Are you having cravings?"

I kept my eyes on the sky as I answered him. "A little, but I think I've gotten through the worst of it."

Please let me stay.

Please let me stay.

He nodded, seemingly pleased by my answer. "You feel like you need a fix, come to me or one of the guys."

Wait—what?

I stared at him in confusion. "And do what exactly?"

He seemed to catch the implication of his own words and his mouth tightened into a flat line. "I just meant that one of us can help you through it. Redirect your focus—take your mind off of it. Shit. You know what I'm trying to say."

For some reason, the more agitated Charm got, the more amused I became. I tried and failed to hide the smile on my face. "So, if I feel like I want a hit of coke, I should find one of the bikers to sleep with? Is that right?"

He growled and stood up abruptly. "No—fuck. I just meant you might want someone to talk to—keep you like accountable or somethin'. I'm gonna let you stay. I expect you to hold up your end of the bargain though—cooking and cleaning. Are we cl—"

I ignored the pain in my side and threw myself into him, wrapping my arms around his massive chest. "Thank you! I won't let you down, I promise. This is going to be a good thing. You'll see."

I was rambling...like usual, and Charm stiffened under my arms before pulling away. "Whatever—don't you have shit to clean?"

I nodded. "I do. And don't worry, if I feel like I need a fix, I'll find a biker to help me 'work through it.' Is that right?"

I had to have a screw loose.

Who messed with the guy who'd just offered her refuge?

This chick, obviously.

"Jesus Christ. I'm regretting this already." He stormed off the ledge and back toward the house as I rolled to my uninjured side, laughing until tears flowed down my face.

———

I could do this.

I'd made it through AP Calculus my sophomore year of high school. This was going to be a cake walk compared to that.

I pulled the rubber gloves back up to my elbows and forced the bathroom door open again.

Nope.

I couldn't do it. I was going to have to break my promise to Charm.

These men were disgusting. So far, Rooster's room was the only one that hadn't left me dry heaving in the hallway and I still had two more rooms to finish after this one. Mine and Charm's. At least I knew that one of those would be simple.

I took in the piles of used Kleenex covering the bathroom counter and floor. Looked like I'd made it to Sneezy's room, and the man apparently wasn't familiar with the concept of wastebaskets. I swept the tissues off the counter and into the large black trash bag at my feet.

Once that was completed, I cleaned the mirror and bleached the countertop. I took my time sanitizing everything; avoiding the toilet for as long as possible. It was no wonder they lived alone—I was willing to bet that even club whores had some standards.

With the rest of the bathroom gleaming, I reluctantly turned my attention back to the toilet and wielded the toilet brush as if it was a weapon before taking a tentative step forward. The thing probably hadn't been cleaned since it was installed.

There was something black on the seat and once I got closer, I realized it was a hair.

I tried telling myself it probably fell from someone's head and not their—

Nope.

I was going to vomit. My eyes watered and I began gagging. It took several deep breathing exercises and a prayer to any god that would hear me before I felt like I was in control again.

I poured a generous helping of bleach over the entire tank, praying that it would kill all the bacteria that was undoubtedly living on it. It took me three tries, with breaks to step outside the room and gag, but I finally managed to get the damn thing clean.

I mopped and vacuumed before moving down to the end of the hall. Checking my watch, I saw that I had time to clean one more room before I needed to get dinner going. I'd mistakenly thought that I'd just reheat the chicken pot pie from last night, but the bikers devoured every bit of it at lunch, leaving me with no choice but to cook something else.

No big deal.

I'd only made my first meal yesterday.

How hard could another one be?

I decided to leave my room for the next day and just get Charm's done. I expected it to be locked, but the silver handle turned easily in my hand and I pushed the cleaning cart inside with only the smallest sense that I was intruding. It smelled faintly of leather and smoke, I noted, as I flipped on the light switch. The bed was already made up and everything appeared to be in its place.

I took my dust cloth and wiped down the dressers and nightstand anyway. It took me less than five minutes. Whereas the other bikers had multiple picture frames of what I could only assume were there families, Charm had one. One picture in the entire room; a picture of him and a woman, resting on his nightstand.

They had their arms around each other and he was smiling— making him almost unrecognizable. The girl was beautiful with dark blue eyes and jet-black hair.

I risked a quick glance at the door before easing the top drawer of the nightstand open. I was just going to see if he had any other pictures hidden away. It was crazy, but suddenly, a small part of me needed to know more about this woman.

For instance, where was she?

The drawer was unassuming enough. There were several hastily scrawled notes left on worn pieces of paper, but nothing that caught my eye. I was just about to slide it closed when I noticed the edge of a leather book peeking out from under the papers.

I debated briefly on whether to leave it and walk away, but curiosity won in the end. It was old; the spine had vertical cracks in it and the brown leather was worn and faded. I flipped to the first page and began reading.

"What'd I tell you about bringing strays back here? Was I not clear on that?" His voice sent a tremor of fear through me, but I refused to cower in front of him.

I'd known that it was stupid to think that I could keep a puppy hidden from him. The grounds around here were never ending, but there always seemed to be someone watching. Someone just waiting to bust me doing something wrong.

The poor mutt had wandered into the grocery store with its eyes matted shut and green gunk caked all over its face. The club whore that brought me was distracted with shooting up on the side of a nearby building, so I grabbed the puppy and hid him under my jacket. It was freezing and I figured he wouldn't last another night.

When I got back to the clubhouse, I found her sitting on an old tire, staring off into space. She'd claimed to be daydreaming, but my dreams never left me looking scared. I dragged her out to the old barn and showed her what I'd gotten for us. With a little bit of digging, I found an old heating lamp and some blankets so the little guy was snuggled in nice and tight.

"He's real small now, but I swiped a couple cans of dog food so we can fatten him up."

Her eyes had widened before she dropped to her knees in front of him.

Her small hands cupped the puppy's body as she cradled him to her chest, rocking him like he was a baby.

I'd wanted to think that I'd saved him that night, but she had. One of the club whores had said that nothing was better than a woman's touch, but I don't think she was meaning it like that. I never bothered to remember their names; they never stuck around long enough for it to matter.

She'd been right about one thing though—my girl had something I didn't and it had kept Bones alive.

That was what she'd insisted we name him because he was all skin and bones when we got him. AJ followed us one day and demanded to be allowed a turn to take care of Bones too.

His hair always stuck out in every different direction like it had never seen a hairbrush and I teased that he looked like a rooster. He was always up at the crack of dawn too; his loud voice echoing off the walls of the clubhouse, waking everyone within a five-mile radius. Luck would grumble that he was going to build onto the edge of the property and throw all of us kids over there, but he hadn't made good on that promise yet.

It wasn't long before taking care of Bones had become an inside operation with us kids—even Matt showed up to help. He never spoke a word; his dad said it was because he was as dumb as his bitch of a mother, but I never saw it like that. He was quiet, but he was far from stupid. He'd write out questions to us on the dirt floor of the old barn and seemed to understand everything that was going on. There was just something in his eyes. You could tell a lot about a person just by looking into their eyes.

Rocky had tried to help, but we figured out really quick that he's allergic to dogs. He's allergic to everything. She gave him another task after he covered Bones in his snot.

Vic stole some medical supplies from the basement and managed to get Bones' eyes completely cleared up. "I'm gonna be a veterinarian, so I need lots of practice. Bonesy, you'll be my first patient."

Bones had just stared up at him, trusting that Vic knew what he was doing. And we had. Well, we'd figured most of it out along the way. She made sure that we all had a shift on the schedule she'd made—even convinced some of the older guys to help out when we couldn't.

Billy complained every time he had to help, but he kept showing up, so it

couldn't have been that bad. His twin, Bobby, showed up every day though—
sometimes, even twice a day. They were nothing alike; some days I wondered
if they'd gotten mixed up at the hospital.

All of us had worked together to get Bones healthy and now, six months
later, we'd been busted. Luck didn't tolerate strays of any kind. As I faced
him, I could only hope that he'd let me take Bones back to town. Miss Pearl
would keep him for us; I just knew it.

I nodded. "You told me, sir. I found him and he was sick. I thought I could
get him better and then take him into town to sell. Maybe earn some money."

I hadn't thought about doing that once, but Luck always seemed to be
pleased when I said I was going to make money.

His eyes suddenly looked sad and I became alert. "I'm sorry I didn't give
you a chance to explain. I should've known you would've had a plan; you're
not such a little kid anymore. You're turning into a man."

My stomach started to hurt as I asked, "Where's Bones?"

He shook his head and pointed up above me.

Into the trees.

"I was going to teach you a lesson. Seems like you've taught me one
though." He left me standing there, staring up to where my dog—our dog—
had been strung up and shot like a criminal. I angrily swiped tears from my
face.

I had to get him down.

Before she saw him like this.

I closed the book and replaced it, suddenly regretting ever picking it
up in the first place. Luck, whoever he was, had killed their dog. I
shouldn't have pried. Now, I was left with a sick feeling in the pit of
my stomach and an unhealthy suspicion that at least a few of the men
had chosen their road names after a stroll down the cereal aisle at the
grocery store.

What was I expecting?

That Charm would've written about the girl who sat by him in
class or what his dreams for the future were?

I was just contemplating who *she* could've been when the door handle began to turn and I immediately rushed into the bathroom where I began throwing cleaning products around, trying to mask what I'd been doing.

Charm froze when he saw me. "What are you doing in here?"

I pointed down at the bottle of glass cleaner as if it was suddenly going to speak up and save me the trouble. "I—you said—I—the door was unlocked."

The corner of his mouth turned up and he crossed his arms over his broad chest. "You came in because the door was unlocked?"

I nodded and then shook my head. "No—well, yes. You wanted me to clean and the door was unlocked, so I assumed you wanted your room done too."

I cleared my throat and looked down at the tile floor, afraid he'd see the truth written on my face.

I know about Bones.

And I'm so sorry.

"Okay then. Well, don't let me stop you. Continue." He went over to a desk in the corner of the room and sat down with his back to me and I fought the urge to go over and hug him.

Instead, with shaking hands, I began spraying down the mirror. His room was probably the cleanest of them all—it looked like he'd had someone come in this morning. He was probably one of those people that cleaned up their hotel room too.

"Hello?"

I jumped at the sound of Charm's voice in the other room, knocking over the roll of paper towels in the process.

"Yeah? You do? No, I'm not surprised. I just didn't expect an answer so soon. It's tonight—send three of yours and I'll bring three of mine. We can work out the details of that later."

I wiped down the counters, trying to do it as quietly as possible so I could hear his side of the phone conversation. I wondered what it was they were into—*was it drugs or weapons?*

"I'm glad you decided to come around. It's a good arrangement."

Maybe both.

This was good. I was focusing on the club's activities and not on the fact that they'd adopted a puppy and nursed it back to health only to have him ripped from them.

I wondered what happened to the guys who helped him. Had they moved away and left him to take over the club? Did he still see them when he met up with the girl from the picture? Obviously, they meant something to him. I knew that just from the way he wrote about them.

"Neve."

Neve?

Like some guy would ever write in his diary about me.

I wondered if men called them diaries—probably journals. It sounded manlier.

"Neve?"

Charm was standing in the doorway when I looked up and I ended up throwing the sponge in my hand at him before jumping back in fright.

He knew.

He probably dusted it for fingerprints while I was lost in thought and—no, that was ridiculous. He'd probably just read my mind. That seemed more plausible.

"Y-you scared me." I clutched my chest and cowered in the corner.

His eyes narrowed. "You enjoy listening in on other people's conversations?"

I shook my head. "No. I wasn't. Just cleaning—see?" I grabbed the bleach spray as if to prove a point.

"I think it's time for you to start dinner. You can finish tomorrow."

I nodded and began gathering everything up. "I'll um, I'll just be downstairs."

He stepped back to let me through. "You might wanna pick up the pace, Sweetheart. You'll never get this place cleaned at the rate you're going."

He slammed the door shut behind me and I couldn't resist turning around and giving it both middle fingers.

Asshole.

11

CHARM

"Please don't hurt me."

That one sentence was all it took. I'd gone to bed convinced that I'd made the right decision, only to wake up in the middle of the night, feeling like the world's biggest asshole.

So, I dragged her out of bed to watch the sunrise. By all rights, she should've been on her way to a bus station by now, but something happened. We'd just made it to the ledge when I realized that she thought I was going to kill her. She'd cowered as if expecting me to hit her. In that moment, it was no longer her in front of me.

It was Raegan.

When she hugged me, it had taken everything in me not to throw my arms around her and cry like a pussy. I would've given anything to have another moment like that, so I made a selfish decision. I wanted her to stay; if for nothing else other than the glimpses I got of the woman I loved. Maybe she was just another junkie and god knew those were a dime a dozen, but I suddenly felt like I'd been given a second chance. A way to set things right.

Something's shifted and while I can't quite put my finger on it, I know that I never want her to feel that kind of fear again.

She's defenseless.

I've told myself that repeatedly today, but I can't help but think it's the other way around.

*T*he men went quiet as she placed a large bowl of spaghetti in the center of the long table. Several strands of hair slipped free from her hair tie, covering her face as she leaned down and scooped some out into a bowl. She walked over and placed it in front of me with a small smile.

My chest tightened. *The resemblance was uncanny.*

The hair.

The eyes.

I'd seen it this morning as we watched the sun rise.

I'd questioned my decision to take her out to the ledge right up until I watched her entire body shift into a state of peace as the light hit her face.

I obviously couldn't ever do it again.

The hug had caught me off guard and with the similarities, I was liable to do something stupid. Like let her hold onto me until she was good and sober.

I glared at her until the smile faded and she disappeared back into the kitchen—as if the resemblance was something she had control over. The others praised the food before every head turned toward the head of the table, obviously awaiting my verdict.

I stabbed it with a fork, taking my time to chew and swallow. "It's edible. Eat up. We've got church."

Up until this afternoon, I'd believed that she was just another lost junkie, but I knew for a fact that she'd been listening in on my conversation with Blade, which only raised my suspicions.

What if she was running from another club?

It was strange. We hadn't had the support of another club in years, but then she showed up and suddenly I had MCs reaching out to pledge their support. Blade's MC had been heavy into running drugs, but had recently looked into expanding into weapons. Instead of declaring war against us for the territory, he'd suggested a partnership.

Back when Luck ran things, the Hell's Horsemen MC had been an equal partner, an ally. Then, they'd up and disappeared not long after I took over. However, word on the street lately was that they'd made some bad deals and were looking to work with another MC.

Money I had. Well, at least enough to keep my club.

What I needed were numbers.

Shit like this didn't just happen.

I felt like she was behind it all.

I pushed thoughts of her aside and focused on what was important. Working with Blade's club.

It was time for Scarred Savages to rise up again.

12

NEVE

There was a light tap on my shoulder, but I rolled away from it.

"No. Five more minutes."

The tap came again and I reluctantly opened my eyes to see Joker standing at the side of my bed. He brought his hand up and tapped it against his lips.

Food.

I'd been so tired after cleaning and cooking, that I left the men to it and came upstairs to crash. I couldn't even think about food after the things that I'd encountered in their rooms.

I rubbed my eyes and pushed myself up into a sitting position. There was still enough early evening light coming in that I didn't need to turn on a lamp. Joker smiled pleasantly at me before bending down to retrieve a small tray containing a cup of broth and some crackers.

I must've been moving up in the world if Charm was allowing me to have crackers. I held my hand to my mouth and brought it down to the open palm of my other hand, thanking him for bringing it up to me.

He set the tray down and shook his head before signing 'thank you' to me. Sensing my confusion. He held his left hand up and quickly swiped his right hand across it three times.

Cleaning.

He was thanking me for cleaning.

I wanted to hug him in that moment—never mind that I'd come very close to being violently ill while cleaning his room. His face reflected nothing but gratitude and it touched me.

His eyes moved down and widened in alarm and I followed his gaze, realizing that my stitches must've reopened at some point while I was sleeping. Blood soaked through my shirt and into the sheets.

Joker held his hand up and ran out before I could convince him that I was okay, returning with Doc a few moments later.

"Let's see what's happened." He removed the bandages and cursed. "I told him it was too much for you."

I placed my hand on his arm. "I'm peachy. I can handle it."

Joker shook his head and left the room again. This time he came back with Charm in tow. I groaned and placed my head in my hands. "I said I was okay."

Doc pressed against my side and I yelped. "Yeah, you sound like you're well on your way to being fully recovered, Neve."

Charm moved around the bed and leaned over Doc's shoulder to get a better look, leaving me feeling extremely exposed with him standing inches away, breathing on me.

Doc pointed down at something. "See that? The stitches tore away. And this is worrying." He dug his finger in again and I bit down on my lip to keep from crying out.

Charm reached out and touched the skin around the wound. "It's infected."

I took a deep breath. "I—I'm perfectly fine. I just need to sleep and I'll be good as new by tomorrow."

Both men gave me incredulous looks as Joker shook his head near the foot of the bed, obviously in agreement with them.

"Neve, your body isn't healing as well as it should. I'd like to take you downstairs and get you started on some IV antibiotics…drain it and then stitch everything back up."

I tried to sit up, but Charm pushed my shoulders back down on the bed. "Will I have to be tied down again? I don't want to stay down there. Please." He couldn't know, but being down in the basement alone wasn't exactly high up on my list of experiences to repeat.

One night I'd dreamt that Clint came through the door. I'd woken up with my throat on fire, half convinced that I'd been choked again. My body shuddered at the memory.

Charm looked over at Doc. "Why don't we bring it up here. She's obviously not in any shape to make the trip downstairs again."

Doc nodded and looked over at Joker. "Can you help me get what I need?" Joker nodded happily and gave me a thumb's up on his way out.

Once the men left, Charm looked back down at me. "Is there anyone you need to get in touch with?"

I thought about it. The cell phone I had before coming here only worked when we'd paid the internet bill. It didn't have a data plan or anything; just wi-fi only. Even if I did have it, there was no one. No one who would miss my presence—no one who would worry over my disappearance.

I laughed weakly, shaking off the negative thoughts. "It's just a little infection. I'm not dying, man."

Charm's jaw ticked and he held my gaze for a moment longer than necessary. "Then you shouldn't have any trouble holding up your end of the bargain."

He looked like he wanted to say more, but instead, stalked out of the room.

I sighed and leaned back against the pillows. I probably should've milked this long enough to get out of cooking and cleaning—at least for tomorrow, but there was something about Charm.

I knew he expected me to fail—to relapse and ruin everything. Something about knowing that made me want to prove him wrong.

I wanted him to have to eat his words.

I needed him to...because I didn't have a plan B. This had to work out until I could figure out what to do with my life.

Obviously, going back to Clint was not an option. And my parents...I couldn't think about that right now.

I was going to have to make this biker my friend.

End of story.

I woke with a start, my body coated in a fine sheen of sweat and I couldn't tell if it was the sound of motorcycles or the nightmare that had pulled me back to consciousness. I lay still and listened as the rumble from the bikes gradually faded into white noise.

I wanted to go back to sleep, but my mind was restless.

I couldn't stay cooped up in this room, regardless of what Doc recommended. The IV tubing ran from my hand up to an almost empty bag. Trying not to cause any damage, I pulled off the tape and gently removed the needle, before slipping out of bed.

I pulled on the sweatshirt that Charm had loaned me the day before and my shoes before creeping silently down the hallway. I felt like a felon breaking out of prison, alternating between elation to be out of my room and an intense fear of being discovered.

Once outside, I leaned against the side of the lodge and breathed a sigh of relief. The crickets chirped, but otherwise, everything remained still. I realized three steps into my journey that I didn't have a flashlight or any way of knowing if I was headed in the correct direction.

I kept picturing myself reaching the stone ledge and walking right off of it because I was flying blind.

Just in case, I kept my hands outstretched in front of me as I continued taking cautious steps forward. Just when I was convinced that I was going in the wrong direction, I saw a small light glowing up ahead. I took another couple of steps forward and the light swung around in my direction. It was the glowing ember from a cigarette. I tried to back away, but the person moved too quickly.

"Running away already?"

I didn't recognize the voice, but refused to cower. I held my chin high, even though I knew that he couldn't see me. "I needed some fresh air."

The ember bobbed up and down as the man nodded. "Get that way sometimes myself. Twitch." A hand bumped mine and I instinctively shook it.

"Neve."

"Heard a lot about you—got Charm all twisted, that's for sure." He laughed as he said it, even as I cringed. I guess it was no secret that their Prez was not a big fan of mine.

I sighed. "Yeah. In my defense, I never asked to be rescued though."

Twitch laughed again before blowing out a ring of smoke that was just becoming visible in the early morning light. "You're alright with me, kid." He gestured back toward the ledge. "Care to sit?"

I was going to decline when I realized that I had nowhere else to go. "Sure."

He took my hand and led me up onto the rock where we sat quietly, waiting on the sun to make an appearance.

"Do you come out here often?"

He took another slow drag before replying. "Every once in a while. Seeing the sun rise—it's a nice reminder."

The sky lightened a little more and I could see that his hands were trembling. I pressed. "A reminder of what?"

He looked out over the ledge. "That you made it. You get another chance—a chance to do things right."

I was taken aback. His response was unexpected, to say the least. "You've made a lot of mistakes?"

Twitch stubbed the cigarette out on the sole of his boot before tossing it into a small metal bucket near the corner of the ledge. He caught my stare. "Fires. If you're gonna light up, make sure to throw the butts into one of these metal bins or else the whole fucking forest'll go up."

I nodded and waited for him to elaborate on his cryptic 'second chance' message, while also appreciating his Smokey Bear mindset. He went back to staring off into the distance though, so I cleared my throat. "Um, have you made a lot of mistakes?"

He blinked and then looked back over, as if just remembering I was still here. "Kid, you and me? We're cut from the same cloth. The greatest enemy we'll ever face is ourselves—" He stopped talking and eyed me closer before amending, "Well, most of the time our greatest enemy is staring at us in the mirror."

It hit too close to home, leaving me defensive. "How are we the same?"

He gestured between us. "Kid, a user can spot another user from a mile away. It's like a fucking neon sign flashing over your head."

I mulled over his words while chewing on my lower lip. To be honest, his words stung a bit. I knew that I hadn't even been sober a full week, but I really felt like I already looked different—healthier.

Twitch reached over and patted my hand gently. "Don't take it personally, kid. I've fallen off the wagon more times than I can count. What matters is that I've woken up the morning after, watched the sunrise, and got my ass back on it."

I shook my head confidently, even as my teeth continued to work on my lip. "I'm not going to fall off. That's not an option for me."

He laughed so hard that he had to lean over and clutch his thighs. "That's a good one, kid. Jesus, you almost had me goin' for a second there. I hope, for your sake, that you're right. You better be prepared for when the shit hits the fan though."

I shook my head again, and reiterated, this time with a little more anger. "No. I refuse to fail. He's expecting that. I'm going to prove him…and you wrong."

He pulled the pack of cigarettes from his pocket and lit up another one before offering the pack to me. I shook my head and he took a couple of drags before responding. "Who's expecting you to fail? And what was your poison? That's telling, you know."

I pulled the sleeves of the sweatshirt down until they covered my hands, stalling. I hadn't meant to tell him about my plan to prove Charm wrong. "Uh…it was coke."

He nodded slowly. "And the man expecting you to fail?"

"Charm. He doesn't want me here, but I don't have anywhere else to go. I have to make this work. My boyf—well, ex-boyfriend tried to kill me and my parents are—" My words were cut off by a strangled sob and it took me a minute to regain my composure. "I—I need this to work."

The sun began to rise and conversation between the two of us stopped momentarily. I focused all of my energy on the pink and purple sky; closing my eyes briefly as the sun crested, blinding me.

Twitch took my hand in his and my eyes fluttered open. "Have you taken the time to work through those emotions while sober, kid?"

I blinked against the tears and looked away, but he persisted. "If you're set on proving the asshole wrong and not relapsing, you need to take the time to properly grieve your dead. Work through the shit, so you can move on."

He was right.

I knew it.

I just couldn't bear to think of that night.

13

NEVE

One week later...

$\mathcal{I}$ waited until the last of the motorcycles faded from view. They were gone for the day, leaving me to complete my chores in peace. My side appeared to be healing the way Doc wanted and I'd been given the okay to resume cooking and cleaning.

Charm always left two prospects behind to guard the clubhouse while also watching me closely, as if I was in any sort of shape to run away. Axel was nice enough; the other guy hadn't spoken a word to me since I arrived and responded to any of my questions with grunts.

Once I was sure that the two of them were preoccupied with biker things, I pulled my hair back into a high ponytail and threw on what was quickly becoming my favorite outfit— Charm's sweatshirt and a pair of black sweatpants. I couldn't seem to stay warm even though it was the middle of July. I just didn't have enough body-fat, no matter how much broth and *Ensure* I drank.

Doc had assured me that I would put weight back on in time; I'd just been hopeful that it would've been a faster process.

I hurriedly cleaned the rooms, finding that I didn't need to pause for breaks as often. As often—meaning that these men were surprisingly still capable of destroying bedrooms and bathrooms in less than twenty-four hours.

Amongst the mound of tissues on the dresser in PD's room, were several condom wrappers and I stared in confusion at them for far longer than was necessary.

"There are no women here!" I exclaimed with a small giggle. "But, at least we're all practicing safe sex."

I had to be losing my head. Charm had specifically stated that they weren't that kind of club, hadn't he?

Did the whores just show up on specific nights?

I tried not to dwell on the fact that I would've heard someone having sex from down the hall and pushed on until I got to Charm's room.

I'd sworn I wouldn't look again, but after a cursory sweep with the duster, I found myself digging through the top drawer of his night-stand and sinking down to the carpet, needing answers.

Matt's old man broke his arm today. Then, he took him out to one of the cabins back in the woods and left him there. Said he could come back when he learned how to use his voice, like a man. Us kids were told to not even think about helping him get food or water either.

She came to me in the middle of the night, shining a small flashlight in my face. "We can't leave him to die out there. You and I both know that he ain't ever gonna be able to talk."

I tried to tell her all the reasons we couldn't when she said, "Please. We already lost Bones. I can't lose Matty too."

I hadn't been able to tell her about what really happened to Bones. Instead, I told her that he got off his rope and ran away. She still looked for him every day and often sighed that she hoped someone nice had found him.

I knew she was right, so we waited until the bikers left the next day before hitching a ride into town for supplies. As usual, the other guys caught up with us when they figured out our plan. She disappeared while we snagged food and water, but showed back up when it was time to leave.

By the time we got out to him, Matt was rocking in a corner, his broken arm clutched to his chest. Sweat ran down his face even though the room was freezing. Vic felt his head and nodded. "He's got a fever—probably from infection. I'm going to have to reset the bones."

Most kids wouldn't have known the first thing about fixing broken bones. Most kids weren't us though.

Vic set it while AJ and I held him down.

If ever there was a time for Matt to speak, it would've been now. His mouth fell open and he tried to fight us, but no sound came out. I knew then that it wasn't a matter of him not wanting to talk. His voice just didn't work. Eventually, he passed out from the pain and Vic got it done.

Rocky showed up with a syringe and proceeded to inject antibiotics into him after disinfecting the skin around his hip. "What? I've seen my ma shoot up hundreds of times," he'd explained as we all stared at him in awe.

Vic stepped back and looked Matt over. "I wrapped it the best I could, but his arm isn't going to be perfect. He went too long with it broken."

Bobby and Billy carried him over to an old bed in the corner and wrapped him in blankets. I thought we were ready to leave him for a little while when she went over and sat next to him, patting his hair until his eyes opened.

"Matty, I got us another book at the library. You wanna read it with me?"

He nodded, but winced when he tried to move. We could've stolen pain medicine, but they would've found us out for sure then. She climbed under the blankets and opened to the first page.

"Today, we're going to do an easy one. Thank you." She put one hand up to her mouth and then down to rest on the palm of her other hand. "Now, don't use your bad arm. Just do what you can."

He did exactly as she showed him as we all stood along the wall like some dummies. She'd been teaching him sign language. While we'd all been fine with messages scribbled in the dirt or written on scraps of paper, she'd wanted him to communicate with us.

"Now, don't y'all go running off. I'm gonna teach you next."

It was stupid, but I wanted to do whatever she needed. She kept us all together and made things seem okay.

I brought my hand to my mouth to stifle my sobs. While I was still no closer to finding out the woman's identity, I now knew one of the men's identities.

Joker was Matt—it had to be. I wasn't sure how I'd missed it before. I'd wondered how someone who lived like he did had learned sign language. It was the elusive *she*.

If she and the woman in the picture were one and the same, I couldn't imagine Charm ever letting her go. He was gone a lot, sometimes on his own. It wasn't too far-fetched to think that he would've gotten her away from the club.

I was also grateful that he hadn't made me stay out in one of those cabins.

I wouldn't have lasted a night.

"Neve!" The prospect, Axel, called up the stairs. "Are you finished cleaning yet?"

I slid the book back under the papers and straightened up just as he came into the room.

"Hey, I just finished. What's next on the agenda?" My heart beat wildly in my chest, leaving me lightheaded from the exertion.

He gave me an odd look. "Uh, I'm just supposed to make sure you don't get into trouble."

Right.

I knew that. I dutifully followed him back downstairs, doing my best to push away thoughts of little boys with broken arms.

What in the hell was wrong with me?

When Charm hadn't shown for dinner, I'd casually asked if I

should save a plate for him. Doc informed me that he'd left on club business and that should've been the end of it.

Except it wasn't.

I'd tried to fall asleep. I'd counted sheep...motorcycles...you name it. It didn't work. My mind had existed in this limbo of using and trying to quit that it hadn't considered much else in quite some time. There'd been nothing to challenge it, until Charm's journal.

As much as I didn't want to, I couldn't stop thinking about it. I needed the identity of mystery girl almost as much as I needed my next breath.

To what end, I still didn't know.

So, instead of fighting it, I picked the lock on Charm's bedroom door—a little something I'd learned from Clint—and snatched the book before heading downstairs. The place was quiet; once again, nothing like what a motorcycle club should be.

I passed by the large stone fireplace, wanting nothing more than to curl up beside it, but the chances of being caught were too high. Instead, I went into Charm's study and turned on the small desk lamp before sinking into his chair, the book cradled in my hands reverently.

I skipped ahead to where they were older.

I'd gone in there ready to throw her ass to the wolves, but then she looked up at me with those damn doe eyes and every ounce of determination fell away.

"Look at you, my knight in shining armor." Her eyes sparkled with amusement. It was the first bit of life I'd seen from her in longer than I could remember.

I blew on the soup and pressed another spoonful to her lips. "Just drink this. It'll help calm your stomach." She'd been vomiting more frequently and I knew it wasn't some fluke. I'd let her keep her secret for a little while longer though.

I wanted to be excited, but given the circumstances, wary hope was all I could manage. Six months ago, I would've been over the moon. Now, I was just scared. For all of us.

She reached up and cupped my face in her hand. "Why are you so good? Look at me, I'm a mess." When she smiled, the skin stretched tight over the bones in her face, further revealing how much weight she'd lost over the past few months.

She'd become a walking skeleton.

I brushed her thin hair back and pressed a soft kiss to her forehead. "You're not a mess. You're perfect. You just need to eat a little more and then you'll be back to your old self."

She gave me another weak smile. "I think I'm starting to feel better already."

She wasn't.

I stopped when the lines began to blur from my tears.

She'd gotten sick—she'd also been pregnant. He hadn't come right out and said it, but it had been hinted at pretty strongly. Maybe she'd just had morning sickness—*but, that didn't explain the weight loss and thinning hair.*

And Charm had fed her broth...just like me. He'd even said something similar about it being easier on the stomach. At the time, I'd struggled to make sense of it. Now, I was just struggling to cope with the fact that his story might not have ended well; which devastated me.

I needed a happily ever after—I'd let mine slip away years ago and all but given up on anything working in my favor, but I'd wanted to believe that she and Charm had made it work.

Had he not only lost her, but his child as well?

Tears fell faster at the thought and I struggled to capture them all on the sleeves of my sweatshirt. Heavy bootsteps from the hallway had me shoving the book into the large front pocket of my shirt before feigning sleep. I worked to make my breaths slow and even as I heard the faint creak from the door opening.

"Neve?"

I made a show of blinking my eyes before looking around the room in confusion. "Charm? Where am I?"

He scratched at his chin, the suspicion never leaving his face. "You're in my office. Care to tell me why?"

I had no excuse and sleepwalking seemed a little too out there to be believable. I settled for a version of the truth instead. "I couldn't sleep. I thought I'd look around for something to read."

I decided to get up before he had the opportunity to think of any other questions regarding my nocturnal activities.

"Stay." He pointed at the chair and I reluctantly sat back down. "Were you crying?"

I shook my head. "No...must be something in the air that's irritating my eyes. Did you know that mold spores and grass allergies are high during the warm summer months? It's true. In the spring, you have trees pollinating, but that tends to lessen in the—"

Charm's eyes widened and he shook his head slowly, as if doing a double take. I tended to have that effect on people when I started one of my longwinded stories.

"What do you like to read?"

I opened my mouth to answer when I realized that I had no idea anymore. I settled for, "I read a lot of books on pathophysiology and neuroscience in school. I have to admit that I haven't read for pleasure in years though."

His face twisted up. "You read what now?"

I laughed. "C'mon, surely you're familiar with neuroscience?" At his blank expression, I elaborated, "The study of the brain? Pathophysiology is just the study of abnormalities associated with various diseases. It sounds lame, but to me it's fascinating."

A hint of pain flashed in his eyes and he stared down at the hardwood floor as I realized my mistake. I'd said diseases and unwittingly dredged up memories of his sick wife.

Charm finally looked up at me again. "That's some pretty highbrow reading material for a junkie. You sure you wouldn't prefer a book on the history of cocaine?"

His words were like a slap to the face and I angrily retorted, "You sure you wouldn't like a how-to manual for removing the stick that's wedged up your ass?"

I clapped a hand to my mouth, but the damage was done.

Instead of stalking from the room or knocking me on my ass,

Charm laughed. It was more frightening than the grim expression he normally wore. I didn't know if that laugh meant he found it funny or if he was amusedly thinking of ways to kill me.

Suddenly he stopped and I sat up straighter in the chair, silently awaiting my fate.

"Fair enough," he drawled. "Why don't you head upstairs and try to get some sleep, Neve. It's late."

I scurried around him and up to my room before he could change his mind. It wasn't until the pain in my side lessened and my breathing evened out again that I remembered I still had the journal and no way of getting it back into his room tonight.

14

CHARM

I ain't been to the city in over a year—never liked being in crowds.

Yet, here I was, walking down 16th Street like I did it all the time. It took three different stores, but I finally found one that carried some books she might like.

I got some strange looks when I sank down into one of their fancy leather chairs in the self-help section, but no one asked me to leave. I imagine it wasn't every day that a biker showed up requesting science textbooks.

So what if I'd pretended that they were for me?

People shouldn't judge books by their covers; especially when they worked in a goddamn bookstore.

I didn't have anywhere to be for another hour, so I settled in and began thumbing through them both. You know, just in case she wants to talk about her reading with someone.

"*R*ooster, you know that scientists can split the brain hemispheres and make them function without the other?"

He frowned and finished loading his saddle bag before responding, "Uh, can't say that I did. Why the fuck would they want to do that?"

To be honest, I hadn't gotten to that part of the book yet. I was a slow reader and only managed a few chapters before I had to head out to meet Blade.

I wasn't going to let Rooster know that though. "Oh, it's good research for stroke victims. They lose control over one part of the brain or some shit and the other could pick up like nothing happened."

"Is that what happened to you? You have a stroke? When the fuck did you start caring about science and research?"

I shrugged. "I don't. It's just good to read the news...stay on top of current events. You should try picking up more than a *Playboy*, asshole."

He leaned against his bike with a shit-eating grin. "Yeah, you're right. I'll go get me some learnin'...maybe run for public office next. Jesus, Charm, you had me going there for a second."

I laughed it off, but inside I was seething.

What was I doing?

Taking an interest in something she liked? Well, that wasn't exactly true. I'd found what I read fascinating and it made me think of Raegan. I wondered if she would've benefitted from research like that. All the notes I'd scrawled on the back of an envelope were just for me.

It had absolutely nothing to do with Neve.

15

NEVE

"Did you wash your hands?" The men at the table gave me puzzled looks, as if I was speaking a foreign language. As if we hadn't had this exact conversation every night for the past month. "Hands," I pressed. "You can't eat with dirty hands."

Rooster glanced down at his. "Mine aren't that bad."

I swatted his arm. "Up. All of you. No supper until you've washed up." I looked at the empty spots at the table as the men began standing. "Where are Charm, Gunner, and PD?"

Guardrail paused with his hand on the back of the chair. "Gone. It'll just be us."

I frowned, feeling let down for some inexplicable reason. This was the problem with reading the damn journal. I'd ignored reason and immersed myself in Charm's world, thinking I was going to gain insight into what made him tick. Instead, I found myself looking forward to seeing him at the end of the day. He'd make some insulting comment and I'd throw one right back at him.

I'd made him smile twice, so we were making progress.

Toward what I still wasn't quite sure. After what I read that night

97

in Charm's study, I'd gone back to the beginning, refusing to skip ahead again. Today's entry left me feeling even more confused than before though.

I caught her with Bobby today. They were out behind the old pumphouse. She claimed it was just an innocent kiss and that it didn't mean anything, but I didn't see it that way. Bobby and Billy both enlisted, and shockingly, the club allowed it. They even decided to throw them a farewell bash before they leave for boot camp tomorrow.

Unfortunately, Bobby was going to be sporting a nasty black eye for his first week.

The funny thing was that he didn't even fight back. He just took it like a man. Billy said that he'd deserved it and Bobby had agreed. We were good after that, but she swore in front of everyone that she hated me and would never speak to me again. The words were like a sucker punch to my gut.

AJ tried to reassure me that she didn't mean it, but I'd seen the hateful glint in her eyes. I bet she wished it was me shipping off to boot camp so that she could cozy up to Bobby without interference.

The club had the beer flowing and no one paid much attention as we helped ourselves to it. I was feeling a lot better about things after a few cups and was actually considering whether or not to take a club whore back to my room. I was angry and I wanted to take my frustrations out somewhere. Luck said those girls could take anything and would just keep coming back for more.

Thankfully, the decision was made for me. She got drunk and saved me from making a horrible decision. I made my way over to her and was immediately pelted in the face by a nearly full cup of beer before Bobby stepped in and offered to take her up to her room. She accepted his offer and flipped me off as he led her up to the clubhouse.

"There's always been this unspoken rule when it comes to her, but you know he loves her, right?" Billy observed as he handed me a towel. "You've got some shit to figure out while we're away."

I was losing her and I didn't know how to fix it.

She cheated on him and he'd made it apparent that he had wanted to cheat on her too. And Billy was absolutely Gunner—it just fit. I wondered if the cheating was why his twin was no longer around. Had he been sent overseas after boot camp? Had he died in war? It would certainly explain why Gunner was always in such a foul mood.

"Where'd they go? Will they be back later?"

Rooster called over the running water in the kitchen. "Club business, Darlin'. They won't be back for a few days."

One by one, the men washed up and then came back to the table. I sat morosely near the end and picked at my mashed potatoes, hoping that the club business had been important because mashing the potatoes by hand had done wonders for the pain in my side.

"Somethin' wrong, kid?" Twitch asked through a mouthful of food.

I shook my head. "Just tired. Eat up. I'm just going to head upstairs and get some sleep."

Doc's chair scraped loudly against the wood floor as he moved to stand up. "I'll come with you—I need to change your bandages and see if we should do another round of antibiotics."

I gave him a forced smile and headed toward the stairs with him right on my heels. Never mind that I was looking forward to some alone time. Time spent in a hot shower, weeping over the path my life had taken.

I still hadn't let myself dwell on Twitch's words. There was no way I was ready to face that yet. The journal had provided the perfect distraction. I would focus on the ghosts of Charm's past, while ignoring the demons from my own.

"Neve?"

I looked back at Doc before opening my bedroom door. "Hmm?"

The men got keys, while my room remained unlocked when I wasn't in there. I mean, it wasn't like I had anything of value, but it would've been nice to have the privacy regardless.

"I asked if you took it easy today. Did you feel any sharp pains?" His brow was furrowed in concern.

"No, Doc. I told you—I've been feeling much better lately."

He closed the bedroom door behind us and directed me to the bed.

"Let's get a look at it today. If the infection is gone, then we may be ready to remove the bandages. If it's not, I'm going to have to take you into the clinic in town. If we throw enough cash at them, they won't need your ID."

I lay back and lifted the edge of my shirt up. Doc's hands poked and prodded near the wound, but the pain was bearable compared to a month ago. "It's looking a lot better today. It's still leaking a little fluid, so I'm going to keep it covered for a few more days. You need to take it easy, but I think you're out of the woods."

"See, and I thought I was still very much in the woods." I deadpanned.

The corner of his mouth turned up in a smile. "She jokes. I gotta say, Neve. I prefer this side of you over the girl who told me I could go fuck myself with a hot poker while she was detoxing."

I winced. "Um, yeah. Sorry about that. I—"

He cut me off. "You don't owe me an apology. I'm sure I'll get fucked up in the near future and you can be the one to deal with me. Then, we'll call us even."

I smiled. "Sounds fair enough. So, have you always known that you wanted to be in medicine?"

Doc gave the stitches another check and began reapplying the bandages before answering, "Uh yeah, I guess so. Originally, I wanted to be a vet. I've always had a soft spot for animals."

I'd found Vic.

Before I could ask the questions that were swirling around in my head, there was a light knock at the door. He placed the last bandage and pulled my shirt back down as Rooster and Joker came in, holding a deck of cards.

"You up for a game?"

I studied his face with a frown. "I'm not playing strip poker with you, Rooster."

He glanced over at Joker. "I told you she wouldn't go for it. You're going to have to find another way to get her naked, bro."

Joker's eyes widened in shock and he began shaking his head 'no,' while signing wildly.

I laughed until tears ran from my eyes. "You didn't say it was for Joker. That changes things, doesn't it?"

I leaned forward and placed a kiss against the mute's cheek and he turned red from the top of his head down to his neck. All three of them stared at me strangely.

"What the actual hell just happened here? You'd go through with it for him, but not me?" Rooster complained.

I shrugged and took the cards from his hands. "You're too obvious about it, Rooster. Everything about you just screams, 'player.' You've got to work on that."

He nodded thoughtfully. "And how would I go about doing that?"

I took my time shuffling the deck. "Well, for starters, calling someone a 'club whore' after just meeting her is probably not the best way to get into her good graces—unless she is an actual club whore. Then, I don't know."

Joker ran a finger across his own throat and smiled, while Doc sat back in a chair and kicked his feet up on the bed. I pushed him off the bed and pointed to his boots. "No shoes on the furniture, Doc."

Rooster burst out in laughter. "Jesus, Darlin.' You're gonna have us all whipped into shape by the time Charm gets back, aren't ya?"

Doc grumbled, but began unlacing his boots and I hid a small smile as I began dealing cards.

'What are we playing?' signed Joker and I grinned wickedly.

"You boys ever hear of a little game called 'Go Fish?' I don't want to brag, but I'm pretty much the best at it."

––––––––––––

Five rounds later, the three men sat in their boxer briefs, glaring down at their cards. All three had the Scarred Savages emblem tattooed somewhere on their chests, and I wondered if it was a requirement when they patched in. Minus the hideous skull, their torsos were a colorful blend of ink.

Meanwhile, I sat comfortably on the bed, still fully dressed.

Should I have mentioned upfront that I had the memory of an elephant?

Maybe. I didn't let the guilt stop me though.

They were playing Strip Go Fish with the best here.

Joker held up four fingers and pointed at my deck and I kept my expression somber as I replied, "Go Fish."

This was a little too easy.

He frowned and picked up a card. When he did, I noticed his left arm bowed out near the wrist; a sign of a break that hadn't healed properly. I'd been correct—Joker and Matt were one and the same. I almost said something before remembering that there was no way for me to have known about things that happened to them when they were kids.

Rooster eyed me suspiciously over his cards. "Darlin', I'm thinkin' that a round of Strip Texas Hold'Em might wipe that smirk off your face. You do realize that if you win this hand, you're gonna have three naked bikers on your bed, right?"

My smile faded almost immediately. "I'm getting a little sleepy actually."

Joker's grin stretched almost to his ears and he shook his head.

I nodded again. "Yes—my side's hurting. I probably need to rest. Right, Doc?"

Doc placed his cards face down on the comforter and looked me over. "Nah... you've made it this far. You can get through another round." He tried and failed to hide a smirk.

They were enjoying this a lot more than they should've been.

Okay, I'd play their game. All I needed to do was lose this hand and then—then, I'd only be dealing with two naked bikers instead of three.

I suppressed a groan. *How did I not see that coming?*

My voice came out much higher than I wanted. "Could we- I mean, could we play for money?"

Rooster cocked his head to the side. "You got any money, Neve?"

I chewed on my lip. "Well, I could pay you back."

Doc shook his head. "Nope. No IOU's."

"Never mind then." I rearranged the two cards in my hands and refused to make eye contact with the guys.

Doc asked Rooster for Aces and laid down his hand with a big grin. "I'm out of cards. What does that mean again, Neve? It's been so long since I've done it."

I rolled my eyes. "It means I let you win, ya big jerk. I hope you're happy."

His grin widened. "Not as happy as you're about to be."

Rooster stood up and began working his boxers down.

"I—no, that's not necessary!" The glint of metal had me lowering my hands and leaning forward. "Is that a—"

Oh, it was. Rooster had his dick pierced.

"See somethin' you like, Darlin'?" It was his turn to smirk at me.

Joker hooked a thumb in the waistband of his and winked at me.

"Oh no, everyone keep your clothes on. The game's over—" I squeaked when he dropped them anyway.

Doc leaned back in his chair, shaking with laughter. I slapped his legs. "This is your fault."

He choked out, "Mine? You're the card shark here. This is all on you."

My cheeks burned and I tried to keep my gaze on the bedspread. "Are we done yet?"

Rooster answered. "Nope. You didn't take off anything. Way I see it, me and J will just stay like this until you do. Oh, and we get to pick what you remove."

I lifted my head with wide eyes. "Oh...so, I can't choose to take off a sock?"

The three of them shook their heads and looked me over. Joker held both of his hands just under his waist before curling them upward. My eyes followed his hands down, earning me yet another eyeful.

When Rooster and Doc looked to me for interpretation, I sighed, "He votes pants."

They nodded and replied at the same time. "Same."

I stood up and quickly shimmied out of my sweatpants. The room immediately fell silent and I realized they weren't all taken aback by my beauty.

No, they were seeing the burns and scars from the skin grafting for the first time. I'd gotten so caught up in the game that the truth of my past had slipped my mind. For the first time in a year, I forgot that I bore the marks of my sins for all the world to see.

"Jesus Christ." Rooster's hand came up, pushing the long hair back off of his forehead.

Joker looked away and Doc stood frozen, his eyes laser-focused on my thighs. "Who did this to you, Neve?"

I blinked rapidly and looked up at the ceiling before answering softly, "Can we be done now?"

The men were in various stages of dressing when I worked up the courage to look down. Doc handed me my pants and I wordlessly slid them back on.

"Neve." Rooster leaned down into my line of vision. "You tell us who did this and he's dead. Simple as that. You're under the club's protection now."

Joker took his right index finger and ran it under the palm of his left hand.

Kill.

I was speechless.

The two of them embraced me before leaving and I turned to Doc. "I think I know of a way you could help me."

"Anything you need; it's yours." Doc leaned in and I told him my plan. He gave me several puzzled looks. "You're sure? And that'll help you?"

I nodded confidently before sending him out. Then I shut off the lights and lay down. The clock illuminated the room, reminding me that I was going to have to be up in just a few short hours.

My mind was restless though. I tried counting sheep, but they kept turning into bikers jumping over fences. I wanted to shut my brain off, if only for an hour or two, but it was futile.

I didn't even know these men and they were willing to risk their lives for me. It was disconcerting. The last time someone had vowed to protect me, I just ended up hurting them.

I was no good to anyone.

I rolled over to my good side and tried to relax. Twenty minutes later, I knew that I was up for the day, and rolled out of bed. I put on my sweatshirt and headed downstairs, suddenly in need of some fresh air.

I grabbed the flashlight sitting on the porch near the back door with a smile. Twitch had left it the day after my run-in with him. Poor guy was trying to avoid a fright-induced heart attack no doubt.

I clicked the light on and headed down the path toward the ledge. I found that I knew exactly where to go this time and breathed a small sigh of relief when I saw that the spot was empty. I needed to be alone with my thoughts for a while.

Twitch wanted me to confront my past...

Doc, Rooster, and Joker wanted me to name my abuser...

This.

All of it was why I'd avoided sobriety; because, when I was sober, terrible things happened. It was too much for one person to work through. So, I'd remained blissfully numb in a cocoon of coke.

I knew the men were right; it was time to deal with it—I was well overdue.

I closed my eyes and willed myself to go back to that night.

"I thought I'd find you out here." The male voice startled me out of my reverie and I swung the flashlight up, connecting with a face. He cursed and I realized who I'd just attacked.

"Charm?" I jumped up and began patting his face awkwardly.

*Make friends with him...*well, this was certainly not going according to plan. I'd just done the exact opposite by assaulting him.

He reached up and grabbed my hands, pulling them down. "What the fuck, Neve?"

I tried to move my hands back up to his cheek, but he held them pinned down near my waist. "I'm sorry—I wasn't expecting anyone. You weren't supposed to be back yet." I winced at the sharp pain in my side. "If it helps, I think I hurt myself just as much as I hurt you."

He led me back over the ledge and pushed me into a sitting position. "Let me look." He released his hold on me and his hands skimmed up my ribs. I bit down on my lip to keep myself quiet.

He pushed the sweatshirt and my t-shirt up, exposing the stab wound. "Can you manage to hold on to the flashlight or you gonna try to take me out again?"

"I can manage." My hands were shaking, but I held the flashlight in a death grip as he looked me over. His face was scruffier than the last time I saw him and, as I moved the flashlight slightly, I could see his cheek was rapidly swelling.

He reached up and held the end of it steady. "Looks like the wound is still closed. Maybe try and avoid attacking anyone else for a couple of days though."

He stood up and I pointed the flashlight at his head. "Hold still. Let me see your cheek."

He shrugged it off. "I'm good."

I bit back a smart-ass comment.

Be his friend.

I stood up on my tiptoes and cupped his chin in my hand, while inspecting the damage. There was a small jolt that I was absolutely going to blame on static electricity. "You're going to have a bruise. I'm really sorry."

I'd made a grave mistake coming out here; even bigger than reading the journal. Touching him made me wish for things that could never be. See, now I that I knew how fiercely he could love someone, I found myself wanting to be on the receiving end of it. I wanted him to look at me and see something other than a junkie.

Charm took a step back and I belatedly realized how we must've looked—with my hands on his face, it sent the wrong message. It was too intimate. This was quickly turning into a most uncomfortable situation.

I dropped my hands down to my sides, mumbled another apology, and went to sit back down on the ledge. To my surprise, he joined me.

"Your hands were cold." He kept his focus anywhere, but on me.

I pulled the sleeves down over my hands and apologized again.

"Stop doin' that." He grabbed the sleeves of my sweatshirt and pulled my hands free, before wrapping them up in his own. "Stop apologizing for everything."

Warmth spread throughout my body, leaving me off kilter. I

nodded. "Sor—" He glared at me again and I amended, "So, you're back early. Did it go well?"

He nodded. "I think it'll be a good partnership. How's it going here?" He continued to rub my hands in between his, even though they hadn't been cold for the past few minutes. If anything, they were growing sweaty from the contact.

"Things are excellent here—did you get your shipment that night?" I'd been struggling for a conversation topic, but even in the dim light, I could see his eyes as they turned thunderous.

"What do you know about that?" If a voice could come out sounding like a growl, then Charm had mastered it.

I swallowed and squeaked out, "Um, I may have overheard your phone conversation when I was cleaning your room that day."

He stiffened at my confession and released my hands, letting them fall back into my lap. "Anyone else you've shared that information with?"

I shook my head quickly. "No, I swear—in fact, I don't even know why I brought it up. I just wanted to make conversation."

I was waiting for him to stand up and throw me off the edge of the ledge, but instead he nodded slowly, as if calming himself back down.

Charm eyed me thoughtfully. "I got you something when I was out. Stay here."

He returned a few minutes later with a small package and thrust it into my hands. "Here. Open it."

"Okay." He held the flashlight as I tore at the cardboard to find *Pathophysiology: The Biologic Basis for Disease in Adults and Children* and *Tales from Both Sides of the Brain: A Life in Neuroscience*. My heart suddenly decided that it was participating in the 200m hurdles, leaping around in my chest as it raced toward the finish line.

"This is amazing, Charm. Really. Michael Gazzaniga. His studies on how separating the right and left brain—"

He cut in. "Would create two separate minds within the same head? Yeah, I read that. It actually creates a lot of contradictions within one person."

My mouth fell open. "How did—you read this?"

The flashlight bobbed up and down as he shrugged. "I read some of it. I take it you're familiar with his work though."

I began rambling on about my lifelong love of discovering how things worked, specifically the brain, while he lit up a cigar and blew smoke rings in the early morning light.

"Where are you from originally?"

I swallowed the saliva that had pooled in my mouth. "Um, Santa Cruz, California. I've lived in Colorado for the past four years though. What about you? You don't sound like you're from around here—"

Charm gave me an exasperated look. "It's Colorado, Sweetheart. No one sounds like they're from around here. What was your plan?"

When I gave him a confused look, he elaborated. "For your life— your goal."

I watched the sky turn all the familiar shades that indicated the sun was about to rise, but I didn't feel joy like I had the other times. "I would've been a doctor. Now, I'm just a nobody."

"Ain't no way you're a nobody. You woke up breathing, I'd say that means you still got purpose. Another day to turn it around." His voice remained steady, melodic.

My shoulders relaxed as I listened to him. I wanted to lay my head against his chest and feel the vibrations of his voice against my cheek. "Maybe…"

"Everybody gets dealt a shitty hand, Neve."

I started laughing, and not in an amusing sort of way, but more of a *this chick's off her rocker* manner. I managed to wheeze out, "You sure about that? Because you seem like someone who was born with a silver spoon in his mouth; always on the right side of the law."

My laughter continued, even as it moved into tears. I was slap happy—I'd moved beyond exhausted and straight into delirium.

The sun illuminated his face, which was set into a hard line. He began messing with the scruff on his chin. "You know, for someone who's relying on this club for everything right now, you've sure got a smart mouth on you. Sometimes, you get thrust into something you never wanted in the first place."

I stopped laughing and wiped at my streaming eyes. "Is that what happened to you? You had to take over?"

I hadn't gotten that far into the journal yet. I was still trying to figure out why he'd stayed and patched in instead of running away the minute he turned eighteen. He could've taken her and started a life somewhere.

The mask fell back into place and the real Charm disappeared again. "I've got a lot of shit to get done today. You ever been on a motorcycle? I'll have Gunner take you out today; get you used to it."

Make friends with him.

I touched his arm lightly. "Why don't you take me?"

He stood up and moved away from me. "You should go with Gunner. He's better at this sort of thing."

Instead of agreeing and letting it go, I decided to blurt out, "But I want you."

You ever say something and instantly wish for a net to reel all the words back in?

Yeah, that was me in that moment. Charm's eyes widened and I started backpedaling. "I just meant—if you had time—I can go with Gunn—"

He cut me off with a loud sigh. "Fine—get some clothes on and meet me out here in ten."

I was in a lot of trouble. I wanted to blame it on Stockholm Syndrome, but the men had made it clear that I was free to go from day one.

I wasn't delusional—I knew that this was an unrequited crush and nothing that I said or did would change that for him.

His heart was with her...wherever or whoever she was. Jealously reared its ugly head again over a woman with no name. I was falling for the president of a biker gang. One who arguably had just done the nicest thing imaginable for me.

I'd been warned about drugs my entire life, for all the good it did me, but never once had I been told to look out for one with a beating heart and whiskey colored eyes.

16

NEVE

I clicked the mouse, enlarging the image on the screen in front of me before taking another bite from the chocolate chip cookie on my lap. I recalled that sugar worked very similarly to blow inside the brain and had decided to work on becoming a Type 2 diabetic by Christmas. On a positive note, it was definitely helping me to put weight on faster. My sweatpants were growing snugger by the day.

Doc had come through for me with not only a laptop, but a wireless printer too. I realized during the card game that the men didn't know sign language. The journal had mentioned that she was going to teach them, but maybe she'd never gotten around to it or it hadn't stuck. Regardless, I wanted to fix that—everyone deserved to be heard. These signs were pretty basic, but it was a start.

My motorcycle ride with Charm never happened because, just as we were about to leave, Gunner came outside. He told Charm that they had 'club business' to discuss and the two disappeared. I thought things would get better between us, but, if anything, they'd gotten worse. While I'd been disappointed that Charm never came back out to take me for a ride, I didn't think much more of it with all the work I had to complete.

My crush was just going to have to wait until the chores were completed. Unfortunately, the pull of the journal was too strong and I found myself yet again in Charm's room; crouched beside his bed, poring over his words.

Vic enlisted in the Army and leaves in a few days for basic. Billy and Rocky gave him shit for not joining the Marines like them, but I'm proud of him. He's getting out of this hell-hole. The club threw the obligatory farewell party with booze and club whores, but I didn't feel much like celebrating. He caught me outside and asked if I thought it was strange that the only way out of the club is through battle.

I'd never considered it before, but he's right. We were born into this and it was always assumed that we'd take after our old men and slip on the kuttes at eighteen. I don't want this to be my life and I sure as hell don't want this life for her.

Things have grown even more strained between us since Bobby left last year. She seemed to be better for a little while, but then he got deployed over to Afghanistan and she fell apart. I'd hoped that his absence would bring us closer, but she's changed. Luck says it's because she's a woman and women are notoriously flighty with their emotions.

I can't help but think that there's more to it than that.

Mac came back to visit his ma and offered me a job as a mechanic in his shop down in Denver. The club allowed him to leave under the terms that he help them transport whenever needed. It was a good arrangement for him—he got his freedom and the club financed his shop. Well, that and his drinking habit.

I took her out on my bike and we headed to the river where I tried and failed to convince her to leave Kasselhessen behind.

"It's the only home I've ever known! What if he comes back for me and I'm not here?"

I'd gotten furious with her and said things that I wish I could take back. Told her that Bobby was some silly crush that she'd forget all about soon enough.

She'd laughed and said, "Everyone knows that if a crush lasts longer than four months, it's love. I love him—and I know this hurts you, but I can't turn it off to make you happy."

I can't leave without her and if she's refusing to go—well, I'll be stuck in Kasselhessen until the day I die.

I'd left the journal in his nightstand, but could still clearly see the sloped letters of his words as I lay in bed that night. My dreams had been nothing short of a disjointed nightmare. In it, Charm had navigated the winding roads easily, leaning one way and then the other as we rounded the curves. It was exhilarating. The wind whipped across us, tossing my long hair up around the helmet as I'd kept my arms wrapped tightly around his waist.

My thighs had clenched around him with every curve we took, the bike vibrating beneath us. I remembered that even in my dream, he smelled like leather and smoke.

He'd taken me down to the riverside and asked me to run away with him. Unlike her, I'd immediately agreed. It would've been okay had that been the extent of it, but just as he leaned in to kiss me, Clint broke through the trees and Charm pulled away.

"You love him?"

I told him I didn't, but he hadn't listened. He just got up and stalked away, leaving me with the man who wanted me dead. The whole thing made me question my feelings. I'd woken early to watch the sun rise and when he didn't show, I felt let down.

My heart had started pounding when he walked into the kitchen at dinner time that next night. *Lust*, an emotion I hadn't experienced in quite a while, reared its head. Suddenly, he was all I thought about. I tried to tell myself that my brain was just reprocessing the day's events and that it meant nothing, yet the feelings persisted.

If that wasn't a clear indicator of just how messed up in the head I was, then I didn't know what was. I was attracted to a man who had, at the least, shown indifference toward me.

At most, he'd—well, he'd bought me books based on what I told him I liked. I consoled myself with the knowledge that if the mysterious she was right; the feelings would fade over the next four months. This was nothing but a silly crush.

In the meantime, here I was, nothing but sweaty palms and a racing heart anytime he showed up. It didn't help that he now had me doing the laundry as well. Knowing what he was wearing underneath those jeans wasn't helping my situation. I had to stick to the plan of making him my friend, while keeping my adolescent feelings under lock and key.

I clicked a button on another illustration and the printer immediately fired up. It had taken a little over a week for Doc to get me everything I needed and another week to find the illustrations I wanted to use. I couldn't wait to see the look on Joker's face when he saw them.

While I was online I'd done a quick search of my name, but unsurprisingly, nothing turned up. No missing person's reports had been filed because I never went any place enough for anyone to notice my absence.

I put the papers into a small stack and carried them downstairs. After some digging and a little cursing, I found a roll of scotch tape in one of the kitchen drawers.

I took my time and had just finished hanging the last one when the back door opened.

"Darlin', did we miss arts and crafts time?" Rooster squeezed my shoulder as he looked around the lodge.

I grinned. "Do you like it? Now everyone can learn what Joker's signing."

He pursed his lips just as Gunner came through the door. "Good God, what happened here?"

"Neve here was just learnin' us some sign language, Gunner."

I nodded at Rooster and turned my smile on Gunner. As usual, he didn't return it.

"Charm's gonna have your ass over this one."

I exhaled slowly and began walking toward the kitchen. "Thanks for the vote of confidence, Gunner. I can always count on your cheery disposition in my time of need."

"Fuck off, Neve." He clipped out before stomping up the stairs.

Well, there was the one biker who would not be getting a friendship bracelet from me in this lifetime.

I pulled the ingredients I needed for dinner from the fridge; cooking wasn't an intimidating task anymore. I'd just make a menu ahead of time and one of the bikers would go get everything I needed. At some point, maybe they'd even consider letting me do the weekly shopping.

I'd been here six weeks and was slowly finding my groove. I'd wake up and watch the sunrise. Sometimes, Twitch was there and sometimes, it was just me. Charm hadn't shown up since the morning I hit him with the flashlight. Then, I'd work my way through the lodge, cleaning and starting laundry. Either the rooms were starting to improve or the guys didn't have enough time to destroy them. I didn't care—it left me with more free time in the afternoons; time that I'd spent reading the journal.

Doc rounded the corner, clutching his face, and headed straight for the freezer. He grabbed an ice pack and held it up to an eye that was almost swollen shut.

"Doc? What the hell happened?" I tried to grab his arm, but he moved out of reach.

"Club business."

I was quickly growing tired of those two words. As if that answered all my questions. Rooster raised an eyebrow, but didn't say a word.

I'd just picked up a cutting board when the front door slammed shut and loud footsteps stomped up the stairs.

"Let me guess—club business?"

Rooster chuckled and pulled a beer from the fridge. "You know I'm not saying one way or another, Darlin'—but you might wanna stay down here for a bit."

17

NEVE

*A*rms circled my waist as I placed the hot casserole on the stovetop and for a nanosecond, I imagined that it was Charm, turning my insides turned to mush. Thankfully, the rational side of my brain kicked in to inform me that I was an idiot.

I slowly turned around to face Joker. His eyes were shiny, as if he was about to cry, and he pointed at the various signs on the wall. He touched his chin and then the palm of his other hand.

Thank you.

I smiled. I knew he'd love it. "You're welcome—*ahh!*" He picked me up and spun me around in a circle, before gently setting me back down and checking me over.

"I'm fine. I'm fine. You just surprised me."

The look on his face—I hoped that I never forgot it. I thought only children were capable of expressions like that. Joy and innocence. I imagined that he'd always looked like this and it wasn't hard to see why his friends had risked their own wellbeing to help him.

The journal hadn't mentioned what had become of his father, but any other references to Matt were generally positive, given the circumstances. That was the thing about reading Charm's writings— he was always so quick to help his friends, often sacrificing his own happiness in the process. It said a lot about his character and made those lustful thoughts I had that much more difficult to get rid of.

"Neve!" Charm growled and I jumped out of Joker's arms guiltily. He followed me out of the kitchen and into the dining room where Charm was scowling at the signs on the walls. "What the hell is this?"

There are points in space with so much gravity, that not even light can escape. They're known as black holes.

I would know—I was staring directly into one.

I swallowed the lump in my throat. "I—I just thought it would be good for everyone to learn sign language." I pointed to Joker. "That way we can communicate with him, um, better."

Gunner leaned over the railing upstairs, a grin on his face.

Jerk.

He was probably the one who told on me.

Charm sat down at the head of the table and leaned back, one leg casually crossed over the other. His hands rested on his thighs, making it impossible to determine if he was upset or getting ready for a power nap. "Neve, look around. This look like a fuckin' elementary school to you? You gonna get a blackboard next? Post the damn alphabet up on the ceiling? Maybe the lyrics to *Twinkle Twinkle Little Star*?"

I clenched my hands into fists and almost smiled as I did it. He'd done it. The bastard had cured me of my little infatuation. In fact, I could picture myself calmly walking back into the kitchen and picking up the butcher knife I'd used to chop vegetables. I could even see myself plunging it into his chest while reciting nursery rhymes.

And if ever there was a case where the left and right hemispheres of the brain could function independently of the other, Charm was it. *What other explanation was there?* He was so absolutely perfect at times that he melted my heart, but before I could get used to it, the cold exterior was back.

The man was a walking contradiction.

I opened and closed my mouth several times, while my brain worked to get my thoughts in order. "Noted, you friggin' black hole," I bit out before walking out the back door and slamming it shut behind me.

I walked until I came to the ledge and then I did the only thing I could, given the situation. I screamed until my throat was raw, before sinking down onto the smooth rock in tears.

Damn him and his black hole tendencies.

Damn the Dr. Jekyll and Mr. Hyde act.

"You alright, Neve?" I spun around and Guardrail took a hesitant step backward; he'd probably been warned about my fighting skills. It was humorous to see such an intimidating man frightened by someone like me.

He had to have been six and a half feet tall with jet black hair that fell past his gauged ears. His beard was so long that it rested on the collar of his cut-off. He was built like a bear—in fact, I wouldn't have been a bit surprised to find out that he killed small woodland creatures with his hands. He was older than the other guys and acted as the voice of reason; well, when he was sober anyway.

I waved him off before turning back around. "I'm good. Go on in and eat. I just need a minute."

"He means well—it's not easy being the Prez. Definitely not a job I'd want." He came closer to me and sat down. "Luck wasn't exactly the easiest person to get along with and this club is nothing like what it was when he ran things."

Boy, was that the understatement of the year.

I somehow managed to keep a poker face. "Oh, so Luck was a better Prez?"

He shook his head. "Not even close. My mama taught me not to speak ill of the dead, but I think I speak for almost everyone here when I say that not many tears were shed when he went to ground."

Went to ground...as in killed?

We watched the sky grow dark as we sat in silence. "So, Charm took over then?"

Guardrail nodded. "He took over, tried to turn the club around— we lost seventy-five percent of our members. A lot of men liked the club the way it was before—so they left, joined up with other chapters."

It made sense. I wasn't entirely familiar with MCs; my only knowledge was based on television shows and brief interactions through Clint—but even I knew that this was the cleanest group of outlaws in existence.

"Well, that explains there not being any club whores around. I guess it also explains why I'm not referred to as 'bitch,' which I greatly appreciate, by the way."

Guardrail closed his eyes and nodded. "He's got a lot to manage and he's just doing the best he can to handle it all. The club was on the brink of financial ruin when Luck died. Charm pulled out of some deals, losing allies in the process, just to get the club back on solid ground. It cost him a lot to get us here."

I watched the older man, as he sat with his eyes closed, reliving a past I knew little about. "Wanna tell me what really happened to Doc's eye?"

He eyed me warily. "Not especially. I like my teeth in my mouth, thank you very much. All you need to know is that it's club business."

Of course it was. "Fair enough."

The biker patted my leg. "Let's go in and eat. As much as I'd love to sit out here and shoot the shit, I'm starving and exhausted."

I sent him on ahead and stared into the dark for a few minutes longer. Being friends with Charm wouldn't be easy, but it was necessary to ensure that I got to stay. I also knew a little about what it was like to have the world resting on your shoulders. I'd spent a good portion of my life afraid of letting the people I loved down. So, I'd placed unreal expectations on myself, always needing to be seen as the go-getter.

Well, I'd gone and gotten myself right into trouble with drugs. And the saddest part was that I hadn't seen it coming. I'd convinced myself that the work I piled on myself was making me stronger. The truth was that I'd gotten burned out by the time I hit eighteen, but the trap had been set and I'd become too afraid to speak up.

I needed a long-term plan, but with no identification and no money, there weren't a lot of opportunities for me. I dusted my pants off and made my way back toward the house.

"You should do yourself a favor and keep your nose out of club business."

My head turned toward the voice. Gunner was leaned up against the side of the lodge, smoking a cigarette. I refused to make eye contact with him and instead focused on the plumes of smoke.

When I tried to pass by him, he moved in front of the doorway, blocking me. "You hear me, Neve?"

I nodded. "Got it. Can I go now?"

Gunner blew smoke right into my eyes and they began watering. "You're not one of us. You're nothing but an outsider, and it won't be long before Prez wises up and sees that. Then, you'll be right back in the woods where you started."

I laughed, even as his words struck terror into my heart. It was the very thing I feared. "Thanks for the pep talk, Grumpy—I mean, Gunner. Now, if you'll excuse me, I've got things to do."

I bumped him with my shoulder as I went inside, hurting myself a lot more than him in the process. It seemed that everything always hurt me worse in the end.

When Charm called for church, I snuck past Axel and retrieved the journal before retiring to my room. I'd grown bolder over the last month and had resorted to taking it any chance I got.

I flipped through it until I found the incident with Luck that Guardrail had been referring to, and once again, I was left with emotions I couldn't decipher and an ache in my chest that wouldn't go away. Something awful had happened and it had changed everything.

"You challengin' me for the throne, Charm?" Luck laughed and spat a mouthful of blood onto the cracked concrete floor, his hands resting lightly on his hips.

I didn't answer—just watched as he continued his macho posturing around the room, keeping an eye on his gun with every step.

"I fuckin' asked you a question—you really think that you're capable of running a motherfuckin' empire? You're soft…weak. They'll eat you alive." He smiled, his teeth stained red with blood, like an unhinged vampire.

That was what he was, wasn't he? He'd taken everything that was good and sucked the life right out of it. He could boast about an empire, but he was surrounded by scorched earth and ruins. I knew it. The other bikers knew it. And it wouldn't be long before our rivals were in on the secret too.

I had to set things right.

Two of my brothers stepped in and forced the man to his knees before me. He looked up at them in shock before directing a furious glare back toward me. "Is this because of the drugs? It comes with the territory and there ain't no way to run this club without 'em, Charm. It'd bankrupt the entire town. Trust me, I don't like what happened either, but it's just the way of things."

I clenched my hands into fists, rage slowly taking a stronghold within. I pushed it back down below the surface and bit out, "You've done just fine all on your own to destroy the club financially. I'm going to set this right. Now, I asked you a question. Who was behind it?"

He ground his teeth together before lifting his chin defiantly. "I'll tell you...when your ass joins me in Hell."

I raised the gun with a slight tremor in my hand. I'd killed before, but never once raised a weapon against my Prez. Against my father.

"This is for her. It's always been for her..."

Rae.

18

CHARM

She said it quietly, but the words stuck with me.

A black hole.

I'd known it was an insult, but had to wait until everyone went to their rooms for the night before I could gauge just how much of one it was. Apparently, she saw me as something that sucked in everything around me, refusing to allow anything to escape.

A light destroyer.

Well, she hadn't been too far off.

I shouldn't have blown up at her like that—shouldn't have made this her fault. I fucked up.

Doc came to me and told me about the scars on her legs.

Burns.

When he admitted to coercing her into stripping, I saw red and without any hesitation, drove my fist into his face and demanded to know who else was there. He refused to give that up though.

Who else had seen her like that?

My feelings were foreign to me; I was suddenly possessive of a woman that I'd tried to throw out only weeks before.

I'd planned to go to her and vow that none of my men would ever put her in that position again, but I found the signs first.

Those signs.

Just like Rae's.

Instead of comforting her, I fucking destroyed any shred of hope she might've found here over the past few weeks. I saw it on her face.

I can't help but recall that I've been called a monster once before; I never saw the truth to it until now though.

19

NEVE

"Axel, do you know who Rae is?"

The prospect froze. "Where'd you hear that name?"

I shrugged and continued folding laundry on the couch, avoiding his stare. "I just heard someone mention it and I was curious. There are no women hiding out around here besides me, are there?"

I risked a glance from underneath my lashes and saw that he'd gone pale. He took several steps in one direction before turning back to me. "I wouldn't mention that name again if I were you. Now, if you're looking to make a friend, I've got just the person."

With that, he promptly left me and the laundry, off to conjure up a friend for me.

Damn.

I'd thought that with him still being a prospect, he'd yet to take the oath to 'keep Neve from knowing anything.'

In a river of tears, I was quickly and irrevocably being swept downstream in a swirl of emotions. It was moving beyond a simple crush; I was falling in love with Charm's words and the passion that I saw displayed on every page. Like a firefly, I wanted to capture it and make it my own.

And I hated myself for it.

She loved him in ways I'd never be able to—they'd had decades together and with that came a familiarity that he'd never have with me. I was just some junkie they rescued and nursed back to health.

Like Bones, the dog.

And my demise would be much the same. My heart had led me into no man's land—afraid to move forward due to uncertainty and unable to retreat. Instead, I remained stranded—paralyzed with fear.

Bobby came home today. He's not the same man that left years ago— injured in combat, he'd been medically discharged and sent home. Gone is the prankster who rigged a little metal kitchen playset up to a generator, shocking the hell out of Rae when she touched the faucet.

In his place, is a ghost; a shell. He took shrapnel to the knee, ending his military career in an instant. He was lucky they said—his best friend came home in a pine box. Billy just said it was bad; he never told us the extent. I haven't heard him speak once; he just hobbles around on the crutches, trying to avoid being near anyone for too long. I both hated and loved him simultaneously. He was a brother to me, but he'd fucked up everything by going after her.

She stood at the top of the stairs, watching him silently. He doesn't know it yet, but she's changed too. The club sank its claws into her and she has no desire to break free. Her heart hasn't been mine for some time now; but, sitting here watching her, I know that he never left her. It was even more apparent when Bobby felt her stare. He stumbled back and looked up at her as if he was surprised that she was still here.

If that's love, then I'm a novice.

I wanted to make her happy—to keep her safe. I patched in and worked my way up to officer to ensure that nobody laid a hand on her.

I thought I was the hero.

I was only the villain.

"Neve!" Axel called from the stairs and I hastily shoved the journal underneath my pillow, heart beating double-time, as his bootsteps approached my door.

"I'm in here. Just cleaning up a little." These near misses were becoming quite the high for me.

Axel came in, closely followed by a woman I didn't recognize. "Neve, this is Amber. Amber, Neve. Thought you two could keep each other company this afternoon."

She tucked a strand of bleached blonde hair behind her ear and extended her hand toward me. "Hello."

"Hi." I took her hand in mine, grateful for the distraction. Axel left us and went back downstairs. "Does Charm know you're here?"

Her blue eyes widened. "Absolutely. Axel wouldn't do nothing without the Prez's approval."

I nodded, my mind working to come up with how she fit into this world. "And you know the club..." I trailed off, hoping she'd fill in the gaps.

Amber smiled widely, her blindingly white teeth on full display. "I'm a club whore."

She announced it much like one would if they got all A's for the semester; such pride in being a plaything to a bunch of bikers. Amber didn't look like what I imagined a whore would look like. Her makeup was expertly done, giving the appearance that she wasn't wearing any, and her clothes were modest—tasteful even. She could've blended in on any college campus in America. Her speech was the only indicator that she probably hadn't completed anything beyond secondary.

"Oh," I tried to choose my next words carefully, so that I didn't offend her. "And you enjoy that, um, line of work?"

She grinned again, as if she found my words entertaining. "Neve, I'm just fucking with you. I've been with Axel since freshman year of high school. He's patching in, so this club has become like a second family for us, you know?"

I nodded, even though I had no idea what she meant. I'd been here going on two months and nobody had tried to adopt me. Amber continued to chatter on about her experience with the club and growing up in Kasselhessen, while I counted the hours until I could read the journal again. It wasn't that her stories were boring; I had just become addicted to that leather-bound book and needed another fix.

She finally paused to take a breath before eagerly asking if she could give me a makeover, further solidifying that it didn't matter the age, we women could always bond over beauty.

My body jerked, startling me awake. I rubbed my eyes and looked over at the clock. It was just after two. I needed to get at least another hour if I wanted to be productive. Amber had left me just before the men got back and by then, it was time to start dinner. The journal was returned to Charm's room and I made excuses to turn in early. I really just wanted to be left alone with my thoughts.

A light caught my attention and I turned toward the source. The mirror on my dresser flickered as if it was a television screen and I sat up and stared at it dumbly.

My reflection disappeared and the mirror became a window. It was Clint's house. He sat on the worn couch, snorting lines, oblivious to the fact that I was watching him.

I slid out from under the sheets and padded over to it, trying to make sense of what I was seeing.

Maybe I'd relapsed.

If that was the case, why couldn't I remember using?

I brought my hand up and touched the glass. As I did, Clint's head popped up and he stared right at me. There was something wrong with his eyes, something unstable. He grinned and stood up, taking slow uneven steps toward me.

I jumped back in fright, nearly tripping over my own two feet.

"Hey, baby. I've been looking everywhere for you." He continued advancing closer and I bit back a scream.

"You're not real. You're not real." I shook my head back and forth, as if clearing the image of him. The back of my calves connected with the mattress and I fell onto the bed, but I continued to scoot away until I hit the headboard with a low thud.

Clint reached the glass and stopped. "I thought for sure a bear had gotten to you—maybe even a mountain lion. I never imagined you were shacking up with eight men. You know fairy tales aren't real, right? You find yourself living in the woods with seven men and their leader, you're not a princess, Neve. You're nothing but a slut."

He moved his body and then his hand pushed through the mirror as if it was made of water. Once he knew that the mirror wasn't a boundary, he began crawling through onto the dresser. It was like something out of a horror movie, but no matter how many times I pinched myself, I couldn't wake up.

I started screaming then. "No...no!"

He slid all the way through and dropped onto the carpet. Now, he was blocking me from my only exit. The mirror shimmered behind him, flames erupting across the glass.

I clutched my chest. *It couldn't be.* Clint followed my gaze and turned toward the destruction. "Careful, it's hot!" He laughed and moved his hand away from the mirror before looking back over at me, cowering in fear.

"I can't—I can't." I clutched at my throat, feeling the familiar tightness wrap its way around my vocal cords.

A family portrait grew black from the smoke before the fire devoured it. Trinkets and collectibles gathered over the years were no exception and quickly fell victim to the destructive blaze.

Clint held his hands up and I realized they were covered in blood. "Oops...guess I made a little mess." He dipped his hands into the mirror and when he pulled them back out, both were in flames.

I screamed until my throat was raw, the smoke becoming heavier to breathe through. It was like trying to inhale through a damp blanket.

Clint touched the bed and flames began racing up the sheets, scorching my skin. "Trial by fire, Neve. Let's see how you fare."

The walls began to bend inside the house stuck in the mirror. The fire had weakened the entire structure and I had to turn away. It hurt too much.

"Neve!"

I looked back at the mirror and I could see them, at the top of the stairs. They were terrified. And it was all my fault.

"I can't stop it! I'm so sorry!" I hoarsely yelled to them.

"Neve!"

I shook my head. "I don't know how to get you out."

The woman blew me a kiss before getting caught up in the inferno. "Neve, honey, open your eyes! Open your eyes. It isn't real!"

Clint pounced on top of me, knocking the air from lungs. His hands sought out my throat and I thrashed wildly to keep him away. "I'm not finished with you...where's the money?"

The fire faded and the window closed again, leaving a mirror in its place. I was still trapped in a burning room with Clint though. I'd been so preoccupied with that damn book that I hadn't thought to keep myself safe.

"Neve, honey. Wake up!" Rough hands gripped my face and my eyes flew open. I immediately tried to sit up, only to collide with a wall of muscle.

"You're okay. Shhhh...it's okay."

I was hyperventilating through the tears. I could still see them clearly in my mind, stuck in a burning house.

"I couldn't stop it. I'm so sorry..." I repeated the words softly to myself.

The hands moved up and brushed the hair off my damp cheeks. He whispered, "It's okay, it's alright. Just breathe. You don't have to be sorry for anything. I've got you."

I lay my face against his chest and wept until a soft knock sounded at the door. A sliver of light cut across the dark as Rooster poked his head in. "Is she okay?"

I stiffened. If Rooster was at the door, then who was holding me?

"Ain't nothing, but a bad dream. She'll be alright." His hands were still holding onto my hair, so I couldn't move away.

Charm.

Rooster closed the door and left the two of us alone again and I wiped at the tears on my face. "I'm sorry I woke everyone up—"

"What'd I tell you about apologizing?" He grumbled.

"I—I think I'm good if you want to go back to bed." I shifted, but his hands remained where they were, pinning me against him.

"What was it?"

I inhaled a ragged breath. "House fire. I just—" A sob worked its way free and I tried to cover it up by clearing my throat.

Charm was silent for a moment. "Did you start it? You kept apologizing in your sleep as if you were the one who set the fire."

I thought back to that night and a small tremor passed through my body. *Hadn't I?* "I don't know why I was apologizing." I cleared my throat again.

What else could I say—that I'd worked so hard to get clean—only to lose everything? That the feelings of anguish were so strong I was certain they'd incinerate me, from the inside out? That I tried to overdose, but found the numbness a better alternative?

I couldn't admit that to anyone.

Love was the same as addiction—destructive.

Charm tightened his hold on me, using his hand to push my head against his chest. He didn't do the awkward thing people do—where they apologize as if they had something to do with it. In fact, he didn't say anything at all. His hands just made small circles across my back and I began to drift off. His voice startled me awake again.

"When I was five, my mother took me to the grocery store with her. I remember that I'd always beg to ride the mechanical horse at the front of the store or even to play the crane game. We walked in and she handed me a small bag of quarters—told me to enjoy myself while she shopped.

"It wasn't until it began to grow dark out, that I got worried. I found a store employee and we looked for her. She'd been gone for hours by then—knew if she took me, my old man would come after her. So, she dropped me off in the front of the store and never once told me goodbye—never gave me any indication that she was leaving for good."

My arms broke out in goosebumps as he softly spoke. It was something that he'd never written about, but it had impacted his life. I didn't understand why he was telling me though; didn't know what it meant. Knowing the things that Luck had put him through, I couldn't fathom how she could've left him with a man like that.

Luck had been a monster and there wasn't a doubt in my mind that his mother had taken his childhood when she abandoned him in that grocery store.

"Charm?"

He shifted. "Yeah?"

I took a deep breath. "Thank you—for waking me, I mean. Would you, would you mind staying a little longer?"

He exhaled softly. "I'll stay—try to get some sleep."

Maybe his presence chased the demons away. Wrapped up in his arms, I realized I'd gotten a piece of what I wanted. I had the man from the journal—if only for the night.

20

NEVE

I blinked slowly, letting my swollen eyes adjust to the light in the room. When I rolled over, I realized the other side of the bed was empty and let out a small sigh. I didn't know what I expected—that the stone-cold biker would've had a change of heart? That the man who wrote about Rae with such admiration and passion would see me in a similar light?

Nice one, Neve.

I looked at the clock and was surprised to see that it was already eight-thirty. Reluctantly, I slid out from under the warm sheets and padded into the bathroom to get ready for the day.

I took my time washing and drying my long hair before pulling on another outfit that didn't belong to me. Today's shirt featured the word 'Juicy' in large letters across the chest area.

Classy.

Maybe the men would allow me to shop for myself and I could buy clothes that didn't have adjectives on them.

I walked downstairs, lost in thought. I had a couple of loads of laundry that needed to be done—I was also going to have to make a grocery list. I opened the door to the refrigerator while tapping a finger to my lips. If I got moving, I might have a little time left over to read the journal.

"Mornin'."

I clutched my chest and spun around. "Jesus, Charm. I thought everyone had left."

He was leaning up against the kitchen cabinets, with a cup of coffee in his hands. "The men are gone—I have business around here today."

I nodded. "Okay. Just tell me where you need to be and I'll stay out of your way."

Disappointment filled me. If he was hanging around, it meant that I wasn't going to be getting any reading done.

"You're my business today, Neve." His eyes narrowed as if he expected me to challenge him.

I closed the refrigerator and turned to face him fully. "Me? What kind of business could you have with me? I told you I'd stay out of your way. And if this is about last night, I'm sorry. I'm peachy now though. See?" I twirled in a small circle and pasted a smile on my face.

He downed the rest of his coffee and placed the cup in the sink next to him. "Ain't about last night. You need to get used to being on a bike. I figure now's a good time to learn."

I moved around him and poured myself a cup. The first sip scalded my tongue, but I kept drinking. I hoped the caffeine would reach through the fog and help me understand this shift in him.

He watched me impatiently. "Is that a yes or are you ignoring me now?"

I set the cup down on the counter. "I don't really have a choice, do I?"

Charm scratched at the back of his neck. "You've always got a choice. I just thought since I had time…"

His voice trailed off and we stared each other down. "What about the stuff I'm supposed to do around here?"

"It can wait." His tone implied that it was his final answer on the matter.

I nodded. "Am I okay in what I'm wearing? Should I change?"

His shoulders dropped as he relaxed. "You're good. Let's go." He walked outside, leaving the door open behind him. I jogged after him as he strode across the gravel and out to a large metal building.

"Wait here." He disappeared inside and I kicked rocks with the toe of my shoe. What did he have hidden in there that he didn't want me seeing?

Charm came back out a few minutes later, pushing a baby blue Harley. He tossed me a spare jacket. "Put this on. I'm gonna grab you a helmet." He grabbed one and tossed it over to me, before going over and messing with something on the back of the bike.

"Okay, let's go over the rules."

I snorted with sudden laughter before slapping my hand against my mouth. "I didn't think bikers had rules," He glared down at me. "Sorry. Continue."

He pointed back to the bike. "See these? These are footpegs. Keep your feet on them at all times. Always get on from the left side—just throw your right leg over and then slide up into the seat. Your hands should be on my hips," I sucked in a breath and his eyes narrowed. "Somethin' wrong with that?"

I shook my head. "No, I just thought there were handlebars or something."

It was Charm's turn to laugh. "There are—for me. Motorcycles turn by leaning, so lean the same direction I do. The best way to do that is to look over my shoulder in the same direction as the turn— your body should always be in line with mine."

My mind went haywire during the last part. He wasn't smiling though, so a 'that's what she said' joke would've probably been in poor taste. Probably.

C'mon, Neve.

Think of mangy dogs and elementary school signage.

"Anything else?" I choked out.

He nodded. "Yeah. If I brake suddenly, use the footpegs to keep from sliding into me. And if you see animals, tap me on the shoulder. If they're on the right side of the road, right shoulder. Left side of the road, left shoulder. It ain't rocket science. Oh, and don't get any bright ideas about leaping off the damn thing and we'll be golden."

I looked back at the bike. What seemed like a thing of beauty a minute ago, now seemed like a steel deathtrap. In my dream, I hadn't had to worry about wildlife or leaning the right way, I just held on and enjoyed the ride. "I really have a lot to get done today. Maybe another time."

I attempted to hand him the helmet, but he kept his hands at his side. "You scared, Sweetheart?"

I laughed weakly. "I'm thinking I'd be better off with the coke. That's all."

His mood darkened instantly. "You can wait and learn with Gunner or you can go with me now. It's your choice, but one way or another, your ass will be on the back of a bike."

"Great." I slipped the helmet on, while cursing him under my breath. He grabbed the chin strap and tightened it. Knowing he wouldn't see, I stuck my tongue out at him from beneath the visor.

My maturity level was on par with that of a kindergartner right now.

"Let's go." He climbed on and started the bike up and I kept my left foot on the ground, while extending my right leg over the seat, doing exactly what he'd shown me. He turned toward me. "Hold on tight. If you get scared or want me to stop, hit me. Don't do something stupid that'll get us both killed though."

I nodded and reluctantly gripped his hips as the bike moved forward. I would've been lying if I said that my muscles weren't taut with fear those first few minutes. The roads up here weren't straight. They were winding, meaning that there was a lot of leaning involved. I kept a death grip on Charm until my body got used to the movements. It was a little like riding a roller coaster and I began to feel giddy.

I stopped focusing on the flaming skull on the back of Charm's vest long enough to appreciate our surrounding and my hands relaxed slightly as he expertly navigated the twists and turns, the wind whipping through his hair.

Gradually, I became aware of the vibrations from the bike and those pesky feelings of lust fought their way to the surface again.

Nope.

Not going there.

I'd seen the picture in his room. I'd read their life story. As much as I wanted to believe that he'd had his own version of unrequited love with her, it was obvious that they'd worked things out by the time she got sick. She'd been pregnant, for crying out loud.

Charm was crazy about her.

What kind of person would ruin that?

I might have been a lot of things, but a homewrecker was not one of them.

Not me.

I just had to reign in my feelings and focus on the task at hand–which was friendship.

Period.

End of story.

Anything else was madness.

21

CHARM

I'd been colorblind my entire life and then she came along—like a fucking rainbow, saturating everything around her.

I'd fallen in love.

Sure, I'd fought against feeling anything toward her, but I think I've known from day one that she's different. This is more than just wanting to sink my dick into her; although that's also at the top of my list. I want to be the one to make her face light up in pleasure and feel her body clench around me as her nails dig into my skin.

Watching her has become something of a hobby for me. I like catching her unaware—like when she's curled up in one of the chairs on the porch, that big ass science textbook lying open on her lap. I can see her from the window in my office and it's different. When she has no idea that she's being watched, the worried look in her eyes is gone and her body is relaxed. She pores over each page with a slight frown on her face, pausing every so often to brush the hair back off of her forehead and every day that I've seen her do it, I've fallen a little more.

I'd understood maybe a fraction of what I'd read, yet she devours the books the way most women do Nicholas Spark's movies.

How had she ended up here?

How had someone as fucking smart as she was ended up hooked on blow?

I'd lost count of the number of fantasies I'd had and I wondered what she'd do if I made my presence known. If I went out and asked her what it was that made her lips turn up in a small smile, would she see how much I wanted her? If I took the book from her hand and backed her up against the wall, would she feel what I'm feeling?

She'd probably just apologize for enjoying herself.

I was back to being a kid, watching the club whores with Luck's bikers. I'd sneak around, wondering what it would be like to be with a woman, while trying to decode their mystery.

The trouble was that I'd never been with any woman the way I wanted to be with her.

I kept my distance though; afraid to push her into something she might not be ready for. It had become my mission to find the person responsible for the bruises on her neck. I wanted to see the look on the guy's face as he died by my hand for the brutality that she'd suffered at his.

I'd convinced myself that I could look without touching, but when she had a night terror it changed everything.

I heard her screams from all the way downstairs. Sleep never came easily for me; not for some time now. When she cried out, I was up the stairs in seconds, gun in hand.

She thrashed around under the blankets, fighting demons I knew nothing about, but it was obvious that she was under the grip of some heavy shit. Her dark hair tangled in the sheets as she struggled and, without another thought, I slid into bed and pulled her to my chest.

My body reacted immediately.

I wanted to fuck her until the nightmares were forced to the back of her mind and all she could see was me.

It was so fucking wrong, yet nothing had ever felt more right.

I stroked her cheek with the back of my thumb, enjoying the softness without apology. When she came to and began babbling, I realized that it hadn't been just some nightmare. She'd lived through it.

I crushed her up against my chest, deciding then and there that I wasn't going to fight it anymore. I wasn't going to force myself to stay away. Her demons and mine were the same; perhaps they were even close friends in another realm.

I want her on the back of my bike. The only woman who ever rode with me was Rae, but it's time. I feel it and I hope she does too.

Neve has fought for life in ways that Rae never wanted to and I can't keep comparing the two. I've got to let one of them go.

I'm going to take her to the cliffs and then I'll tell her everything.

22

NEVE

"Where are we?" I slid off the bike. Charm had taken so many turns that I'd become disoriented and doubted that I could've found my way back to the lodge even if he paid me.

We were surrounded by trees in every direction and had gone off the main road a few miles back, ending up in the middle of the wilderness.

He put the kickstand down and grinned. "You'll see. C'mon." He walked off the narrow road and disappeared into the trees.

I set my helmet on the bike and reluctantly followed him in. There was a small path that wasn't visible from the road and we walked along in silence until we reached a clearing with a lake surrounded by stone. It was nature's version of an in-ground pool. The sunlight made the surface shimmer and Charm turned around to study my reaction.

"Oh my god, it's beautiful. I've never seen a lake like this before."

His lip turned up in a small smile, but he remained silent.

I didn't do well with silence, so I talked to fill the space. "I was thinking, maybe I could start doing the shopping—that is, if it's okay with you. I'd kind of like to get myself some clothes too—not that I don't appreciate what I've got. No, I just thought—"

"You ramble when you're nervous, you know that?" His face was unreadable as he continued, without waiting for a response. "Who was in the fire, Neve?"

I looked away and whispered, "Pass," but he hooked a finger under my chin and brought my face up to meet his. I didn't want to talk about it, but seeing as to how I already knew most of his secrets, it was only fair to give him one of mine.

I swallowed, feeling as if I was choking as I replied, "My parents."

His eyes searched my face and, for a split second, I could've sworn I saw sadness in them. "It wasn't just a dream, was it?"

I blinked at the sudden tears that formed and shook my head. "No…it wasn't."

Charm nodded, as if he'd known the answer all along. "You blame yourself—why?"

"Because I got out and they didn't!" I blurted and then immediately covered my mouth. I hadn't ever spoken the words aloud. I'd spent the last year with a dull ache in my chest and guilt that never lessened.

The fire had been my fault.

"Miss, can you hear me?" The man asked, as he knelt beside me.

Light flickered at the corner of my eye and I turned to see my childhood home engulfed in flames. They'd gotten out—surely they'd made it out. Paramedics yelled over me and I wanted to tell them to go back inside and make sure my parents were safe.

It was nothing more than a little smoke inhalation.

An oxygen mask was strapped to my face as I struggled to sit up. The yellow man pushed me back down and this time, I didn't fight him. I only caught a quick glance, but it was enough to keep me from moving. The skin on my thighs was blackened and curled up, revealing the muscle underneath.

I felt nothing.

"You ever been cliff jumping?"

I shook my head and frowned at him as I came back to the present. *What the hell was he talking about?*

One minute, he was asking me about my dead parents. The next, cliff jumping. I was going to get whiplash just from his conversation skills.

He pointed toward a grouping of rocks on the other side of the lake. "Roaring Springs River feeds into this—it's actually a rock bowl, not a lake. And back over there, is a small trail leading up to the cliff."

I continued to stare blankly at him until he grew frustrated and began shouting while pointing. "Cliff jumping, Neve. You and me, we could climb up and jump off—it's about a twenty foot drop and the water is frigid, but it could be fun."

I held up my hand. "You want me to jump off a perfectly good cliff and into freezing water?"

He nodded earnestly. "Yeah."

I frowned again. "But I don't have a swimsuit."

Or a last will and testament typed up and ready.

He grinned and began walking toward the hiking trail. I called out after him, "I wasn't agreeing!"

He continued and I had to run to keep up, which then made me realize how out of shape I was. The trail began to inch upwards and I could see the river on the other side of the cliff. The rapids swirled violently and I resisted the urge to cling to the back of Charm's cut-off.

One misstep and I'd be at the mercy of unforgiving waters. I shivered and looked away. When we reached the top, Charm stripped off his vest and shirt. Dark ink connected in swirls across his muscular body—obliviating everything around us, and leaving me gasping for breath as if I'd already gone under.

"Um, is that necessary?" I squeaked out.

His head cocked to the side. "You wanna ride home in wet clothes?"

I shook my head slowly. "I sort of thought I'd just stay up here and watch you do it. I wasn't planning on getting in though."

He laughed, showing nearly all of his teeth. "Oh, Sweetheart. You're going in."

Most men could say sweetheart in a complimentary way; with Charm, there was always this condescending undertone.

I shook my head vehemently and took a tentative step backward.

He moved toward me. "How about this? You jump and I let you start doing the shopping on your own. That would include a budget for new clothes."

I almost agreed, until I remembered the reaction I'd gotten before when the other bikers had seen my thighs. "I—I can't."

His gaze dropped down and I cringed. One of the guys must've already told him. "How about this? I go first and then you. I'll come back up and get your clothes right after and you can stay in the water."

He unfastened his jeans and then stopped, clearly waiting for me to answer. I forced my gaze away from his hands. "Okay. You have to go first though."

Charm nodded and took off his boots and socks before sliding the jeans down his hips. He kicked them into a small pile and then grinned wickedly at me. I was just contemplating what his reaction would be if I threw caution to the wind and fell into his arms as he stepped to the edge and jumped off.

Holy hell.

He didn't even give me a warning. I was lost in thoughts of him being an underwear model in another life and then he was gone. I stepped over to the edge and he waved up at me. "Your turn, Sweetheart!"

I turned away and raised my middle finger in the air, resisting the urge to scream in frustration. I'd made the mistake of looking down... all the way down.

That was only twenty feet?

With shaking hands, I pulled Charm's jacket and my Juicy t-shirt off and then reluctantly removed the rest. Here I was—standing in my underwear on the edge of a cliff during the last week of August.

I stepped to the edge and took a deep breath. *I could do this.*

"Neve! I'm freezing my ass off down here! Hurry up!"

One.

Two.

Three.

I prayed that I didn't land on Charm or any sharp rocks and

stepped off. My stomach jumped into my chest, giving me the same sensation I'd had on the bike of being on a roller coaster. It was terrifying, but as icy water flooded my nose and jolted my system, I suddenly wanted very much to do it again.

As I pushed my body up to the surface, coughing and spluttering, I realized that I'd experienced the same feelings as when I was high.

I'd felt something while sober that I would've thought impossible. *Happiness.*

"I did it," I breathed.

"You damn sure did, honey." I opened my eyes to see that Charm had not gotten out to go get our clothes, as he'd promised, but was instead swimming closer to me, a big smile plastered across his face.

Five.

I'd made him smile five times now.

My teeth chattered from the water and I kicked my feet to try and warm myself up. "I'm dying of hypothermia over here. Weren't you going to get our clothes?"

Please don't come any closer.

I wasn't capable of fighting my feelings anymore. Not when he looked at me like that.

Charm grinned as he moved ever closer. "You're shivering. That's a good indicator that you're not hypothermic."

My mouth dropped open. "How did you know that?"

He reached out and pulled me closer to him, rubbing my arms to get the blood flowing. "I've been doing some reading lately—you know, science stuff."

I bobbed my head and murmured, "Science stuff."

Something softened in Charm's expression as he watched me piece it together and I suddenly felt hot in spite of the frigid water.

His hand came up and cupped my cheek and then his mouth was on mine. It didn't matter how many times I'd imagined it; nothing lived up to the reality of him kissing me. It was like jumping off of that cliff all over again. He kissed like he wrote—with a fiery passion that I'd never experienced before or ever would again in my lifetime.

My lips parted as his tongue pushed its way past my lips, taking anything and everything I had to offer while his hand held my head immobile. The stubble on his face was abrasive, but I was lost in the moment, too far gone to care. He reluctantly pulled back and my numb fingertips trailed across his pecs, as he lightly kissed a trail down the curve of my neck.

I forgot about the cold and guided his mouth back up to mine, wrapping my arms around his neck as I pulled him closer. My legs locked around his waist and my hips rolled forward, seeking. His hands explored my body before connecting with my ass. With a low growl against my lips, he dug in, crushing me up against what I'd sought only moments before.

I could've stayed like that for an eternity, but then I thought of the girl from the notebook and the heat that had flooded my body was replaced with guilt.

Rae.

I forced myself to use her name. She wasn't just some girl; she possessed something that I never could—his heart.

And this was wrong.

I abruptly pulled away. "I can't."

He leaned back, panting, as beads of water ran down his face. I expected him to argue, but he didn't. He just stared down at me, as if waiting for an explanation.

I continued rambling. "It's just that these stitches—Doc said not to submerge them and well, I'm pretty sure that this counts as submersion."

I'd been cleared for weeks and the stitches had dissolved even before then, but I couldn't give him the real reason without revealing my duplicitous behavior.

Charm nodded and began paddling toward the edge. "I'll just grab your clothes."

He climbed out and shook himself off, still refusing to make eye contact with me.

I was trying to lighten the somber mood that had settled over us, so I said the first stupid thing that popped into my head. "That water is ridiculously cold, isn't it?"

He glanced down at the front of his boxer briefs and then scowled. "It wasn't that cold."

I hadn't meant it like that, but I snorted with laughter regardless, before slipping underwater. When I resurfaced, Charm was trudging angrily up the trail toward our clothes.

"Come back. It's cool." I called up to him with a giggle as I pulled myself up onto the warm rocks near the edge. Thanks to a steady diet of sweets and the effects of the artic water, my breasts were fighting to break free from the confines of my bra.

I laid back and let the stone warm my back, my teeth still chattering, from both the water and my close encounter of the Charm kind. I'd messed everything up. Why couldn't he have just been an asshole? Why'd he have to go and show an interest in my life? And where was Rae? She'd gotten sick, but that didn't mean anything. I hadn't built up the courage to skip ahead in the journal again.

Maybe deep down I didn't want the truth.

A shadow passed over me and I sat up as Charm tossed my clothes over. He was fully dressed again, as if nothing had happened. "Get your clothes on and we'll head back."

I turned so he couldn't see my legs and began the arduous task of pulling denim over damp skin. "Did you warm up?" I peeked over my shoulder and his expression turned murderous.

"Jesus, Sweetheart. It wasn't that bad."

I choked back a laugh long enough to say, "That's what she said."

He stared me down, his lips remaining in a solemn line.

Tough crowd.

I turned away and pulled my shirt over my head, fighting to keep the giggles in. Once I was fully dressed, he started back down the trail toward the bike, not bothering to see if I was keeping up or not.

"You know it's okay, right? Fifty-two percent of men will—"

"Don't make this harder than it has to be," he growled.

I clapped my hands and jumped up and down. "That's what she said—no, wait. That's what he said? That's what one of them said!"

I liked frustrating him. Like an annoying little sister. A guy like Charm needed someone to bring him down a few pegs. And the quickest way to forget the most amazing kiss of my life, was to convince myself that I could never be seen as anything more than the annoying junkie who'd shown up and killed the bachelor vibe at the clubhouse.

I kept pace with him, even though it was obvious he was trying to get away from me. "Slow down. Let's talk about it."

He walked faster, so I added, "I'm sorry."

"Fuck off, Neve," was his response.

"Wait up," I panted as I jogged behind him. "Let me be your friend."

I'd meant it as a joke, but it came out laced in desperation.

He reached the motorcycle and tossed me the helmet. "With friends like you, I damn sure wouldn't need any enemies. Let's go."

I nodded stupidly and put my helmet on, thankful yet again that he couldn't see my face as my cheeks burned with embarrassment. I'd tried to make friends with him and put my personal feelings aside, but that kiss had only confused things further.

He belonged to someone else and a man like Charm couldn't be shared. The problem was lying in the pleasure center of my brain. I'd had a hit of him and there was no coming back from that.

I was a full-blown addict now.

23

NEVE

There were several bikes parked in front of the clubhouse when we pulled up. I slid off the motorcycle just as PD came down the path toward us.

"Got some company, Prez. Neve." He nodded at me in greeting.

Charm took the helmet from my hands. "Neve needs to run to the store and get some new clothes. I want you to take her. I'll let you know when to come back."

I protested. "Can't I change clothes first?" My underwear was still wet and the thought of shopping in wet clothes was not appealing in the least.

Charm looked toward the lodge. "Where are they?"

"Your office."

He sighed. "Fine. Take her to change and then go. Do not let her out of your sight."

Who did he have in there? Al Capone?

I stuck close to PD's side as we made our way inside and upstairs. I could hear men's voices coming from the hallway downstairs, but luckily, the coast was clear.

PD stood guard outside the door while I changed and then all but dragged me back downstairs. We'd almost made it to the truck when we ran into trouble.

"Who's the bitch?" I immediately turned around, ready to fight, while PD moved in between me and the man. The voice sent chills down my spine.

"This doesn't concern you, Blade."

The man took a step closer. He had a scar running down the side of his face and messy black hair that fell around his shoulders. He might have been attractive were it not for the permanent sneer on his face.

"Seems to me that Charm's been holding out on us. He went and got himself a club whore. Where's he been hiding you?" He reached out to touch my hair and I spit in his face.

"I'm no one's whore, asshole."

He reared back, as if he'd never been told off, before cracking his neck and taking another step closer. "You're a feisty bitch, I'll give you that. You just need to be broken."

"I. Am. Not. A. Bitch. Do you hear me, asshole?" I forced each word out in a snarl and lunged toward the man. PD was quicker this time and his hands shot out to wrap around my waist. Axel came running from around the side of the lodge, gun drawn.

"Neve, you okay?" He looked at the three of us, never taking his gun off of Blade.

I nodded shakily and moved toward him.

"You mess with her, man, and Charm will unleash hell. She's off limits." PD said everything matter-of-factly, but his voice held a warning.

As if backing up his statement, the other bikers lined up outside the lodge, arms crossed over their chests. Well, not Gunner, but whatever.

"We got a problem, PD?" Rooster called out.

PD shook his head. "Not anymore. Isn't that right, Axel?"

Axel grinned and winked at Blade. "I think we had ourselves a little misunderstanding with our friend here."

Blade looked ready to self-combust, but he nodded. "Yeah. She's off-limits. Got it." PD nodded to the other bikers and they followed Blade back inside. Axel holstered his gun and pulled me into his side in a rough hug before helping me into the truck.

Once we were safely on the road, PD turned to me. "Do not ever try any shit like that again, Neve. Let us handle pricks like him."

I pouted. "But he called me those names."

He nodded, focusing on the road. "I know, but in case you've forgotten, you weren't in great shape when we found you. It can't be crazy to assume you've encountered men like him before, yeah?"

I shrugged. "I mean, sure, but I guess I've gotten used to not dealing with it here."

He patted my leg. "And you won't. If it happens, let us take care of it. It happens and we're not around, then come find us. Nobody is going to fuck with you unless they want to fuck with the entire club. Got it?"

I nodded. "Got it."

He pulled a handkerchief from the pocket of his pants and began blowing his nose. That's all the man ever did. I hadn't seen the handkerchief in with his laundry—probably because he never washed it. I grimaced and turned away.

I knew that there was an attractive man buried under the mound of Kleenex and handkerchiefs that seemed to be permanently attached to his face. What I had seen, in those rare moments that he wasn't sneezing, was enough to make me do a double take. He was just as tall as some of the other guys and made up of mostly lean muscle. Except for those biceps—holy cow, those arms—he could crack walnuts with them.

He kept his beard neatly trimmed; I knew that from all the hair I found on his bathroom counter every day. PD really did keep himself looking nice, apart from the phlegm.

"Damn allergies. Can't ever catch a break."

I suddenly knew who I could help next. We drove through town before turning into the parking lot of a strip mall. There was a small grocery store, flanked on one side by an outdoor apparel shop and a women's boutique on the other.

He put the truck in park and turned to me. "I figure you can get groceries and a few things for yourself." He handed me a wad of cash as his cell phone began buzzing in his pocket. "Go on ahead; I'll catch up with you."

"Thanks." I mouthed as he answered the call.

My vision was blurry on my way into the grocery store. It was such a silly thing to get emotional over, but I hadn't had money for shopping in longer than I could remember.

It seemed every penny Clint made had gone right back up our noses.

I gathered the items I needed fairly quickly and meandered over to the cosmetics and health aisle. Before I was an addict, I was a beauty junkie with quite the collection. Amber had brought me some basics, but I added some mascara, eyeliner, and eyeshadow to my cart before looking longingly at the lipstick.

My kryptonite had always been lipstick.

I finally narrowed my choices down between the colors of *Ruby Redbird* and *Where There's Smoke, There's Fire*. I stared at them for a few minutes before tossing both in the cart.

Surely Charm wouldn't notice that on the bill.

Like a jolt of lightning, the craving hit me out of nowhere. With hands tightly gripping the shopping cart handle, my body hunched over in agony. I needed a hit, everything in me demanded it. I was furious with myself—I'd gone almost nine weeks without it. Why was my body betraying me now?

My vision narrowed until all I saw before me were white mountains of blow, just waiting, and my heart thudded in my chest with excitement.

I forced myself to walk over to the allergy medicine, finding what I needed in the homeopathic section. I grabbed the box with shaking hands.

I could do this.

"Hey, lady."

I dropped it into the cart with a yelp and looked up to see Amber standing a few feet away, a blue hand basket draped on her forearm as if it were a designer purse.

"Hey," I managed weakly, heart still pounding.

She was over to me in a second. "Are you okay? You're looking a little pale."

I shook my head. "I—I need to get out of here, I think."

She grasped my shoulders in her hands and studied my face. "I know what you need. You don't have to act like everything's fine, Neve."

I looked down and focused on the cough drops lining the bottom shelf—anywhere but her face. "They told you?"

She laughed lightly and leaned down into my line of vision. "Sweetie, they didn't have to. I've been sober for two years now. So, what do you say we check out and get your head right?"

"You all done?"

I jumped again and guiltily turned around. "PD—you scared me!"

He laughed. "Hey, Amber."

She arched an eyebrow. "Hey, yourself. I ran into Ali the other night. She was asking about you."

PD suddenly found the contents of the shopping cart very interesting. "Whatcha got in there, Neve?"

Smooth. He was just going to skip right over that.

"Just things that were on the list," I pushed the cart up toward the front, while forcing thoughts of coke back down into the darkness. "Do we have time to shop for clothes? Oh, and Amber and I were thinking of doing something too—if we have time."

He nodded. "We've got time to shop...see a movie...you name it. What'd you have in mind, Amber?"

She grinned wickedly. "Are you coming with?"

His smile faded. "Why? What are you planning?"

Amber latched onto the front of the cart, pulling us toward the checkout, while gleefully calling over her shoulder, "I take it you can't let Neve out of your sight, so I hope you like yoga."

PD groaned. "Anywhere but there. Shit, I'll take you to every clothing store in town if you want."

I caught Amber's eye and she winked. "Guess who owns the yoga studio."

Ah. That made a lot more sense. We paid for the groceries, but arranged to pick them up on our way back to the lodge. PD was quiet on the drive over to yoga, while Amber peppered me with questions about my knowledge of yoga and meditation.

A half hour later, we were cobra and tree posing our way to a restful state—well, some of us. Others were standing near the front door, looking as out of place as a hooker on Rodeo Drive. Ali, to her credit, remained unfazed and carried on as if there wasn't a massive biker standing in the corner, scowling at everyone.

That glower had certainly disappeared when she demonstrated firefly pose for the class. His look didn't convey anger—quite the opposite really. The more I was around the bikers, the more confused I became. PD was obviously into Ali, yet acted as if she meant nothing. Charm was hung up on Rae, but no one dared mention her name.

How did eight men—ten, if you counted Axel and Joseph—live like monks?

And why?

The class ended, but I remained sitting on my mat; pleased that I'd still been able to master almost every pose, especially since I hadn't practiced in over four years. My side was almost completely healed, minus the occasional twinge from scar tissue forming. For the first time since I arrived in Kasselhessen, I took the time to appreciate how far I'd come.

I had been sober for eight weeks and one day.

I'd learned how to cook.

I had found a job that left me feeling exhausted, but productive at the end of every day.

I'd fallen in love and, while not the healthiest of choices, it proved that Clint hadn't damaged me beyond repair.

I was still here.

And the cravings that had seemed so overwhelming an hour ago, faded until I was in control again.

Before I could get lost in my positive affirmations, strong arms lifted me up and toward the door.

"Time's up. We need to get you some clothes," PD hissed as he stalked toward the door, with Amber rushing to keep up.

"Goodbye. It was great to meet you, Neve. Say hello to Charm for me," Ali called.

I extended my hands toward her. *"Namaste, Ali. I'll be back, I promise."*

Once we were safely back out on the street, PD turned to me and Amber. "You two ready for shopping now? Let's do all the shopping— fuck." He gave me a pointed look. "Don't say a word, Neve. Not today."

I quickly realized two things. One—Ali was more than just some fling. She'd gotten under his skin and I was going to make it my mission to get to the bottom of it—*that's what she said.*

I was completely hopeless sometimes.

Okay, time to be serious.

The second thing was that Charm must've been the one who called PD as we got to the grocery store. He obviously wanted PD to stall.

But why?

"Hey, PD," I casually began, earning me an immediate eyeroll.

"Jesus fuck, Neve. Let it go." He began walking toward the stairs and I did my best to match his stride.

It was unfair really. I'd waited a full twenty-four hours to discuss this; thinking I'd give him some time to cool down. I deserved a medal for the restraint I'd shown.

And, maybe it wasn't the conversation I wanted to have, but the other party in my situation had gone AWOL; leaving me to ponder that cliffside kiss on my own.

I was going to work up the courage to confront him; I was.

I was going to come right out and ask, *"Charm, what happened to..."*

Or I'd say, *"Look, Charm. I know about..."*

Well, I still had time to figure out how to put all the words

157

together into one coherent thought. I just wondered if my heart was going to be capable of accepting the answer.

"PD—wait. Just hear me out, please."

He stopped at the top of the stairs and resignedly turned around. "Are you slow? Did anything I said yesterday stick? I don't want to have this fucking discussion with you. Is that clear?"

Each word was enunciated loudly. A normal person would've fled the landing; unfortunately for him, I hadn't been 'normal' in quite some time.

He stomped down the hall toward his room and I dutifully followed after him again. "Just look me in the eyes and tell me that you're not in love with her."

PD's shoulders sagged as he stopped at his door. With his back to me, he replied, "I said to drop it." He let himself in and closed the door quietly behind him.

I debated for a fraction of a second before going in after him. He refused to acknowledge my presence; choosing instead to shed his vest and empty his pockets onto the dresser as if I wasn't standing a mere three feet away.

"Did you know that penguins are monogamous?" When he didn't respond, I continued, "It's true—when a male penguin falls in love with a female, he searches far and wide to find a gift. And not just any old gift, but the most perfect pebble on the beach. He then presents it at her feet—it's a little like kneeling to propose, but they're penguins. I don't even know if they're capable of kneeling, come to think of it. I would think they would just waddle around all penguin-like—"

PD sat down on the edge of the bed and pinched the bridge of his nose. "Jesus, you talk too much. Are you going to make a point or just continue spouting off random animal facts?"

I shoved my hands down into the deep pockets of my sweatpants and rocked back on my heels, looking more like a fidgeting toddler than an individual with an above-average IQ. "I just meant that penguins mate for life—for instance, they would only seek out another partner if their mate were to pass. And that's probably only young widower penguins. Older penguins are just content to remain single and play bridge at the penguin retirement center."

He pressed his lips together, fighting the smile that was suddenly creeping across his face. "Is that so? And that relates to me…how?"

I sighed. "Isn't it obvious? Ali might be your penguin. I saw the way you looked at her and it wasn't just because the woman's basically a human pretzel. What happened there?"

He stiffened and I placed a hand on his shoulder. "I'm not trying to pry, I swear. It's just sometimes when you see two people who would be perfect together, you kind of want to just smack their heads together until they see it too. You know?"

The grin widened on his face. "I know exactly what you mean. Sometimes, we get in the way of our own happiness, don't we Neve?"

I sat down next to him and nodded. "Sure, I guess. I just don't want you to spend the rest of your life regretting the decision to not be with her if she makes you feel even the tiniest bit of happiness. If she appreciates your interests and takes the time to get to know what makes you tick, then don't throw it away. If you have nothing holding you back, then go after her, like the badass biker you are."

He watched me amusedly before sneezing into his handkerchief. "You have a lot of experience in this department?"

I snorted, "What? An unhealthy obsession with other people's love lives? Guilty." I waved my hand toward him. "But, that's neither here nor there. I have a plan to help you. So, when I was at the store yesterday, I got a Neti Pot. It's supposed to help with severe allergies and congestion. You just pour it into your nose and it flushes everything out. I think this—"

"You want me to do what? Oh, fuck no." PD's eyes widened and he jumped up off the bed, heading toward the stairs.

I retrieved the box from my room and ran down after him. "It'll help with your allergies—I promise."

Rooster looked up from his phone and clapped his hand on his thigh before jumping up from the dinner table. "Oh, this I gotta see."

PD shook his head. "No way, Neve. I'm not letting you shove something into my nose."

I'd grabbed the Neti Pot, along with some honey straws I saw in the checkout line. I'd read somewhere that local honey could help with allergies and with all of PD's sneezing and carrying on, I was willing to try anything at this point.

Him? Not so much.

The front door opened and I turned expectantly. I quickly tried to hide my disappointment when I realized that it was only Twitch. I really needed to discuss things with Charm—sooner rather than later —I was like a rubber band that was about to snap.

"How's it hangin', kid?"

I pointed to PD. "Twitch, tell him to suck it up and let me fix his allergies."

Twitch came over and took the box from my hand. "Oh, PD—this is nothin'. I use one myself from time to time."

I looked at him in surprise before nodding authoritatively. "Good. See? Nothing to worry about. What do you have to lose?"

PD poured two fingers of Jameson into the glass in front of him and then downed it. "Fuck—alright. But only Neve is allowed in there."

Rooster's booming laugh filled the room. "Fat chance of that, fucker. I'm getting a front row seat to this."

Twitch rubbed his hands together. "I can give you some pointers. You okay with that, kid?"

I grinned mischievously over at PD. "The more the merrier."

PD flipped me off and stomped up the stairs. "Let's get this shit over with."

The two men gleefully followed him up, while I stayed back to warm the water. I hadn't been sure if tap water was okay or not, so I'd grabbed a case of bottled water before we left the store. I warmed it up and added the salt before carefully walking upstairs.

We gathered around the sink in PD's bathroom as I read over the instructions. Twitch gave a few suggestions, but PD just stood frozen with the pot in his hands.

"Um, PD? You have to put it in your nose and lean over," I offered, but he didn't move.

I was going to have to distract him to calm his nerves. "So, how'd you get the name PD? What does it stand for?"

His features relaxed and he gave me a slow smile. "It uh- well, it means, *Pussy Detective*. Because—"

Rooster cut him off with a loud chuckle. "Oh hell no it doesn't. Nice try. It stands for *Pollen Detector*. Charm said he could sniff out all the pollen in Colorado."

A vein bulged on PD's forehead and I patted his arm. "If you try this and it works, then you're free to call yourself PD: Pussy Detective again. Imagine what Ali will think."

He inserted the tip of the pot into his nose and leaned over, breathing through his mouth, as the saltwater flowed from his other nostril. Once he exhaled enough to clear the one side, we reheated more water and did the other side, all of us gathered around like anxious schoolgirls awaiting fresh gossip.

"So?" I asked, once we finished.

He nodded. "It didn't suck. And I can breathe through my nose— which is pretty fucking awesome."

I grinned widely as Rooster hip-checked me on his way to the sink. "My turn."

24

CHARM

I thought she was in the same place.

We were going to be freezing our asses off and then I was just gonna come right out and tell her everything. Instead, she'd looked at me with those eyes, pulling me under her spell and destroying any chance of my words coming out right.

When I leaned in, she hadn't pulled away—fuck, she'd practically wrapped herself around me. I'd been working up the courage to tell her about Rae and how I'd ended up here when she ended it; leaving me pretty goddamned confused. When she started rambling off dick jokes, I got the impression that I'd misjudged the damn thing entirely.

I should've just let her enjoy the jump—but now that I've had her mouth, I want the rest of her too.

I am completely fucked on this one.

"*D*o you need a few more minutes to write in your diary or can we get this fucking meeting started?"

I snapped the journal shut and leaned back in my chair to face Gunner. "What the fuck are you doing in here? What meeting?"

He exhaled slowly and leaned against the doorframe of my office.

"The meeting you called yesterday. I've got Blade's crew outside, but he's getting antsy and I'm getting close to putting hands on him."

I pinched the bridge of my nose. Jesus Christ. I'd fucking lost my mind over this Neve situation. "Show him in."

Blade sauntered in with a lit cigarette hanging from his mouth. "Charm."

"Blade."

We'd had to move the meeting to the warehouse down by Boulder —PD had confronted me over allowing other clubs in with Neve there; apparently Blade had assumed she was there to be used by anyone.

I clenched my fists under the desk. Savages didn't abide by rape; obviously, not every club was on the same page.

He pulled out his switchblade and began cleaning under his nails, oblivious to the fact that part of his blade was coated in dried blood. "Been thinking about your offer and my club's in. What? You surprised?"

Surprised? I was shocked.

This wasn't just a partnership. I'd proposed a merger—his club joining ours under my command.

I hadn't expected him to go for it though. "Not surprised—it's a good deal. I guess I just thought that you'd need more than a couple of days to think it over."

He put the knife down and leaned forward. "How is this gonna work? Back in the day, you guys were the Mother. Do we bow down to you now or some shit?"

There was wariness in his tone, and rightfully so. He'd only dealt with Luck in the past. He was right not to trust me or my club fully.

That would come with time. But first, we were going to go over my club's rules—and that included the fact that Neve was and would always be off limits. If I didn't have the entire town relying on me, I would've called the whole thing off for the mere fact that he'd tried to fuck with her.

She might not have been mine, but I was going to keep her safe and out of the hands of men who thrived on abuse.

25

NEVE

Things have changed, and not for the better. She's sick. I have no idea how long she's been hiding it from us. Bobby found her unconscious on the stairs with a large gash in her forehead.

In a clubhouse like this, it's a miracle that no one touched her. Luck wouldn't have done a goddamned thing about it, but I sure as hell would have. Mac stood on guard outside while Vic sewed her head up.

When she came to, she didn't remember a damn thing. She just told us that she'd felt a little off this morning when she woke up, but that was it. Bobby wouldn't make eye contact with me after that. He knows something; I can feel it.

I'd wanted to press the subject until one of them cracked, but it was obvious that she needed some space. I decided to take her to Pearl's for some clothes; everything seems to be falling off of her lately, even more of a sign that something terrible is happening.

I feel helpless.

In all my years, I've never not had a plan or something to fall back on. I'm completely out of my depth here; everything I love is slipping right through my fingers. The tighter I hold on, the faster everything falls away.

"*N*eve." The whisper woke me with a start and I bolted upright with a pounding heart and a sense of dread.

"What's wrong?" I searched for the voice in the dark.

"Sorry to wake you, Darlin', but we got ourselves a situation downstairs. Guardrail had a few too many."

I sighed and fell back into my pillow. "He's always had a few too many, Rooster—what else is new?"

He pulled the blankets off of me. "He crashed his bike."

I sat up again. "Oh my god—is he okay? Where's Doc?"

He grabbed my hand and pulled me from the bed. "Doc's still gone with Charm and Gunner on a ru—club business, I mean. You've spent enough time shadowing him; can't you patch him up?"

It wasn't until we reached the last stair that I woke up enough to realize what he was asking me to do. Sure, I'd followed Doc around from time to time when my work load allowed it, but to fill in for him? I was nowhere near ready for that.

We reached the basement and I could hear the groans coming from the biker I'd come to regard as a father figure. I turned to Rooster. "You sure we can't take him to a hospital—preferably one that caters to outlaws?"

He shook his head. "I'm not sure that sort of thing even exists."

I tentatively approached the metal table, wishing like hell that I was still in bed. Joker and Twitch held Guardrail down by his arms, but the man continued to thrash and moan.

"Hey, friend," I offered lightly, "What happened here?"

Sweat lined his brow from his struggle and he forced out through clenched teeth, "Had a little trouble navigating. My left foot took the brunt of it."

I grabbed a cloth and ran it under cold water before applying it to his forehead. "Were you drinking?"

He nodded and looked away. "It's just the way things have always been, Neve."

I checked him over, starting at his head, working my way down. He'd been wearing his helmet and gloves so he fared better than he should've with what he'd had to drink. When I got down to his ankle he jerked away from my grasp.

"Easy there. You're going to have to let me look at it." His pants had been torn away from both legs when he crashed and he had road rash on the skin that was exposed on his left leg. I gave the other bikers their tasks and got to work; grabbing Doc's go-to kit from the cabinet. I patiently picked pieces of gravel and debris from his skin with a pair of tweezers, while Rooster acted as my assistant, getting me whatever I needed to complete the job.

"You know," I said quietly as I worked, "an estimated eighty-eight thousand people die from alcohol-related causes every year. It's actually the third leading preventable cause of death." I continued cleaning the wounds as best I could, falling silent after deciding that my speech on responsible drinking was falling on deaf ears.

"What are one and two?" Twitch asked, as he applied pressure to Guardrail's shoulder, keeping him flat on the table. When I gave him a blank look, he elaborated, "The two leading causes of preventable—whatever you said."

I smiled. "Oh. Uh, nicotine and sedentary lifestyles, respectively. Alcohol is a coping mechanism, obviously, and is still the most widely abused drug out there."

I applied antibiotic cream and petroleum jelly before bandaging up his calf, while he looked at me in a way that was hard to describe; as if he was trying to figure me out. "How do you know so much about all of this?"

I shrugged, while taking in the damage to his foot. "I love statistics and I guess it just stays with me." Thankfully, someone had the foresight to remove his boot, or we would've had to cut it off. His ankle was grotesquely swollen and already turning blue and purple from bruising. I gently palpated along his foot, just as Doc had shown me, to feel for broken bones.

"Do we have an x-ray machine?" Not like I would know what I was doing if we did, but it didn't hurt to ask.

The men shook their heads, waiting for me to make my diagnosis. I took in a slice that ran along the inside of his right calf. "Okay, I'm going to need the sewing kit to stitch up this cut. I'm not feeling any broken bones; but I think it's safe to say that you've got a sprained ankle," I paused as I remembered high school gym. "RICE—rest, ice, compression, elevation. You're going to have to stay down here for a while unless the men can move you upstairs."

He clenched his jaw. "Whatever you think, Neve. So, you really think alcoholics are in the same category as drug addicts?"

Rooster handed me the kit and I pulled what I needed from it. I'd been practicing my stitches on bananas and oranges. This was my first human case. Obviously, I was going to keep that to myself—no one wanted to be the first patient.

I swallowed my fear and began disinfecting the leg wound, using his question as a distraction. I didn't take offense; most everyone saw themselves as better than an addict, never realizing that with one slip they could find themselves in the exact same boat. "Well, yes. Every addiction started somewhere; some moment where things got over-whelming and instead of facing it, you turned to a vice—a drug."

He winced as the needle connected with his skin and I paused. "Just get it over with," he forced out. "I'm gonna talk to keep myself from coming off the goddamned table, okay? Is that how you ended up here?"

I bit down on the corner of my lip and bent over; carefully placing another stitch with shaky hands. *Wasn't that how I'd ended up lost in the woods? An unhealthy desire to be the best?* "Something like that," I muttered distractedly.

"I enlisted the day I turned eighteen. That's what the men in my family did and that's what I wanted to do—uh, can you guys give us a minute?" The three shuffled out into the hall, leaving us alone and Guardrail continued, "Thing is, I was gonna break away from tradi-tion and not come back. This club? It wasn't ever in my plans."

I paused again and straightened up, stretching the muscles in my lower back. "What happened?"

The journal had never mentioned anything about Guardrail—at least, not that I'd been able to decipher. It was hard to know when they were only mentioned by their real names.

He frowned. "I made it as far as the medical exam; it turned out that I had a heart defect. BAVD—Bicuspid Aortic Valve Disease—a fuckin' mouthful to say. That alone wasn't a disqualifier though and I thought I still had a chance. The aortic stenosis they also discovered was what ended my career before it even began. A fucking birth defect killed everything."

I returned my focus to his leg and the stitches, afraid to break the spell that had gotten him to open up. "Did they surgically correct it?"

"Oh yeah, the club paid for that shit too. Got myself a nice mechanical valve. Lay your head on my chest and listen."

I did as he asked and heard the click; realizing that I'd heard it before, but had attributed the sound to white noise.

"I lost my chance to serve and found myself indebted to the club all at once. They let me open a body shop down in Denver, but it was just another front for Luck's running."

Something pricked my memory as I moved back down to his leg.

Mac came back to visit his Ma and offered me a job as a mechanic at his shop down in Denver.

He was Mac; and obviously, he hadn't been able to hold on to even the smallest bit of freedom that the club had allowed him. "How'd you end up back here?"

His nostrils flared and he clenched his jaw. "Some things went down that required me to give up Denver and come back home. Are we almost done here?"

I'd struck a nerve and any good that had been done seemed to unravel until Guardrail had completely closed himself off again.

"Let's move you up to your room. That way someone's close enough to check in on you every few hours."

He agreed and the other guys came back in just as I placed the last stitch.

It hit me out of nowhere.

This time, the craving for cocaine was stronger than before, muffling the sounds of the men around me, until all I could focus on was my need for it.

I wanted to run over to the cabinets and begin throwing doors open to look for blow. I knew they had to have some around here somewhere. I'd wait until they went back to bed and then I'd ransack the whole damn clubhouse if I needed to.

"You alright, kid?" Twitch eyed me curiously, "You zoned out on us."

I nodded absentmindedly and ended up knocking the tools needed to be sterilized into the floor. "Yeah, just tired—that's all."

Rooster placed a hand on my arm. "Why don't you go on back upstairs? We can take over from here. Joker, you mind getting Neve back to her room?"

The mute shook his head and offered me his arm and I wearily took it, even though I wanted to run screaming from the room—to claw at my skin until I could shed it. Anything to not feel like this. I'd been giving Guardrail advice as if I'd somehow mastered the art of staying sober.

I was nothing but a fraud.

Joker helped me back into bed and then left, closing the door softly behind him. I focused on each inhale and exhale while waiting for the clubhouse to settle into silence. I willed my mind to relax, but nothing seemed to work.

I was damn near salivating at the thought of getting high.

I listened as the men carried Guardrail up to his room and then doors began opening and closing. The sounds of their voices faded, but I waited an extra thirty minutes just to be safe.

I hated myself.

Loathed my need for this drug.

I didn't understand it—I'd kicked the habit.

I shoved the blankets off my legs in frustration before roughly running my hands over my face. I needed to stay in bed—just close my eyes and get some sleep.

I lasted thirty seconds and then I was up, creeping silently across the carpet in my room. *I was just going to look around; not use.* I turned the door handle and took two steps into the darkened hallway before falling over a figure in the dark.

"I thought I might get some company if I camped out in the hallway," the voice whispered to me as I crawled over him and pushed myself up onto my knees.

"Why are you out here, Twitch?"

He offered me his hand and pulled us both up off the floor. "I could ask you the same thing, but I think we both know the answer to that. C'mon."

He led me downstairs and out toward the back deck before gesturing to an empty chair. "Have a seat." He started pacing across the deck as if he was arguing with himself, but stopped abruptly and turned back to me. "How bad is it?"

"Truthfully?"

He sighed. "Only way to be, kid."

I chewed on my lip. "I want to crawl out of my skin. I just want to feel happy again. To not feel anything, but mind-numbing pleasure."

Twitch nodded, immediately understanding what I meant. "Charm'll probably have my ass, but I can get you something to take the edge off."

I wiped my sweaty palms on my sweatpants, resisting the urge to bounce my legs in excitement. He stepped back inside long enough to grab a glass pipe before sitting down in the chair across from me. He must've noted my wary expression because he held the pipe up toward me. "Hash pipe, kid. Jesus, you think I'd bring crack out here? Charm might be pissed that I'm giving you weed, but he'd have me strung up over crack."

I watched as he packed the bowl, using the porch light to see. He lit the end of it and took a few puffs before offering it to me.

"I've never done this before."

He nodded. "You prefer a bong or a joint?"

I clarified, "I mean, I've never smoked pot before. Like ever."

Twitch's eyes widened. "Fuck me. I just assumed with your... history...well, it doesn't matter." He showed me how to inhale and we passed the pipe back and forth a few times.

He was right—the marijuana diminished the cravings until I could think clearly again. It was a completely different high than what I'd ever experienced with blow—cocaine left me feeling jittery, but with the weed, I felt relaxed.

Calm.

My mind wasn't racing with thoughts of the past. I was in control again; quietly existing alongside Twitch. It was nice—just sitting here with him. I felt like we could stay right here forever. We wouldn't worry about what tomorrow would bring; the two of us would just enjoy the scenic view from the porch.

The fog from the cocaine withdrawals left my system and my brain—not content to remain idle—went right back to focusing on Charm and all the reasons why he kissed me and then took off. I closed my eyes and let the back of my head hit the chair with a small sigh.

New plan—I would sit out here forever until I unraveled the mystery that was Charm, Prez of the Scarred Savages.

"Better?"

I opened one eye and nodded at him. Twitch might've only been a few years older than me; it was hard to tell. The parts of his face that weren't covered in wild facial hair were smooth and clear, indicating youth. His beard was straight out of the nineteenth century, with thick mutton chops connecting into a full beard near his chin. He was underweight, a side effect of his drug use, most likely. It was his eyes that made it impossible to guess; they were hard...aged. As if he'd seen more than one person ever should in life.

I didn't know how many times he'd fallen off the wagon, but judging by the visible track marks on his arms, it must've been a lot. His arms were sleeved in tattoos, but the scars were still visible through the ink. There were several on his wrists that looked a little like slashes.

He surprised me when he reached up and tucked a strand of hair behind my ear and I brought my eyes back up to his face. His hand lingered near my cheek. "You're a good person, Neve. I think you'll make it."

I leaned into his palm and smiled. "So are you, Twitch. Thanks for looking out for me tonight—maybe we could keep this between us though?"

He stroked my cheek. "Yeah, kid. Just me and you." His eyes were half-open and he looked like he was on the verge of falling asleep. He set the pipe down and grabbed me in a tight hug. Just when I expected him to release me, he pulled me onto his lap.

I looked at him questioningly. "What are you doing?"

"Shhhh…" He whispered. "Just let me hold you. I won't try anything, I swear. It's been a long time since I've just been close to someone else. Do you ever feel like that? Like you just need to feel another human being to not feel so fucking alone?"

I settled against his shoulder and closed my eyes. I nodded because I knew exactly what he meant. I'd yearned for that very thing since my parent's deaths. There were times that I'd been sitting in the very same room, mere feet from Clint, yet felt as though I was locked inside a prison cell. I couldn't imagine that being with the Savages would've given him many opportunities to meet someone and fall in love. "What did you do before this, Twitch? Have you always been with the club?"

He shifted me over before answering. "Grew up in the club. I joined the Marines after high school, but got injured in combat in Afghanistan—blew out my knee. That was it."

He continued talking, unaware that I'd gone stiff in his arms.

What were the odds that there would've been two men who'd gone overseas to fight?

Two men who would've blown out their knees, ending their military careers early?

It couldn't have been. Charm hated him—he never would've allowed him into the club.

I pulled back and stared down at him in disbelief, finally seeing a truth I'd missed. They weren't identical, but those eyes were the exact same as his twin's. In spite of what he'd witnessed in battle, he still had a kindness about him that Gunner lacked.

"Bobby?" I whispered, as my hand traced down the side of his face and he went white.

His own hand came up to cup my cheek, his voice quivering as he said, "I knew you'd find your way back. That first morning, I sat out there, praying you'd come back to me."

A tear slipped from my eye and I began shaking my head. "Twitch, no. It's me. Neve. I'm not her. I'm so sorry."

He released me and stood up, knocking me over in the process. Somehow, his hand shot out and caught me right before I hit the porch though. I expected him to say something, but he just kept studying my face, as if it might morph into hers.

Finally, he took a step back and ran both hands over his face roughly. "How? Jesus fuck, is this a joke? You knew who I was. Your hair—your eyes..." He paused and watched me helplessly.

I ran the back of my hand across my eyes as more tears fell. "I read Charm's notebook. I didn't mean to, I swear. I just put two and two together from that. I'm sorry." I admitted it all, realizing that these weren't just characters in a story. They were men who'd grown up in a bad situation that had only gotten worse as time went on. I may have come in and read their stories, but I didn't really know them.

And, in that moment, what I'd done felt wrong—even disrespectful somehow.

He surprised me when he pressed his lips to my temple before backing away slowly. "I'm just gonna head up to bed. You sure you're good now? Not feeling any more cravings?"

I shook my head. "Twitch, I'm fine. You don't have to leave, I can go."

His lips flattened into a straight line, disappointment radiating off of him before he left me alone on the porch. I waited a few minutes before going in to retrieve *Tales from Both Sides of the Brain*; if ever I needed a distraction, tonight was it.

I curled up in the chair, struggling to focus on the words. The author had written about his daughter marrying his second wife's brother, which should've held my attention, but my heart just wasn't in it.

The words blended into gibberish as I struggled to make sense of Charm allowing Twitch to patch in. The sounds of summer surrounded and lulled me into a state somewhere between awake and asleep. Every few seconds, my body would jolt back to consciousness, only to drift off again.

"Neve..."

I shifted, convinced I was dreaming because there was no way I was hearing that voice.

"Neve, honey, wake up."

I sat up, unaware of how long I'd been out. The sky was still dark, but I was no longer alone. Somehow, I'd slept through the rumble of motorcycles. "I'm awake, sorry."

Charm took in the book on my lap and the blanket I'd snagged from my bed. "Doing some late-night reading?"

I shook my head. "No, I was actually about to go off on a moonlit killing spree in the woods. Care to join me?"

He squeezed his eyes shut even as a grin lit up his face. "Jesus Christ, Neve. Some of the stuff that comes out of your mouth. What have you been up to since I left?"

Emboldened by the smile on his face, I said, "Left? Don't you mean ran away?"

Charm's smile faded. "It wasn't like that. I had—"

"Oh, I know. 'Club business.' *What does she win, Johnny?* Neve, you're the proud owner of a new car!"

I was on a roll. I didn't know whether it was the pot or just my pent-up emotions over what we'd shared at the cliffs that day.

He sank down onto the chair in front of mine. "Are you high right now?"

I focused on his right ear as I answered. "No. Are you?"

He stiffened, even as he leaned forward. "Why are you so mad? You made your feelings known and I've stayed away. End of discussion."

I sputtered, "End of discussion? You kiss me out of the blue and it's just end of discussion?" I got up and began pacing the length of the porch, frantic energy coursing through my veins.

Charm took the opportunity to stretch his legs across my vacated chair, firing me up even more. He had no right looking like he was about to fall asleep, while I was over here still waiting for answers.

"What do you want, Neve? You were there and I took a chance. Ain't nothin' to talk about, Sweetheart. It didn't mean shit."

I took a step backward, as if his words had physically slapped me across the face, instead of just emotionally. "So, if it meant nothing, did you tell your girl?"

He scratched at his beard and frowned. "My girl? What the hell are you talking about?"

My eyes stung with unshed tears, but I wasn't doing that. I wasn't going to fall apart over something that had obviously been nothing more than an opportunity that presented itself. I tried to phrase the words in a way that in no way implied that I'd been reading his journal. "I saw the picture in your room, of you and a woman. I couldn't destroy a relationship. You seemed so happy and I don't wanna be the person who messes that up."

That's what I did, wasn't it? Destroy things that were once good?

So, maybe I'd made him smile a handful of times. Rae had probably done the very same thing hundreds more. It was naïve of me to think that what we had between us had been special. Hell, he'd just come right out and told me that it hadn't meant a damn thing.

Charm leaned back in the chair, his arms crossed over his chest, giving nothing away. "So, your only reason for pushing me away is because of the picture you saw? And if you hadn't seen it, then what?"

Well, I read the journal too...so, I'm pretty sure that I couldn't live with being your sloppy seconds when I've read about how fiercely you loved Rae.

Obviously, that was something I could never vocalize.

I sighed. "Well, I probably would've done the same thing. If I let my personal feelings cloud my judgment, then what happens when things fall apart? I really like it here—these men have become like brothers to me. I don't want to do anything to jeopardize that."

"You think I'd throw you out if it didn't work out between us? I wouldn't do that to you, honey. You've proven yourself to be a part of this club."

Honey.

He'd said it before, when I had the nightmare, and then again when we went cliff jumping. It was such a small word, yet it stirred up big feelings inside of me. Feelings that I could never act on. When he called me 'sweetheart' it was different. He'd always said it conde-scendingly.

I hurriedly rushed out, "This is all hypothetical—it's not like it matters."

But, it had mattered.

Every second spent with him left me wanting more. I mashed my lips together in an effort not to cry.

Charm watched me carefully. "Neve, maybe you should go upstairs—try to get some sleep. Things will be better in the morning."

I nodded and he stood up. Just before I made it to the door, he intercepted me. "I—" He stood there frozen, his massive hands grip-ping my shoulders to the point of pain.

I didn't mean to, but the hint of cigar smoke that clung to him hit my nose, igniting memories that left me unsteady. I leaned in and inhaled and then his hands were on my face, backing me up toward the side of the lodge.

I'd never wanted to be someone without a conscience, until now. I wanted all of the pleasure and none of the guilt.

Charm's mouth hovered inches above mine, so close that his hair tickled along my cheek. All I had to do was stretch up onto my toes. One small movement and we'd be connected.

His exhales were ragged, but warm against my face. I tilted my chin up even more, begging him to make a move, while my mind waged a war with morality.

"Goodnight, Neve," he whispered, and the spell was broken. He held the door open for me on my way inside, but refused to make eye contact again before disappearing down the hall to his study.

I moved up the stairs faster than ever before and slipped back into bed with a pounding heart and an incredible sense of guilt. I was still in the process of steadying my breathing when I was struck by the full impact of Twitch's words.

If he was under the assumption that I was Rae reincarnated, then there hadn't been some last-minute miracle.

Either Twitch's mind was gone from years of drug use or Rae was dead. Neither was a particularly positive conclusion.

And there was no way that I could stay much longer. Perhaps there wasn't any place in the world where I'd be immune to the effects of Charm, but I wasn't willing to compete with a ghost for his affections.

26

NEVE

I had a dream last night that she was gone. I shrugged it off as a nightmare, but I think it was a premonition. Vic and I have tried everything to keep her well, but nothing seems to last. She's lost even more weight and sleeps all the time.

I wanted to ask her about the baby, but the words refused to come out. Maybe, on another level, I don't want the truth. It would only make a terrible situation worse.

Bobby has fallen into some bad shit.

It's like he wants to go down with her…

Charm was right—things did look different that next morning. For starters, he was gone…again. The days turned into weeks, but my escape plan was still nothing more than a wistful idea.

I simply wasn't sure how to put it in motion and avoid hurting anyone's feelings. These men were no longer my begrudging rescuers, but brothers. I didn't know when the shift happened, but I was dreading the day that I'd leave Kasselhessen—and them—for good.

Guardrail was slowly starting to get up and moving again. After Doc confirmed my diagnosis of a sprain, we'd taken turns helping out with his care. I'd braced myself for the drinking—had even written several statistic-laden speeches in my head, but I couldn't bring myself to lecture him for his coping mechanisms. After that night, it was obvious that I could barely manage myself.

It was inevitable; he was going to go right back to it as if nothing happened, and I was going to bite my tongue in keeping my opinion to myself, knowing he might not be so lucky the next time.

I'd mentally prepared myself as best I could, so when I saw the note in his familiar chicken scratch, I damn near fell over in shock.

Hey Doll, can you pick up some O'Doul's at the store?

I'd considered swapping out his beer with the non-alcoholic stuff, but the desire to remain alive had me rethinking the entire idea. Maybe he'd actually taken some of my ideas to heart. There was no doubt in my mind that he was still getting the real stuff, but it meant a lot to me that he'd at least try.

Charm eventually deemed it safe to come back to the clubhouse, but managed to remain elusive. Gunner acted as his personal body-guard, ensuring that I never got within ten feet of him. I searched fruitlessly for the rare moments when he wasn't on the phone barking orders or out on some mysterious club business, but it never happened.

Never a moment to talk about what had happened between us when we went cliff jumping or even the aftermath on the porch.

Charm had gone back to regarding me with something akin to indifference, yet still found the time to thank me for cooking and cleaning when he came in at night. He hadn't been upset to find me asleep on the couch either when he got in early this morning; he'd just quietly woken me up on the way to his study.

It was what I'd wanted from the beginning...friendship. Now, I found myself suffering from Liberosis—which technically wasn't even a real thing, but I had this desire to care less. To revert back to how I was when I arrived.

I needed a how-to manual for managing my emotions while sober.

PD rode along with me one more time, but after that, I was on my own for shopping trips. *"I'm not getting dragged into another one of yours and Amber's yoga classes,"* had been his exact words. It was refreshing to see that not everyone took my advice as gospel—god forbid, I suddenly get cocky. I was always able to count on PD and Gunner to do the opposite of what I suggested.

Despite my desire to see PD reconnect with Ali, I relished the freedom to do what I wanted; even if it was only for an hour or two a week.

Amber was always willing to drop whatever she had going on to sip a five-dollar cup of coffee while trailing after me down every aisle in the store. Sometimes, we went to yoga. Other times we went and tried on clothes. To an outsider, our activities were nothing out of the ordinary; but to an addict like me, it was a normalcy I hadn't known since high school.

I'd really taken to exploring Kasselhessen; I'd pack the groceries down in an ice chest in the back of the truck and then drive around until something caught my eye.

Yesterday, I'd passed a historical sign and learned that the town had been founded by German immigrants during the Pike's Peak Gold Rush of 1859. The small mountain community had been at the center of the region's mining district before losing half of its populace to the Civil War. Kasselhessen was an oddity though—they hadn't disappeared when gravel mining dried up and their population was low—no, the town had just turned to hard rock mining and kept the town running.

Now, it had a biker gang.

I found a small, family-run thrift store not long after and it had proven to be my favorite stop so far. I'd been sifting aimlessly through a bin while an older couple nearby bickered over a ceramic reindeer figurine when I found the coin. The year was wrong, but the message was the same regardless. I purchased it for a quarter and tucked it into the pocket of my jeans.

This morning, Twitch joined me on the ledge to watch the sunrise. I'd been coming out here ever since the night of Guardrail's accident;

needing to atone for the cravings I'd experienced. They just kept popping up at the most inopportune times—leaving me feeling weak and ashamed.

I was usually alone, but found that it hadn't bothered me. It gave me a chance to work through the storm of thoughts and memories in my head. I'd carried the guilt of my parent's deaths for over a year and, no matter how much I tried to combat it, coke would always be my first choice for coping.

Twitch sat silently beside me—we hadn't encountered each other much since the night he confused me for Rae. I knew that I wasn't going to get another opportunity, so I kept the coin hidden in my hand until the sun lit up the sky and then gently placed it in his. He turned it over in the morning light, studying the words written on it.

The medallion was white with gold trim, nothing fancy. It had a small hole near the top so it could be worn on a chain. 'Out of the Ashes of Addiction Comes Recovery and Growth,' 'Just for Today,' and the words 'Serenity' and 'Peace' were written on one side. The other side featured the Serenity Prayer with the words, 'God, Gratitude, Hope and Healing.' In the center, it said 'Miracles Happen.'

"I wanted to get you something for helping me a few weeks ago. It's not much, but I thought you could carry it with you as a reminder. You know, on days when you can't see the sunrise."

Twitch's jaw clenched as he stared ahead, lips mashed together. He nodded and managed to get out a rough, "Thanks," before he jumped up and took off, leaving me alone again.

"What the hell did you do to Twitch, Darlin'?" Rooster drawled out as he walked up.

I laughed nervously. I'd wanted to surprise the biker, not send him on a bender. "Nothing. He had somewhere to be, I think."

Rooster laughed. "He took off like he'd been shot out of a fuckin' cannon—thought you might've scared him."

I rolled my eyes. "Yep...all sixty-three inches of me are pretty intimidating."

He laughed, but headed back toward the clubhouse, no doubt going after Twitch. I brought my knees up and rested my chin against them, defeated. I'd been able to show four of the men my gratitude, but I still needed to think of something to do for the others. Minus Gunner, they'd all gone out of their way to make me feel welcomed and accepted, and I wanted to return the favor.

Unfortunately, everything I touched turned to shit. One bad decision had turned my life into this and it didn't matter how hard I tried, Gunner had made it abundantly clear that I would always be an outsider. I would spend the rest of my life wishing that I could've changed the past.

"You are pretty intimidating."

I jumped at his voice, ignoring the flush that crept up my neck. "I didn't know you were out here." My voice cracked and I tried to mask it by clearing my throat.

Charm took the last remaining steps until he was next to me. "Yeah—I've got a lot of shit to get done today, thought I'd get an early start. So, you scaring my men?"

I smiled. "Yeah, you know it. Listen, I'm glad you're out here. I wanna talk to you about what happened that night on the porch—"

Charm held up a hand, stopping me. "I already told you that we were good. I actually just came out here to let you know that we're going to host a few other clubs here in a few days. I'm gonna need your help to pull it off. I'm thinking we'll have close to a hundred. I can get you some help in the kitchen, but it'll be a lot of work. You think you're up for it?"

My heart sank. I wanted to tell him that I said what I did before I figured out that Rae hadn't pulled through. I wanted to tell him that I was afraid I'd never live up to his expectations. Most of all though, I wanted to tell him that I was afraid to hurt him.

Loving me was nothing short of a death sentence.

Instead, I answered distractedly, "It might be hard, but I think I can handle it."

He clapped me on the shoulder. "That's what she said."

My mouth dropped open in shock. "You—but I? You—" I sounded like a broken record, skipping over words.

He winked and walked away, calling out over his shoulder. "I'll let the guys know to get you whatever you need."

In that moment, he could've knocked me over with a feather.

Who was this man and what had he done with Charm?

It's...it's over.

I was going to get her out of the clubhouse for the day—I fucked up. I should've gotten her away from here years ago. This club is poison; destroying anything and everything in its path.

She'd promised that things were turning around.

Instead, I'm forever left with the image of her, propped up in bed staring at nothing. She was so cold and I knew it was too late, but I tried resuscitating her anyway. I close my eyes and see the horror on Vic's face as he dragged me screaming from her side. I'm haunted by all the things I could've done differently.

Her blood is on my hands.

Luck shrugged the whole thing off; as if she'd never meant a damn thing to him. It wasn't until I overheard him on the phone that I put two and two together.

She was collateral damage.

Now, I'm not going to stop until this club is mine. And the first order of business will be getting rid of the whores, the drugs, and him.

I sat at the large metal island in the kitchen with a notebook in my hand, but completely lost in thought. I had to come up with a menu to serve a hundred people; there wasn't time to dwell on Charm's reasons for going after Luck when Rae died. I couldn't fathom how he connected her death to the club. Unless, she had lung cancer brought on by being around bikers who smoked. Although, if that had been the case, I couldn't imagine that Twitch would've remained a smoker.

I stared back down at the blank notebook and tapped my pen against it. I had to come up with something. Charm was taking care of the tables and chairs, but there was so much work that needed to be done with only a few short days in which to get it all accomplished.

"How's it going, Darlin?" Rooster poked his head in.

I held up the notebook. "Well, if I could come up with a menu, I'd be doing a lot better. Did you guys take care of alcohol?"

He grinned slyly. "Oh, we took care of the booze. I think we might need another building to store it all."

I laughed and went back to tapping the pen against the blank page. I really needed some inspiration right about now.

Rooster sat down across from me. "What about brisket or chicken? We've got that big ass smoker just begging to be used."

I thought it over. If we did a barbecue rub on them, then I could pair it with potato salad and baked beans. "Okay, that could work. If he's planning on a hundred, then that means we'd need to look at roughly six to eight ounces of meat per person—I'm going to go with the higher number since the majority will be men. Eight hundred ounces—that puts us at fifty pounds. Maybe we could split and do twenty-five pounds of brisket and twenty-five pounds of chicken. I might need to add a couple of pounds in to account for water weight."

Rooster's mouth hung open. "Did you just do all that in your head?"

I nodded. "Doesn't everyone?"

He shook his head. "No one I know."

Doc came in and Rooster filled him on my 'impressive' calculating skills. He rubbed his hands together gleefully. "Okay, ninety-seven people want to drink. If we bought twenty-four cases of beer, will that be enough?" When I gave him a confused look he added, "I'm trying to make it harder for you."

I grinned. "Well, a case of beer is twenty-four bottles. If you bought twenty-four cases, that gives you five hundred seventy-six beers. That means, out of the ninety-seven people coming, each person would get five point nine three beers. And with a hundred people, that leaves you with five point seven six beers per person. I don't know about your friends, but if they drink like you guys, that's not going to be enough."

"Charm, you hearin' this?" Rooster looked over into the doorway and I stopped talking.

"You always been this good with numbers?" His eyebrows furrowed in confusion.

I nodded. "Yeah, I love numbers—especially for stuff like this. It's like a puzzle..."

Seeing the astounded faces, I self-consciously tucked a strand of hair behind my ear and looked away.

"Fifty-two crates."

His voice was so quiet that I had to lean forward. "Excuse me?"

Charm looked me right in the eye. "Fifty-two crates. Let's say that's what I've got—figure I can make twelve thousand on each one."

I didn't ask the obvious question—which would've been, 'What's in the crates?'

No, my inner mathematician came out. "Fifty-two crates at twelve thousand each? So, you'd be looking at six hundred twenty-four thousand. Split eight ways, it'd still leave you with seventy-eight thousand per person. Although you probably wouldn't just split it evenly eight ways—that'd be a little too simple. With you being 'the Prez,' surely your cut is bigger. So maybe we're looking at twenty percent for you —one hundred twenty-four thousand eight hundred dollars. Still, the other guys would walk away with seventy-one thousand, three hundred fourteen dollars, and some change. Oh, but I didn't factor in giving some back to the town—I'm probably completely off—"

Charm's mouth hung open in shock and he held a hand up to stop me from continuing. "That's insane."

I shook my head. "No, it's easy—you just multiply and divide. Anyone can do it."

He laughed bitterly. "Not usually without the help of a calculator. Jesus, Honey. How'd some genius like yourself end up here?"

I shrugged. "I wanted to be the best. I found that I'd have to forfeit sleep in order to do that—got hooked on blow instead and well, here I am."

Numbers had always been easy for me. It was like the problem was drawn out in front of me—I could see all the numbers and then it just became a matter of moving them around as needed to get my answer.

Charm clicked his tongue against his teeth and a flood of heat washed over me again. There was just something about him that left me feeling completely undone.

"Alright, let's get back to work. I think Neve has this completely taken care of—might even save me a little money too."

I found that I wanted to save him more than money; I wanted to save the parts of him that had obviously been lost when Rae died. While there had been brief glimpses of the man he was before, Charm had obviously hardened himself after losing her.

Rooster hung back. "Hey, I had a question for ya. You mentioned before that I was too obvious."

I jotted down a few more party notes before answering. "I did say that."

He spun around on the stool and reached for my hand, demanding my full attention. "Well, say that some chicks show up at the party. How can I avoid coming across like that?"

I grinned. "Are you coming to me for female advice, Rooster? Things must be bad then."

He glared down at me. "C'mon, Neve. Tell me what to do."

I shrugged. "Do you know how to dance? A lot of women love a man that can move on the dance floor."

He pressed his lips together before answering. "I'm not sure what kind of party you're thinking this is gonna be, but we don't usually dance."

"Why not?"

He gestured to his cut-off. "Because we're bikers, Darlin'."

I pointed the pen at him. "That's your problem—too concerned with your image."

When he jumped off the barstool and left the room in a huff, I had to fight the smile that kept creeping onto my face. If I knew Rooster, he was hunting down music so I'd teach him how to dance.

I wasn't wrong.

Ten minutes later he stormed back in with his phone in hand. "Alright Neve, here's what I've got."

He turned on some fast-paced rap music and began moving around the kitchen as if he was having a seizure. I gave up on remaining silent and burst out laughing.

"What? What's wrong with this?"

I shook my head and dabbed at my eyes. "Nothing if your goal is to end up on *YouTube*. If you want to impress the ladies, you need something slower." I took the phone from him and scrolled through his music, finally deciding on some Luke Bryan.

"You know we won't be playing anything like this at the party, right?"

I turned the volume up. "Why not? This is good music."

His head moved along to the beat of the song. "Hell yeah it is. Doesn't mean Charm will let us play it."

I slid off my stool and grabbed his hands. "Okay, put this hand here." I placed his right hand on my hip. "And this one goes here." I held his left hand with my right. "Now, we'll start slow so you can get the hang of it."

Luke Bryan crooned about dancing on tailgates, while we swayed back and forth in the kitchen.

"Now, let's do the steps. You're going to lead, okay? Two steps forward and one step back."

Rooster started off a little rocky, but by the third time the song played, he'd gotten the hang of it—only stepping on my feet twice. We moved around the kitchen to the beat of the song and, as he got it down, added in a couple of spins.

Joker tapped me on the shoulder before signing that he wanted to be taught as well and I winced as he hopelessly stomped across my toes throughout the song. When PD cut in, I gave a silent prayer of thanks. His arms were stiff, as if he was afraid to move and it took several turns around the room before he loosened up.

The kitchen had become our dance hall and bikers streamed in, happily awaiting their turns. Axel had obviously been taught by Amber and moved gracefully around the kitchen, while Guardrail's moves were jerky and robotic; making the lack of a female presence completely apparent.

A throat cleared just as he dipped me backward, nearly taking my feet out from under me. "You givin' lessons?" Charm leaned against the door frame, running his thumb against his beard.

Guardrail pulled me back up and I let go of his hands guiltily. "Why? Do you want to learn?"

He nodded and cut in between us. My heart beat a little faster as he gripped my waist with one hand and my hand with the other. He led effortlessly and I began to suspect that he knew exactly what he was doing. In fact, he could've taught every man here, with the exception of Axel.

Whereas the other men and I had probably looked like a couple of junior high kids dancing, Charm's body was so close to mine that it was impossible to ignore the way his muscles brushed against me as we danced.

He leaned down next to my ear and whispered, "I may have done this a time or two."

I grinned like an idiot as my face turned cherry red before murmuring, "I noticed."

He moved even closer and his breath tickled my ear as he said, "I didn't mention it before now, but if you wanted to go into town and get some clothes for the party, you can."

"Okay. This doesn't mean you're my man though, right?" I laughed easily and licked my dry lips, high off of every inhale and exhale. His fingers tightened on my waist at the words and I bit back a moan.

Keep it together, Neve.

He frowned before tucking a strand of hair behind my ear. "I got zero interest in being your man, honey."

The music ended and I realized that Rooster was the only one still in the room, sitting on a barstool, watching both of us curiously.

"Charm." Gunner walked in. "Got something you need to see."

I waved at him and he scowled in return, giving his full attention back to his Prez.

Charm stumbled as he backed away. "Yep. Let's go. Neve, you good here? Got everything you need?"

I nodded and waited until they left before letting out a heavy exhale of disappointment. It wasn't like a relationship with Charm was even a viable option, but finding out that he had zero interest in being my man still stung.

I had to pull this party off.

They were all counting on me.

I just hoped that I didn't let them all down.

2 7

CHARM

My girl's a goddamned genius. And it's not just her impressive math skills; she's changing them.

Guardrail is all of a sudden cutting back on his alcohol. PD's gone homeopathic—and it's not even related to the Pilates shit that Ali talks him into. I saw Gunner studying one of Neve's ASL signs like it was a treasure map.

Gunner.

Doc swore that she would be replacing him any day now.

And Twitch? I hadn't seen him smile like that since her. I hadn't seen him fight to stay sober in a long time either.

Now, Rooster has her giving him dating tips.

That night, on the porch, I thought we were close. The air reeked of weed and I knew that Twitch was most definitely behind it. Instead of being angry, I'd been caught up in her words.

It had been real to her too and her confession only made me want her more—despite her fucked up past, she had honor and that wasn't something just anyone possessed.

She disregarded her feelings out of respect for Rae.

Neve had looked up at me from underneath her lashes and her lips automatically parted when I led her up against the side of the clubhouse, leaving me feeling—I wasn't even sure I knew how to describe it. I'd never felt it before.

Overjoyed?

Thrilled?

Ass over teakettle for her?

Whatever it was, I've felt it every time I looked at her.

It was irrational—craving her like this.

With any other woman, I would've walked away by now, but she makes life worth living. She's taken eight men—men who had nothing —and given them purpose.

She carries physical and emotional reminders of her past, yet always seems to have a smile on her face.

Little Miss Sunshine.

If I ever work up the courage, I'm gonna tell her about the girl in the picture and then claim her as mine for eternity.

28

NEVE

"Okay, we can set that pan over on the back counter."

Joker grabbed a pair of oven mitts and moved the pan of baked beans from the oven to an empty countertop. We hadn't had a moment to rest. The past three days had been nothing but work.

I spent yesterday morning cleaning the entire clubhouse and the damn thing sparkled from all the elbow grease. I'd taken some extra time cleaning Gunner's room—*okay, I snooped.*

Again.

I'd done something nice for almost all of the guys, but I hadn't been able to think of one thing to do for him.

It had taken me an extra fifteen minutes, but in his nightstand, under a roll of condoms, was a worn picture of two Marines. I studied the picture and realized that one of them was Gunner. When I turned the picture over, there was a name and a date.

I'd known that he was a Marine, but nothing was ever mentioned in the journal about his return home. It appeared that Twitch wasn't the only one who'd lost friends in battle.

Feeling like a thief, I'd tucked the photo into the waistband of my jeans and finished cleaning. Once I was sure that no one was paying attention, I snuck out and drove into town. The men were busy getting the meat ready to smoke—something that was going to take all night from what I understood.

I doubted they'd even noticed I was gone. I parked the truck to find them gathered around the smoker back near the storage shed, drinking and laughing. I'd simply returned the photograph back to his nightstand and set the canvas up on his dresser before heading back to work.

Hours later, I woke to an empty house and realized that the men hadn't even made it back inside. Joker joined me in the kitchen about an hour after I got up and we worked side by side in comfortable silence. I'd made the potato salad up in advance, so all we had to take care of were the baked beans.

I was going to need to nap for a week to recover.

I cleaned out her room today—Luck insisted. Said he had a prospect that was patching in and needed a place. I thought about splitting his face open, but remembered the plan.

Billy showed up and helped; Bobby's still in Psych...something about a mandatory seventy-two hour hold. We didn't talk; just worked in silence, packing her things.

I was proud of myself, thinking that I'd done alright until I saw the book. We all had one—she'd insisted on it. After Matt's broken arm, she was adamant that we learn to communicate with him the only way he knew how. I sank down on the bed and turned the pages, my fingers tracing her drawings, as my chest tightened in despair.

It just hit me that she'll never draw another picture.

I'll never again see her head bent over that damn desk while she furiously sketches a masterpiece.

I lost it and demanded everyone's copy.

I torched them all, but the pain in my chest has only gotten worse.

My love for her is a grave that I can't seem to stop digging.

I wanted to shed my ratty clothes and head upstairs to shower, but I owed this to Charm. I was finally beginning to understand his anger over the signs I'd made. I'd practically rubbed his face in the fact that she was gone.

I turned to Joker. "Hey, I forgot to take the signs down. I'm just gonna take care of that while this finishes up. Okay?"

His face fell, but he nodded.

No one had mentioned them again, but I knew what they must've been reminded of every time they passed by one. The other clubs weren't likely to let it go unnoticed either. I'd just pulled the second one off when his voice startled me.

"What the hell are you doin'?"

I jumped and turned around. "Hey, good morning. I was just getting rid of these before the party."

I wanted to try and fix a horrible mistake...

Charm shook his head before barking out, "Let's put it to a vote. See what the club says."

My mouth fell open in shock. "Are you drunk? You all but told me to take them down not that long ago."

"Guys! Let's go."

The other bikers walked in and sat down at the table, as if it was completely normal to call impromptu meetings in the middle of the dining area.

He walked around to the head of the table and addressed them. "Listen up, Neve here was thinking she should take down the signs before the other clubs arrive. Thoughts?"

PD shook his head. "They stay." He'd been using his Neti Pot faithfully and I hadn't heard him sneeze since. He was much more pleasant to be around; although that might've had more to do with me bumping into Ali as she snuck out of his room one early morning last week.

Rooster gave me a cocky grin. "Stay."

Joker held his thumb and pinky out in a Y handshape before shoving his knuckles forward and down.

Stay.

Guardrail raised an O'Doul's in a toast to me. "I like 'em."

Twitch fingered a chain around his neck and my heart skipped a beat at the sight of the medallion hanging from the end of it. "The kid's stuff stays."

Doc pinched his lower lip between his thumb and forefinger, lost in thought. He looked like he'd done more than just hang out with the smoker—I wasn't even sure how he was remaining upright. "I vote they stay," he said, with a slight slur.

Gunner sat silently at the end of the table. I knew there was no way in hell that he'd be on my side. He cleared his throat and looked around the room. "Well, Neve. I'll say what no one else has the balls to —" I cringed. "The signs class this shithole up. I say they stay."

Charm nodded. "Looks like it's unanimous. You better get those two rehung and then get ready for the party."

The men cleared out to finish setting up and Joker retreated back into the kitchen, while I stood in disbelief with the signs in my hand.

Had Gunner been abducted by aliens?

That was the only explanation for the complete one eighty he'd just done.

"Neve." The voice was soft.

I held my hand up. "Just a second, Gunner. I'm trying to determine if you've been body snatched."

He smirked at me, but his eyes were shiny. He tried to cover it up by running his hands through his hair. "You know there's no mother-fuckin' way that aliens would even think about crossing me."

I smiled. *That sounded like Gunner.*

He cupped my face in his hands and my eyes widened. *This was definitely not Gunner.*

"Neve, I saw what you did—in my room. No one's ever—that picture—honoring Cody like that?" He got choked up and paused. "Let's just say you're not a complete pain in the ass."

If I would've known that enlarging a photograph of him and a Marine buddy was the way to his heart, I would've done it day one. He might as well have told me that he wanted me to have his babies. My mouth was near the floor and he kept my face gripped in his hands before leaning in and pressing a rough kiss to my forehead.

"Thanks."

By the time I remembered to respond with a weak "You're welcome," he was already gone again. A river flowed from my eyes as I rehung the two pictures and, after being assured that Joker had the kitchen under control, I went upstairs to shower.

I let the hot water knead my sore muscles for as long as I could stand it before towel drying off and getting to work on my hair and face. I hadn't worn any of the makeup I got at the store. I hadn't worn anything since the afternoon that Amber came over. There just hadn't seemed to be any point to it with me cooking and cleaning all day.

I wiped the steam from the mirror and smiled at the girl in the reflection. Almost three months of taking care of myself had done wonders. I'd put on some much-needed weight and my face no longer looked skeletal.

I was damn proud of the woman I was becoming, even if I'd endured Hell to get here.

I took my time applying makeup and blow-drying my hair until it hung in loose waves down my back. Amber had told me that these gatherings were a big deal, so I wanted to look my best.

Once satisfied that I'd mastered the beauty aspect, I pulled the dress out of the back of my closet. I'd gone into *Pearl's Treasures* with plans to find a nice blouse, but when I'd told her that it was for the barbecue, she led me over to the dresses and began gathering them up by the armful.

"Let's get you a dressing room started."

She had me try on only one. When I slipped on the vintage halter dress, we both agreed it was perfect. It featured large white polka dots on red material. The bust was white, with cherries and red skulls across it. It was low-cut, but for a biker gathering, I'd fit right in. The best part was that it came down to my knees, so none of my scars showed.

I smiled as I slipped it off the hanger and stepped into it. I was going to match the guys with their flaming skulls. Pearl had tried to talk me into a pair of vintage red pumps, but with it being an outdoor party, I settled on a pair of red flip flops instead.

I applied sunscreen to my arms and chest before giving myself one last glance in the mirror. It was amazing what a good dress and a little red lipstick could do.

I heard the rumble of bikes pulling up as I got to the top of the stairs and I was only slightly disappointed that there wasn't a handsome biker with dark hair waiting for me at the bottom. However, this wasn't *Titanic* and I wasn't a woman of high-class.

With a deep breath for courage, I opened the front door and stepped out into the sunlight.

Rooster was talking to a man from one of the other clubs, but stopped and stared when he saw me. I gave a shy wave and he held his hand up, frozen.

The other guy was still talking as if nothing was amiss when I walked up. "Hey, Rooster."

His eyes pinballed up and down my dress more than once. "Holy fucking hell, Neve. Has anyone else seen you?"

I shook my head. "Is this not okay?"

He excused himself from his conversation and latched onto my arm, pulling me through throngs of people. The biker left behind stared longingly at me and I looked away, suddenly uncomfortable.

Charm was behind the smoker, a beer in hand.

"Charm. Did you want Neve to be somewhere special?"

He didn't look at us. "Uh, no. Just tell her to stick with our guys."

"Why don't you tell her yourself," I suggested playfully and he turned around, nearly dropping his beer when saw me.

Rooster chuckled. "I thought you'd wanna see."

I smoothed the front of the skirt with my hands and waited for him to say something, while Rooster went to grab another beer, leaving the two of us alone by the smoker. If we hadn't been surrounded by dozens of other people, it might've even been considered romantic.

"Jesus, honey. You look fuckin' amazing." He kept staring and I began babbling away to cover up the awkwardness.

"Did you see I have skulls right here?" I gestured toward the bust. "Just like you guys."

He swallowed and nodded. "I—uh—I did see that."

"They're actually considered the center of individuality and archaeologists have found skulls dating back thousands of years ago, some even predate writing systems. This means that we don't even know why they had them on display."

Charm nodded again, the corner of his lip turning up into a slight smirk. "You're doing it again, Neve."

"Doing what?"

He chuckled. "Spouting off inane facts because you're uncomfortable."

Luckily, PD walked up before I had to explain myself. He actually did a double take when he saw me. "Holy shit, Neve. You look sexy as fuck."

Charm growled. "Somethin' you need, PD?"

He frowned and took a step back. "Yeah, actually. I need Neve—we've got a little situation."

I looked around. "Where's Doc?"

PD kicked at some loose gravel with his boot. "Well, the situation is Doc. Guy's been drinking since last night and he is beyond fucked up. Said Neve owed him."

I groaned. "Where is he?"

I was hoping to enjoy the party for a little while before having to take care of anyone.

"We got him up in his room, for now."

Charm gave PD a look and he added, "I'll take you up to him."

I brushed off any feelings of disappointment. I'd given my word to Doc. "Bye Charm. Save me some food."

He gave me that weird look again before agreeing.

The party was in full swing now—there were bodies everywhere. I was busy counting the bikers in attendance when I got the distinct feeling that I was being watched. I turned around and there he was, back by the trees.

Clint.

He'd found me, but didn't make a move, like I'd expected. He just stood there, watching me silently.

I sucked in a breath and PD grabbed me, spinning me around to face him. "What's wrong? What happened?"

I blinked and looked again, but he was gone. *Had I imagined it?* "I'm sorry. Thought I saw something."

It was a hallucination.

That was the only thing that made sense.

"Neve. Neve. Neve."

I took a deep breath and patiently replied, "Yes, Doc?"

"Have I told you how pretty you look?"

"Not in the last five minutes, no." If I'd acted anything like he was while I was detoxing, it was a wonder he hadn't thrown me out into the woods himself.

PD had dropped me off to find Doc hunched over the bathroom counter. *"Kill me,"* He'd groaned. *"Why did I drink so much?"*

From there, he'd proceeded to splash cold water onto his face before giving up and sinking down to rest his head against the toilet seat. I'd patted his back as he repeatedly told me how pretty I was. Apparently, his idea of manning the smoker had involved copious amounts of liquor.

"He's gonna be so fucking pissed at me for keeping you in here," he grumbled to the toilet seat.

I wet a washcloth with cool water and placed it on the back of his neck. "Eh, what's a party without you?"

He continued mumbling to himself. "If I thought the black eye was bad—shit, he's going to murder me."

"Wait, Charm gave you the black eye?"

He nodded slowly. "Yep. I opened my big mouth and told him about strip Go Fish. I shouldn't have done it, but I wanted him to know about your legs—see if we could track down the assholes responsible. Obviously, he didn't take it well."

I shook my head as my face went numb. "But, that was right after I got here. Why would he care about our game?"

He hadn't given any indication that he'd felt anything other than disgust back then.

Doc propped his hand up under his chin and looked at me. "I can see down your dress, Neve. Is that a new bra?"

I slapped the back of his head. "Focus, Doc. Why did Charm hit you? It doesn't make sense."

He laughed until his head fell off his arm and then righted himself. "It doesn't make sense? Are you fucking kidding me? It's been you from day one. Everything changed when you showed up."

I raised a hand to stop him. "He called me a mangy dog. Surely you didn't forget about that."

He smiled to himself and closed his eyes. "Oh yeah. You know how some guys are cards and flowers?" I nodded and he continued, "Well, Charm is whiskey and insults."

I began fumbling with the washcloth in my hand. "I just wanted to return the favor to you guys for helping me, and I wish I could've done more. I never meant for any of this to happen."

His smile faded and he leaned closer. "You say that like you're not planning on being around tomorrow."

"Look at me, Doc." I paused. It was now or never. "How many addicts go the rest of their lives without a relapse? How many live to say they beat it? There's already been so much loss in this place—I can't put anyone here through that again. I'm going to be leaving soon, so you're not reminded of her."

Doc ran the back of his hand across his eyes, like a toddler fighting sleep. "I wondered how long it was going to take before he opened up to you about her. You'll never be anything like that, Neve."

I snorted as a bitter laugh escaped. "Obviously. She got sick—I did too, but in a different way. I couldn't cope with my life, so I medicated with snow. We couldn't be more different."

He propped himself up again and looked me in the eye, all traces of humor gone. "How is it you know so much, but so little? His sister was an addict and there wasn't a damn thing any of us could do to save her."

I grabbed Doc's shoulder and got right in his face. "His sister? I'm talking about the woman from the picture. Who is she?" My voice had taken on that shrill tone that seemed to always accompany hysteria.

Nothing was making sense. It was as if Doc was speaking in riddles.

He shrugged out of my grasp. "The girl from the picture? Do you mean Rae? That's her. That's his sister."

I sucked in a sharp breath. *Sister?* The entire time it had been his sister? There had never been a twisted love triangle involving Twitch. "He has a sister?"

He nodded. "Had. He *had* a sister. Their mom abandoned them when Charm was five and Rae was two. Just left them at a grocery store. He tried to look out for her as best he could when Luck moved them from Texas up here. The club was heavy into drugs and it was really only a matter of time before Rae got in deep herself.

"She would try to clean up, but with that bitch heroin living under the same roof, she couldn't stay away long. When H wasn't available, she did blow. Luck turned a blind eye to it, but Charm? Charm did everything in his power to sober her up. We'd detox her, but she'd crawl right back to it."

"That's why you have the straps downstairs, isn't it?" The hope that had briefly made an appearance, just as quickly left.

Doc nodded. "Yeah, for all the good it did us. When she fell for another biker, we thought it'd straighten her out, but she just dragged him down with her. Rae got pregnant and said she was gonna quit—told us that he begged her to." He paused and roughly wiped at his face just as I did the same. Twitch had tried to save her, only to go down himself.

"We found her dead in her room not long after—she'd overdosed on heroin. Twitch attempted suicide three days later—slit his wrists and ended up in a psych ward. I didn't think he was gonna make it. Hell, there are days that I still don't."

Twitch?

The scars.

I brought a hand up to my mouth, trying to muffle my sobs. He'd loved her, but she'd loved drugs more. It could've been the story of me and Clint. He'd never cared for me the way he did heroin.

Doc continued, "Hasn't been right since then. Lost his girl and his baby at once. He was out on a run, so he blamed himself for it happening—thought she would've been fine had he stayed back. Rae was always going to do what she wanted though; it wasn't a question of if she would OD, it was when."

It made sense; why Twitch had gotten close to me. It was why he'd wanted to hold me the night we got high—because I reminded him of Rae; and in that moment, he had her back, however brief it was. God, he'd even convinced himself that I was her...maybe he'd even thought that he could save me where he hadn't been able to save her.

I stumbled back into the doorway and sank down to join Doc on the floor. "So, what did Luck do?"

Doc laughed humorlessly. "He pinned it all on Charm. Said if he would've done a better job with her that none of it would've happened. The club began to split after that—if the Prez couldn't handle his own daughter, how the hell was he supposed to run the club?"

Charm had pushed me away when I showed up, not out of spite, but because I reminded him of his dead sister.

Hurting people hurt people.

My mom used to say that all the time, but I never really thought much about it until now. Charm put up boundaries because he couldn't relive her death again.

"Charm would drag her out to watch the sunrise—he'd read a book on helping addicts recover. Apparently, watching the sunrise is a natural high. He didn't go out there again though until you showed up."

The entire time I'd wanted to prove him wrong and it turned out that he'd wanted the same thing. I thought back to the first time he took me out to the ledge and the way he'd stared at me; needing me to be different.

"Is that why he took me on the motorcycle? As part of this natural high thing?"

Doc cocked his head to the side, still using his arm for support. "He took you out on the bike?"

I nodded and he continued, "Well, yeah that was one of the things he tried with Rae. He put his role as VP on hold trying to fix her—yoga, meditation, cliff jumping—you name it, the guy tried it."

We slipped back into silence again and the weight on my chest grew heavier, not lighter. Hearing about Rae made what happened at the cliff more complicated, instead of less. Before, it was the thought of a girlfriend standing in the way. Now, it was this intense fear of not living up to his expectations. What if I was no better than her?

If given the opportunity, would I blow my sobriety?

Doc saw my face. "Hey, you're nothing like Rae. Don't try to compare the two. You worked your ass off to sober up and you've remained clean. I don't know that she ever made it past a week."

I shook my head. "But, Charm…he can't have feelings for someone like me. I'm what he despises most—an addict."

What had happened between us was nothing more than lust. I was a female in close proximity; it was bound to happen. Nothing about it was a good foundation on which to build a relationship though.

"Neve, how many times have you driven into town on your own?"

I thought back over all my visits into town. "I don't know—I've gone at least once a week though."

"Eight. You've been into town eight times. Wanna know how I know? Because one of us has followed you every single time to make sure you stay safe. Hell, I think most of us would've done it even if he hadn't asked us."

I pushed myself up, my legs shaking. "I have to go. Doc, can I leave you alone?"

I had to know if it was true and I had a crazy hunch that I knew where to find my answers before confronting Charm.

He nodded. "Probably just gonna upchuck and get it over with the minute you leave."

I wrinkled my nose. "Okay, glad I'm leaving then. I just need to sort this out. I'll come back by later and check on you."

He nodded and stared down into the toilet bowl. "He's gonna

claim you as his Ol' Lady, Neve. If he doesn't, then he's a fucking moron and one of us'll do it."

I could hear him retching as I shut the door behind me and raced down the hall toward Charm's bedroom. I tore open the nightstand and flipped through the journal, but everything in it was about Rae, ending with her death.

I returned it to the drawer with a sinking feeling. What had I expected—that he'd written about me?

Wait a minute.

I slipped out of his room and down the stairs, dodging bikers in various states of drunkenness before letting myself into his study. In the center drawer, buried underneath ledgers, was a shiny red notebook.

29

NEVE

I turned the pages with trembling hands, pausing every so often to brush the tears from my cheeks. I'd initially sworn that Doc had been wrong; had convinced myself that whatever had happened between us at the cliff was nothing but some lust-driven frenzy. He'd made it apparent that he'd loathed the very sight of me.

I brought my knees up to my chest in the leather chair and forced myself to power through, even though everything in me said to run away. And then I read about the most intimidating man I'd ever met going into more than one bookstore just so that I'd have something to read and my emotions ricocheted around the room.

He'd even read through them, so we would have something to talk about.

My wariness gave way to hope.

When the words stopped, I sat back in shock, clutching the notebook to my chest. It was true. He'd fallen for me much like I'd fallen for him.

We'd even encountered the same obstacle in Rae.

I couldn't feel my legs as I left the study; it was as if there was a gravitational pull leading me directly to him. It was madness—pure and simple madness. Yet, my feet continued to propel me forward, even as my mind bounced between reactions.

It changed everything.

It didn't change a thing.

I was getting emotional whiplash just trying to keep up.

Was I cut out to be a biker president's Ol' Lady?' Was that even something he still wanted? What happened to him not wanting to be my man?

I was so caught up in my thoughts that I didn't notice the man at the end of the hall until I crashed into him.

"Sorry," I began as he grabbed onto my waist and spun me around before setting me down gently.

"Well, well, well. This MC might have the best-looking bitch around." He kept his hands on my waist and backed me up toward the wall.

His voice held a hint of malice and I tried, unsuccessfully, to push him away. "I need to get outside."

He clicked his tongue. "That's no way to treat company, bitch. You might've heard a lot of shit from the other whores, but I'll go easy on you the first time. I promise."

"Get your hands off of me." I held my chin high in defiance and when he tightened his grip, I reared up and kneed him in the balls.

"Fucking bitch. I'll make you bleed for that."

He stood back up and lunged at me. I tried to move out of his reach, but he was quicker. He grabbed my arm and began pulling me back toward Charm's office.

"You sure you wanna do that?" A voice asked and I turned, ready to thank my rescuer, until I realized it was Blade—the biker who'd referred to me as a bitch in front of PD.

Their cut-offs shared the same logo, meaning they were from the same club. The man holding me had the Road Captain patch on his vest, while Blade had the Prez patch sewn onto the right breast of his.

Great. I'd managed to find myself in the crosshairs of the *Hell's Horsemen.* From what I'd overheard from the other bikers, these guys were not likely to treat me like a little sister. I'd be lucky to get out of here unscathed.

The man sneered. "You can have what's left of her when I'm done."

I was kicking wildly now to escape, but the man kept a firm grip on my arm.

"That's Charm's Ol' Lady, asshole. He'll gut you if you a lay a hand on her." Instead of feeling relief, my fear intensified. There was something about him that just made my skin crawl.

The man immediately released my arm. "Why didn't you say so in the first place?"

I moved toward Blade, keeping my eyes on the man the whole time. He pulled me into his side and walked toward the front door. "Jesus Christ, you need to stay with your men. Find one and don't wander off—your ol' man might not take kindly to rape, but these other fuckers don't share the same morals."

I nodded shakily as we moved through the crowd of bikers out onto the front porch where Joker was standing with a beer in his hand. When he saw my face. He dropped it and began signing wildly.

Are you okay?

What happened?

I nodded. "Thanks, Blade. I'll stay with Joker, if you don't mind."

He turned to the mute. "Keep her in your sight, got it? It'll be a fucking massacre if something happens to her."

Joker nodded and then began checking me over, before signing, *are you hurt?*

I shook my head, needing to choose my words carefully. Charm had said that I was part of this club; I had to be prepared to deal with bikers like ones in the *Hell's Horsemen MC*. If I made a big fuss now, the party would be over before it really even began and the men might not think that I was cut out for this kind of life.

I took a deep breath to steady myself. "No...some asshole got handsy. I do need to talk to you though."

He frowned and we walked over to the corner of the porch where it was less crowded.

I leaned against the rough wood exterior and exhaled slowly. "Did Charm tell you to watch out for me? To make sure I was okay?"

He nodded as if the questions were no big deal. Then, he linked his left index finger with his right, before reversing it.

Friend.

"He wanted you to be my friend?"

He nodded again and gestured around us.

"He wanted all of you to be friends with me?"

He smiled widely.

I grabbed him in a hug and held on, even more confused than before. His strong arms came up and wrapped around my back.

The card game.

The sunrises spent with other people.

He'd done it all for me and I'd pushed him away because I was convinced that there was someone else. It seemed blatantly obvious now.

Joker released me and pointed toward the bonfire. I nodded and we began walking toward it. He left me standing near Joseph, the prospect, while he grabbed another beer. My eyes scanned over the crowd of people gathered around the fire pit, searching for familiar faces.

Quite a few people were dancing on the slab of concrete we turned into a makeshift dancefloor—proving both Charm and Rooster wrong. *Speak of the devil...* I recognized Rooster as he took slow turns around the dance floor, his head leaned in, talking to a pretty brunette. Judging from the look on her face, he was doing more than counting steps as he whispered in her ear.

Gunner and Axel stood off to the side, acting as the unofficial lookouts for the party, while Guardrail was trying to drink another biker under the table. Cheers of *"chug, chug, chug"* echoed across the grass.

Twitch and PD were involved in a deep discussion near the fire, their heads close together. Ali walked up with drinks in her hand and PD easily pulled her into his lap before resuming his conversation. Amber appeared to be giving makeup tips to a table of club whores, but stopped and gave a small wave when she saw me.

I saw him before he saw me. Charm was sitting in one of the lawn chairs, his eyes searching every face until they landed on mine. He visibly relaxed and a small smile played on his lips.

I held up my hand and smiled back, feeling every bit like a junior high girl waving to her crush. My cheeks grew hot as he watched me.

"So, what's it like?"

A woman with overwhelmingly strong perfume moved into my line of vision, forcing my gaze away from Charm. Her hair had been bleached until it was white and her makeup was caked on in thick layers—she'd even managed to complete the stereotype with lipstick on her teeth.

"I'm sorry?"

She pointed to Charm. "What's it like being his Ol' Lady?"

His eyes narrowed when the woman pointed and I began stuttering. "H-h-he's not mine—"

She cut me off. "That's not what I heard."

I nodded, still staring at Charm. "Excuse me, I'll be right back."

I began walking back toward the clubhouse—I just needed a moment to get my thoughts in order and my nerves under control.

I passed several bikers who praised the food. Before I ended up here, I didn't know my way around a kitchen. I stopped and took one last look around the gathering as Rooster and his dance partner brushed past me on their way into the house. He turned back to wink at me and I couldn't help but smile.

I'd done it. I'd pulled it off.

Somehow, in the midst of withdrawals, I'd managed to help every biker in this club.

Well, every biker but one.

30

NEVE

"*Y*ou did good, honey."

A burst of pride filled my chest as I turned around and saw Charm standing just a few feet behind me. "Yeah?"

It had gone off without a hitch—I'd come a long way in the last few months. These bikers had become my drug—taking care of them my new hobby. And the crazy thing was that I couldn't imagine being anywhere else.

Charm reached out and grabbed onto one of my dark locks, as if anchoring me. "You did a kick ass job."

It hit me—my longing for blow diminished whenever he was near. With that, something shifted and I knew that he felt it too because he closed the distance between us, taking my face in his calloused hands. "Thank you," he said, just above a whisper.

I swallowed the lump in my throat. "I think it's me who should be thanking you. Everything—all of it—was for me?"

He nodded and I looked down at my feet, trying to gather my thoughts into something more than blubbering gibberish.

"Are you mad?"

I blinked slowly and looked up, as if seeing him for the first time. His light brown eyes were half open as if he was under the influence. His beard was unkempt, with each hair fighting to go in a different direction. He was wild, and I found I didn't want to tame him. No, I wanted to run free alongside him. To share space with him.

Finally, I shook my head. "Anger isn't even close to what I'm feeling."

Confusion was closer to the truth.

He stepped closer. "When you told me that the only thing holdin' you back was the girl in the picture, I felt something I ain't felt in a long time. Hope. I thought that I'd give you space, let you see the truth for yourself, but I can't seem to stay away when it comes to you, honey."

"What about you having 'zero interest in being my man?' That was just a few days ago; surely your opinion didn't change in three days?"

He gave me a half smile. "Honey, I stand by what I said the other day—I got zero interest in being your man." My face fell, but he continued, "You don't need a man—you need a goddamn warrior. A gladiator—someone willing to risk it all to keep you safe. A protector —that's what I want to be."

I was wrong.

I'd compared Charm to a gravitational pull, but gravity was weak and easily defied. I could jump and break its force. Hell, airplanes did it every day.

With him, it was different.

A strong nuclear force was the sturdiest of the four forces in nature, but the effects were only felt within a close range. Yet, I felt the effects of Charm all the time, whether he was at the clubhouse or not.

It was obviously an electromagnetic force between us—two complete opposites pulled together. I'd been fighting it since I arrived, but as we'd gotten closer, it had become impossible to resist. The static electricity had built up and I was beyond caring about the zap it would inevitably bring.

"Your sister—it's why you kept your distance."

He ran a hand roughly over his face. "I couldn't watch another person spiral out of control. So, I did what I could and when it got too hard—I had the guys fill in for me. I just need you to know that I'll wait, however long it takes, but you're gonna be mine."

My heart pounded out a steady rhythm in my chest; a reminder that I was still alive, even though it felt as if it should've stopped several times over the last few minutes.

I stepped forward until our bodies were touching and looked up at him. Fire burned in his eyes, but it was obvious that he wanted me to make the first move.

The realization struck me. He was my penguin—he'd searched an entire mountainside for ways to keep me sober and had presented his pebble in the form of sunrises and textbooks. There was no use in denying it anymore.

Charm was it for me.

I was in love with him. Wholly and unequivocally under his spell. I stretched on my tiptoes and cupped my hand against his cheek before taking his bottom lip between mine. "I don't want to wait..."

I didn't get to finish my thought before he hoisted me up into his arms and I wrapped my legs around his waist as he strode down the hallway to his room. "Not out here."

We made it into the bedroom and he stripped his shirt off, before impatiently untying the halter top of my dress. The room was fairly dark and I shimmied out of it, confident he couldn't see the marks on my legs. It was one thing to know about them and another to see them up close. I shouldn't have worried, his eyes remained on mine as he slid his jeans down, before pushing me back onto the king-sized mattress.

I smiled as his mouth made a trail from my neck down to my stomach, each hair on his face tickling my body. A small giggle escaped and he growled before pulling down his boxer briefs. "Fuck, Neve. I need to be inside of you and I don't want anything between us."

My eyes widened in understanding and he added, "In case you're wondering, I'm good."

"That's what she said," I blurted out before a nervous laugh escaped my lips.

Charm rocked against me with a small growl. "Is that a yes? You gonna let me in?"

I nodded, maybe a bit more eagerly than I should have. I hadn't been with anyone bare—Clint might've been strung out, but he always used protection.

The door knob began turning and I stiffened under him. "Go the fuck away!" He roared at the door and the handle stopped moving immediately. I was thankful he'd remembered to lock it behind us.

With a slow thrust, Charm pushed past my every barrier, taking me 'as is' and filling me entirely. With each wall that he demolished, I clung to him, unable to do anything more than accept everything he was giving me. His tongue moved roughly against my lips before dropping back down to my neck…to my collar bone.

I arched up until his beard scraped against my nipples, silently offering them up to his amazing mouth. His hands slid up the back of my legs, stroking them in time with his gentle thrusts.

We were beyond words, completely sober, yet high on each other. The smell of smoke clung to our damp skin and I closed my eyes and breathed it in, committing it to memory. I could almost hear the crackle of the firewood and see the sparks from the embers as they floated down to earth.

He was like the woods surrounding this place and I wanted nothing more than to get lost in him.

His muscles rippled as he held himself above me, the sweat visible on his forehead as it made a lazy descent down past his thick eyebrows. I bit down lightly on his lip and he groaned; the sound reverberating down into my toes, forcing my body to tighten around him, fusing us together.

I had never known anything like this before.

I never imagined that the simple act of sex could convey love, but I felt it with each thrust of his hips. His fingers brushed against my core, while his other hand gripped my ass, anchoring me up against him.

We were no longer Charm and Neve; it had become so much more than that. The faint taste of a cigar was on his lips along with something I couldn't quite place— I never wanted to forget it though.

Moans and whimpers escaped my lips; sounds I'd never heard myself make before. His mouth and hands were everywhere as he rocked into me, as if checking to make sure I was real.

"Honey..." He murmured against my hair.

Charm pushed me closer to the edge with his words, stripping me bare and taking everything I had to offer, before we entered into a freefall. He thrust deeply and poured himself into me while I held him in a death grip to keep from floating away. We lay in silence for a few minutes, the air punctuated only by the sounds of our labored breaths.

"Charm—" there was so much that needed to be said.

"Kane, honey. In here, call me by my name. Out there, I'm Charm. In here, I'm just yours."

It was easy for a man to sum up his feelings in a few simple words and I blinked, trying to force the tears back in, but found it was a futile effort. My words were forgotten. He'd just confessed part of his real identity to me and I knew that I owed it to him to come clean about the truth of my past, but I'd been rendered temporarily speechless.

His rough hands brushed away the tears that made it to my cheeks and he pulled me into his side, my back up against his chest. "Sleep, sweet Neve."

Sunlight peeked through the blinds, pulling me from my dreams. I attempted to roll over when I realized there was a large arm draped across—well, across my breasts, specifically. The other was tucked under my head as a pillow.

I turned my head back to look at the biker who'd stolen my heart. He was still asleep, his breathing deep and even. I wondered what he was dreaming about as his eyelids flickered rapidly.

Moments later, he sat straight up with a gasp, and I rolled back onto the mattress.

He took deep gulps of air before realizing I was in bed with him. Once he saw that I was though, his features relaxed and he grinned down at me. "Mornin'."

"Good morning."

"I thought I dreamed you."

It wasn't some bold declaration of love, but my eyes filled regardless. "I'm real. You know, it's kind of silly to be asking now, but I don't know how old you are."

He popped his neck and stretched before answering me. "I'm thirty —you're legal, right?"

I smiled and nodded. "Yes, I'm legal. Twenty-two, to be exact."

His eyes moved down my body and I shivered until his expression changed. His hands landed on my thighs, softly prying them open. I quickly realized why when he sputtered, "What happened to you, honey?"

I'd known that he would be repulsed; even I could barely stand the sight of them. I was reminded daily that my mistakes had cost me so much more than a college career.

Trying to change the subject, I exclaimed, "I just remembered—I never went back to check on Doc again."

It was a pathetic diversion and we both knew it.

Charm shook his head. "I had one of the others take care of it. Now, tell me what happened."

I froze, like an animal caught in the headlights of an oncoming car. The urge to run was overwhelming, but I owed him honesty, even if doing so meant confronting the ghosts of my past.

I swallowed even though my mouth had gone dry. "The night of the fire, I was there. My boyfriend and I were visiting my parents. I'd worked so hard to sober up because I wanted them to be proud of me —" My voice broke off in a strangled sob, but I fought it and regained control.

"Take your time, baby." Charm was still laying casually on his side, his hands resting on my thighs. The pink and white scars were even more prominent against his tan skin.

I took several deep breaths before continuing, "It was hard, but I did it, and when we were there, it felt like things were back to normal. My boyfriend had never been to California before so we spent the week visiting the beach and our favorite restaurants.

"Our last night there, we went to bed. When I woke up, I was on the front lawn with burns on my legs. My boyfriend got me out of the house just as the entire thing went up. Our room was on the first floor —my parent's—" I paused again. "My parent's bedroom was upstairs. The firemen found them on the stairs. The smoke alarm had malfunctioned in the hallway outside their room and the fire spread so fast. They tried to escape, but couldn't."

Charm moved over me and wiped the tears from my face. "It's okay, honey." He murmured and I shook my head.

"No, it's not okay. I'm the reason they're not here right now." The tears fell faster. I could drown in them, but the grief would remain. I was going to lose him, just like I'd lost them.

His eyes narrowed. "How was it your fault?"

"It was me. I started it. I had a cell phone that my parents had given me as a way to keep in touch and I always kept it plugged in and charging on the bed next to me when I fell asleep. They determined that the fire originated from my phone—it was right next to me. If Clint hadn't gotten me out of there, I would've died with them."

Charm put all of his weight on one arm and brought the other around my neck, pulling me into his chest. "Was Clint the same boyfriend who beat you?"

I nodded and explained how, after my parent's deaths and dealing with the pain from the burns, I attempted to OD on blow. I told him how numbness was the only way I'd been able to live with what happened and the way that blow helped lessen the grief, if only temporarily. I confessed that drugs had woven their way through Clint, twisting and taking root until only the addict remained.

Then, I went through everything that happened to me the day I ended up in the woods, culminating with my rescue by Doc and the others.

Charm sat back on the bed. "That fucker's a dead man. You tell me where he is, Neve. We'll take care of it. You're part of my family now, and no one crosses me and lives to tell about it." His thoughts echoed those of Rooster, Joker, and Doc.

I love you.

The words got hung up in my throat.

He sank to his knees in front of me, running his fingers reverently across my thighs—worshipping that which I'd tried to keep hidden away. "You're so fucking perfect," he whispered as his mouth dropped down to my core. My eyelids fluttered closed and my head fell back as I melted against him.

Charm's tongue lapped at my clit—destroying all rational thought and leaving me lightheaded.

More.

I needed more.

I sat up and took in the sight of his massive hands framing my thighs. It wasn't his mouth that completely undid me; it was those hands. I'd felt it the first time he held mine under the guise of warming me up. They were daunting; I wouldn't have been surprised to find out that he'd killed men with them.

That was just it though.

He'd had more than one opportunity to use those hands against me, but never once had he raised them in anger. Those hands had spoon fed me broth, wiped away my tears, and held me lovingly. Even now, his fingertips traced my scars while his mouth fought to bring me pleasure.

For the first time in a year, I ignored the way the scarring looked silver in the sunlight, and pushed Charm onto his back. He looked up at me in surprise as I settled on top of him, yet his hands slipped easily around my waist, holding me steady. I sank down onto him and we each gave a low groan.

I'd spent my entire life running—toward an unattainable goal or just away—but with him, I felt like I could stand still and just breathe. All of the obstacles that had come up against me were no match for my biker. Without words, we settled into a gentle rhythm; and with each thrust, he chased away the demons.

31

NEVE

December

$\mathcal{I}$ stood up on my tiptoes to add the last gold ornament to the tree before stepping back to admire my work.

Tree number three was complete.

We had one in the living area, one in the dining room, and one for Charm's room. I was just debating whether or not to go out and look for seven smaller trees to place in the other biker's rooms when I heard the door slam downstairs, along with an exclaimed, "Holy fuck, Neve!"

So, I may have gone a bit overboard, but it was my first holiday sober. Amber had talked me into wrapping the banister in garland, claiming that it would give the lodge a cozy Christmas feel. From the sounds coming from downstairs, I was going to have some explaining to do.

The bedroom door opened and Charm strode in, shedding his leather vest on his way over to me. "Honey?"

I plastered a large smile onto my face as I stood in front of the tree, hoping it would convince him that the decorations were a necessity. "Yes?"

The corner of his mouth quirked up slightly, although it was obvious that he was trying to fight it. "Looks like you went shopping today…"

I nodded, refusing to give anything away.

He scratched at his beard. "And we needed all of these decorations why?"

"Because of Christmas. Did you know that you're standing under mistletoe right now? And mistletoe is actually an interesting thing to kiss under, considering—"

"Considering that it's a parasite that drains its host dry? Yeah, that doesn't exactly scream romance."

I stood there, dumbfounded. "You know that? How?"

He gave up the fight and let the grin take over his face. "Oh, honey. I read it in a book. A man has to find ways to keep up with you. Now tell me, do you know why people kiss under the mistletoe?"

I crossed my arms over my chest cockily and opened my mouth just as I realized that I had no idea. For the first time in quite some time, I was stumped. "Well, it's because of—I mean, everyone knows about the thing…"

"Right. Come here." He sat down on the edge of the bed and removed his boots before gesturing for me to join him.

I climbed onto his lap. "Alright, Mighty Bringer of Knowledge, why do people kiss under the mistletoe?"

"Well, it goes back to Norse mythology. Baldr, son of Odin, dreamed of his own death. Turns out, his mother, Frigg, also dreamed of his death. She was afraid that it was prophetic and made every object vow to never come against her son.

"Well, every object obeyed, except for mistletoe. Loki, the trickster god, used that to his advantage. He fastened it to a spear and handed it over to Baldr's brother, who inadvertently used it against Baldr, killing him. Luckily, the gods were able to resurrect him and Frigg declared mistletoe a symbol of love and vowed to bestow a kiss on all those who passed beneath it." His gruff voice lulled me into a relaxed state and I settled my head against his shoulder.

"So, because some god's wife decreed it, a parasite that killed her son is now a symbol of love?" Mythology had always perplexed me. I think it had something to do with the fact that none of it was rooted in science.

Charm pressed a kiss against the top of my head. "I think you're supposed to take away that love can conquer anything, including death."

I slid off of his lap and back onto his bed—our bed— with a yawn. I hadn't slept in my room since before the gathering. We'd slipped into a routine over the past couple of months—and the funny thing was that none of the guys seemed to care. The morning after the party, Charm announced that he'd claimed me and that was it.

In biker code, I guess it meant I was off-limits and no one was to mess with me. My relationship with the other bikers had gone on, much like it had before. They were like older brothers; always teasing, yet making sure that I knew I was safe with them.

Everything else was the same—except, at the end of the day, I fell asleep in the arms of the man I loved. It was a strange thing, being in love. While I'd seen Charm angry plenty over the past few months, he seemed happier when he was with me. The other men noticed it too—so much so, that Rooster began calling me Charm's 'Xanax.'

If he was upset, they'd come find me and send me down to him. His face would light up and his body would relax the minute I entered the room. I swore I could visibly see the tension as it left his body.

He valued my input too. He started coming to me with the club books, asking me for help. I still didn't know exactly what the club dealt in, but he and I had become a team of sorts.

I think he knew that I loved him, but I wanted the first time I told him to be special. I was kind of hoping that I'd come up with some-thing spectacular while it was just the two of us over the next couple of days. The other bikers were going to be riding down to the Springs to help out another MC that had just lost their Prez. From what I'd gathered from the other bikers, they were considering bringing them on.

I rolled onto my side, facing him. "What do you want to do tomorrow? Pearl said we should check out the Parade of Lights over in Cedar Ridge. Have you ever been?"

Charm pulled his shirt over his head and I was momentarily distracted. He lay back with a sigh and stroked my hair. "About that—I think I'm gonna have to go with the guys. We just absorbed the Hell's Horsemen and Blade thinks it wouldn't look good to the other MC if I don't show. You could come with us though, baby."

A wave of disappointment crashed over me, but I gave him a small smile. I'd been looking forward to dominating every second of the Scarred Savages Prez's time; I wanted to act like a normal couple, even if it was just for a couple of days. I nodded. "Yeah, that makes sense. We don't want anyone getting cold feet."

He stopped stroking my hair. "So, you'll ride out with us? Twitch and Joker are out on a run until tomorrow night and Axel can hold the place down until then."

I shook my head and stretched. It was late and all my decorating had left me zapped. "It's freezing outside. If some of the guys are going to be around, I think I'll just stay back and make sure they don't destroy the place. You'll only be gone for a few days, right?"

His mouth flattened into a thin line and he nodded. "No more than three. You'll stay with the guys? No going into town on your own?"

I frowned. "I always go into town on my own," his jaw tightened and I amended, "But I will absolutely not do that while you're away."

Charm shifted and took my hands in his. "You'll be safe; Joker and Twitch will be back early tomorrow night and you've got your phone so I expect a phone call the minute they get back." He moved off of the bed and began pacing. "Screw it—I'm fuckin' taking you with me, honey."

I reached for his hand and pulled him back onto the bed, resting my forehead against his. "You can't drag me along for club business like this and you know it. Trust me, with the way your accounts are, I have plenty to do. When do you leave?"

He glanced over at the clock on the nightstand and sighed. "Gonna ride out in a couple of hours—we've got some club business to take care of before we head down."

I didn't ask and he wouldn't have told me if I had. In cases like this, ignorance was bliss.

I got up and changed into the oversized sweatshirt he'd given me during my first week and settled in under the covers with him. "Go—the sooner you go, the sooner you can come back to me."

He exhaled a low growl, but didn't argue. Instead, he pressed a soft kiss against my lips. "I'll be back as soon as it's done."

I nodded and snuggled up against his warm body. He'd be close to me for a few more hours and I was going to take advantage of every second.

The numbers ran together on the computer screen and I sat back to rub my fatigued eyes. I'd been sitting in Charm's study for the better part of the day, but the books were still a long way from being perfect.

Everything was labeled as shipment or load, nothing specifying what it was they were moving and receiving daily. Regardless, it was easy enough to work through.

I'd found a small package wrapped up and waiting for me when I awoke this morning. It was *Death by Black Hole* by Neil deGrasse Tyson. The note attached to the top brought a grin to my face.

> *To my little science nerd:*
> *I can't wait to see what random facts this book will generate.*
> *-Your black hole*

I'd give myself another ten minutes here and then I was going to be curling up in the overstuffed armchair in the den to devour this book.

The back door slammed and I glanced at the clock on the bottom of the screen—it was only four.

"Twitch?" I called out as I stood up.

It had taken me a while, but I'd successfully tracked him down the morning after the biker gathering. He'd been sitting out on the back patio, staring blankly into the woods and without a word, I'd climbed onto his lap and hugged him.

"I'm so sorry," I'd whispered and he'd nodded, before holding me tighter.

We didn't talk about it after that—I didn't want to do anything that would lead to a relapse for him.

There was no answer so I assumed it was Joker. I walked out into the hallway, but the house remained silent.

"Guys?"

The hair on my arms stood up as I got to the back door and looked out. There was no one there.

"Hey, Neve."

I jumped and spun around, ready to fight. He was sitting on the arm of the couch as if he belonged. "Blade? How did you get in here? Aren't you supposed to be with Charm?"

Something was wrong—*had there been an accident?* If so, why was he not panicking?

He shrugged calmly. "I picked the lock. I thought we needed some time to talk; one on one."

My heart beat out a steady warning and adrenaline coursed through my veins. "You can't be here—the guys will be back any second. They'll kill you."

He laughed and shook his head. "Now that's not exactly true, is it? We run an empire together—he got weapons and I got the drugs."

No.

My legs began to buckle beneath me. It couldn't be—it made no sense. He'd lost his sister to a drug overdose; he ran the club differently to ensure it never happened again.

How could he?

I noticed the small mirror on the table near the couch and my feet instinctively took a step closer, even as my brain urged me to run. Addiction was incredibly naïve—I knew next to nothing about this biker; only that he'd given me a bad feeling the last time I encountered him, but with a pile of snow poured out on the table, all my misgivings suddenly disappeared. "What is all this?"

He pointed to the lines of powder and grinned. "It's blow, Neve. Surely these bikers haven't been depriving you. It's some of the newer stuff I've been getting for Charm. Keeps you feeling high for so much longer, without the letdown after."

My mouth watered; my body suddenly craving a bump. Just a small one—just to remember what it was like. It had been five months.

Twenty-two weeks and four days, to be exact.

3,792 hours.

227,520 minutes.

13,651,200 seconds.

"Neve?" Blade frowned up at me. "You're fucking spacing out on me—did you already take a hit today?"

I shook my head. "You need to leave. They'll be back."

He stood up and came over to me and I cowered against the door frame like a defenseless kitten.

Damn you, Neve.

Blade ran his hand down the side of my head and I froze. His eyes softened. "Don't be scared of me. I'd never hurt you." He pointed toward the table with his hand. "Normally, Charm likes to be the first to sample everything, but I'm willing to make an exception. You like it and you can tell him how good it is."

I wanted to do exactly as he asked; instead, I shook my head from side to side, refusing to make eye contact with him or the coke. It called to me like a siren, but then, I saw Charm's face in my mind and my body relaxed. He was soon joined by the other bikers and my breathing became steady again. I couldn't do this to them.

I clearly heard Twitch in my head. *"Most of the time, our greatest enemy is staring at us in the mirror..."*

I refused to be my own downfall. If I went down that road and began using again, I knew that I would never find my way back again. I'd end up just like Rae.

"Get out." I raised my voice and pushed Blade away. "I don't care what deal you think you have with him, but it's over. He's not buying your shit. Final answer—and your MC is gone. Scarred Savages don't deal in drugs."

Blade clenched his hands into fists and exhaled slowly. "Neve, I don't deal with club whores or Ol' Ladies, so your word means shit to me. I don't give a flying fuck how many of these pricks you're fucking. Your pussy disqualifies you from having an opinion."

He shook his head maniacally, as if trying to revert back to the nice guy he'd been a moment before. "No, it's fine," he muttered before taking a step forward, punching the wood paneled wall with a loud roar. "FUCK! Did you give them the money?"

I took another step backward, stumbling in the process. I was going to have to run...again. Unfortunately, Blade was on top of me before I could regain my footing. I pushed and clawed his face as I struggled underneath him and he brought his fist down against my cheek; violently crunching the bone.

My head swam in confusion and I attempted to fight him off again as he dragged me across the floor. Black spots danced in my vision long enough to stun me as he slammed my face against the surface of the coffee table.

He gripped my arm in a tight hold, squeezing until I was certain the bone would snap and in my agony, I made the mistake of sucking in a ragged breath, inhaling the line of coke beneath my cheek instead. I immediately coughed and spluttered, trying to expel it, but it was too late.

Charm.

I'd let him down.

"Shhhh...it'll feel good in a minute, Neve," Blade said quietly. "I wanted you to get a taste of the good stuff, but I gotta be honest here, I thought you'd be down to snort it. When did you get too good for it? Every time I visited Clint, you were always so strung out; I could've fucked you and you never would've known."

My heart began beating faster and faster—not only from the snow, but because I recognized his voice. He was the one who'd driven the knife into my side and left me to bleed out on the floor. I wanted to run, but the high was indescribable. Within seconds, the pain and fear in my head were replaced by euphoria.

I didn't care.

Everything was okay.

As if testing his theory about fucking me against my will, Blade's hands roamed across my breasts and belly before he reached down and cupped between my legs. I was blissfully numb to all of it. "You feel so fucking good. You let that motherfucker, Charm, inside of you —maybe I should take a turn. After all, you belong to me now."

My limbs were made of Jell-O, but I summoned enough energy to spit in his face. "I belong to me, asshole." The words were heavy on my tongue and I was beginning to feel different; not at all like I'd ever felt before. It was as if I was hovering just above the floor, defying gravity.

Blade wiped the spittle off his cheek and smiled down at me. "Do you know how much work I've put into getting what I deserve? That money was meant for me. It was always going to end up in my hands. Once they were gone, I just had to eliminate you."

My breathing grew shallower as I stared through him and toward the ceiling. "What m-money?"

He rocked back on his heels near my head, pulling his hand free from the waistband of my sweatpants. "You're shitting me, right? The fucking life insurance money, Neve. The inheritance they promised you—all of it. It's mine and I've come to collect."

I kept waiting for the feeling of invincibility to hit as it always did after a bump, but I was becoming weaker as the seconds ticked on. "I don't know about the money," I panted in short little bursts.

"Did you really think the fire was an accident? Clint got in deep with me; swore that he'd pay every dime back. I gave him a deadline and all of a sudden, he wanted to take you to visit your folks. I was prepared to cap him until I looked into it—you were the only child of two very rich fucks. Not only would Clint be able to pay me back; I was going to come out of it a very wealthy man.

"He called me up three days in to tell me that all of the money was tied up in stocks and real estate though. I simply pushed him in the right direction—a little something extra in everyone's drinks—and the whole thing was set in motion. I wasn't worried about the coroner finding Ambien in their systems—they both had prescriptions for it.

Apparently, knowing that your daughter is strung out a few states away makes it hard to sleep at night."

I sucked in a shallow breath as tears ran down my face. *He'd killed them*—he'd taken away the only family I had in the world. *For what—money?* He'd scarred me physically and emotionally over something that hadn't even existed.

Blade continued, oblivious to the pain I was in. "Cell phones overheat all the time—I rigged yours for Clint; the plan was for him to hold a pillow over your face until the fire had spread. You were supposed to be unrecognizable—he was going to stick by your side and marry you, making him the heir to their fortune. You'd fade away from your injuries and we'd be free and clear. Apparently, you thrashed around and your boyfriend suddenly grew a goddamned conscience; dragging you outside to safety like some hero."

I'd blamed myself for that fire—had lived the last year with the burden of their deaths on my shoulders. And this motherfucker was responsible for all of it. I was filled with rage, yet my body was no longer responding.

When I tried to form a fist with my hand, it was as if my limbs were no longer attached to me. Dizziness swept over me in waves, distorting Blade's face until it looked as if he was behind a funhouse mirror. My ears began buzzing and I looked at the ceiling expectantly, waiting for the swarm of bees to materialize.

A window broke near the front of the clubhouse and Blade reluctantly moved away from my body to investigate. I tried to swallow the saliva in my mouth, but my throat had suddenly gone numb and I panicked when, instead of a clear breath, I began gurgling.

My eyes teared up as I struggled and fought for my next breath. My body, sensing that I was choking, forced the contents of my stomach out, but I couldn't turn my head and ended up vomiting onto myself. I was going to die, lying on the floor of the clubhouse. This would be what Charm would find when he got home.

He would think I went back to it.

Just like his sister.

I caught movement out of the corner of my eye and realized it was

Axel. He didn't hesitate to roll me to my side, pounding on my back until I managed a weak breath.

"Fucking hell, Neve. I gotta get you out of here. The alarm tripped at our facility over on Main and I didn't realize until I got there that it was a trap. I drove as fast as I fucking could, but he got here first. Do you know what they hit you with?" He spoke in a harsh whisper, trying to keep his presence hidden.

I caught movement over his shoulder and shook my head violently from side to side, doing everything I could to warn Axel.

He'd shaved his head and there were now open sores on his face where it'd once been clear, but I would've recognized him anywhere. I knew now, without a doubt, that I hadn't imagined seeing him at the biker gathering a few months ago.

Clint.

Instead of ambushing Axel, Clint dropped to his knees and brought his hand toward my throat. I wanted to squirm out of his grasp, but I couldn't get my body to obey me.

"Her pulse is low. We need to move now," Clint hissed the words before prying my eyelids open. "Neve, baby, stay with me."

I tried to speak, but the words got stuck to the roof of my mouth; so, I shook my head, an act that required every bit of my focus.

Why was he here?

And why was he trying to help me?

"What was she dosed with?"

Clint patted my hair, ignoring Axel's question. "Neve, we're going to get you out of here, I promise. I was strung out on some bad shit the last time and I got paranoid. I'm done—no more playing Blade's games."

Axel looked between us, clearly puzzled by Clint's confession. "You know what? It doesn't matter—surely Doc has Narcan lying around. We just need to get enough in you to reverse this shit." He remained calm and lifted me up gently in his arms, my head lolling back onto his shoulder, while Clint grabbed my legs as they carried me toward the back door.

The two of them navigated the porch steps two at a time, doing their best not to jar my body.

I wanted to remind Axel that Doc kept everything in the basement, but it was getting harder and harder to stay conscious. We moved unevenly across the gravel, as the frigid mountain breeze blew directly into my face, like nature's own oxygen mask.

"I'll get you into the truck and then I'll grab the—" Axel stumbled, but recovered and took another step before I heard the popping sound again and then he fell forward, forcing me out of Clint's grasp and crushing me under his weight.

He exhaled and blood ran from the corner of his mouth like tears. He forced himself onto his arms before rolling off of me. "Run, Neve. Run and don't stop." He wheezed as he inhaled, expelling more blood when he let out his next breath.

The footsteps grew closer, but I couldn't move any part of my body. Clint tried to untangle himself from the both of us and I wasn't sure whether it was to offer aid or flee. I also didn't know what exactly was on that coffee table, but I was willing to bet my left leg it was more than just blow.

Axel held my gaze and I watched, horrified as the life drained from his eyes, until he was staring beyond to something I couldn't see. He let out a small exhale, but didn't draw another breath. I wanted to cry out—to scream—anything, but my body remained frozen.

My friend had just been murdered right in front of me.

The footsteps stopped at our feet and then Axel's body was yanked off of me and thrown aside before Blade fired another two rounds into his skull. "I always hated that fucker."

If there were any doubts at all, I was now absolutely certain that he was the man who'd been in Clint's house that night as he leaned down toward me with a menacing smirk. "Not such a high and mighty bitch now that your bodyguard's gone, are ya?"

Without Axel obscuring my view, I quickly realized why Clint hadn't run. Blade held the gun on him, keeping him rooted to the spot. I silently willed him to make a break for it, pleading with my eyes.

Instead of taking the hint, Clint cried out, "What the fuck did you give her?"

Blade rolled his eyes, but never once lowered his weapon. "I had to force it into her, Clint. She was fighting like a wildcat—you never mentioned how feisty she was. I thought she'd be more willing to tell us where the money was with a little snow in her veins."

Surprisingly, Clint didn't back down as he spat, "I've told you she doesn't know where it is."

Blade ground his teeth together, his jaw popping out as he did it. "And you'll forgive me if I don't buy a fucking thing you say right now. We had a deal, you fucked me over. Now, we do things my way."

Clint held both hands out in front of him, as if he thought it would placate him. "I hear you and I will get you the money, but you fucked the plan when you dosed her with that coke. It's laced."

Blade lowered the gun. "What did you just fucking say?"

If I had use of my limbs, I would've chosen now to run as both men were completely distracted. As it was, I was forced to lie on the cold hard ground, fighting like hell for my next breath.

Clint ran his hands through his hair in frustration. Despite the freezing air, sweat ran down the sides of his face. "Uh, the coke—it was laced with fentanyl."

Blade's voice remained calm, but his stance revealed his rage. "Why would my blow be laced, Clint?"

Clint began walking toward him. "You swore to me that we'd get the money and nobody would get hurt—you said you were just going to scare her. You fucking stabbed her, Blade. I finally quit letting you do the thinking and laced your shit. That coke was a one-way ticket to Hell for you, fucker. We need to get Narcan in her. Now."

Blade's eyes widened in surprise. "I didn't know you had it in you. Thing is, I don't deal with you anymore." He calmly fired a round right between Clint's eyes and I tried with all my might to squeeze my eyes shut, but found that it was just one more part of my body no longer under my control.

Clint didn't have a chance to react—he was dead before he even hit the ground, leaving me completely defenseless against Blade.

All this time, I'd thought that he was after Clint. It had always been me though. And Clint's plan, while brilliant, didn't exactly give me a sense of hope that I was going to make it out alive.

The sound of bikes carried through the trees and Blade tugged me up off the ground, dragging me along behind him like a rag doll. "Where's the money, Neve? Oh, that's right—you can't fucking tell me, because he laced the coke with fentanyl. Goddamnit!" He roared the last word and dropped me onto the gravel.

I felt nothing, even as the toe of his boot connected with my abdomen repeatedly. Vomit was forced up again and Blade stopped kicking me long enough to turn me onto my side.

"You fucking bitch—you're not checking out until I get the money. I've been crossed one too many times—Charm ever tell you about how his old man encroached on our territory?

"Dirt bags that had used me for years, suddenly got a better deal with Luck. He'd get 'em hooked on his shit and off they'd go. He took something of mine, so I destroyed something of his—Rae was already strung out. Lacing her H with Apache was the easiest damn thing I've ever done. That fucker knew it was me too; he pulled out and then got himself dead. Guess he never bothered to fill Charm in on that though —dumbass came looking for a fucking partnership before Luck's body was even cold. It's funny—guess he's gonna lose you to Apache too."

I struggled to piece it all together. The thoughts floated around in the air above me along with a few snow flurries; the words looping together into one long strand of gibberish. I opened my mouth. "Prmmm..."

That wasn't right.

Blade leaned down. "What's that, 'honey?' You're gonna have to speak up."

He didn't wait for a response before hauling me back into the trees. I labored through another breath as he dug through his pockets, producing a small vial and a syringe. He measured out the liquid and jammed the needle into my thigh.

His teeth clenched together as he watched me struggle for air.

Within seconds, the pressure on my chest eased enough for me to take several deep breaths, but something was still off.

The ground beneath me rumbled as the bikes pulled up to the lodge and the leaves began swirling violently in the breeze, as if even they were afraid of what was to come.

"Neve?" Twitch called out as the bike shut off. I knew that he'd seen the broken window and the door left open. His boots moved quickly from the gravel onto the porch steps, but we remained hidden in the trees.

Realizing I only had one shot, I took a deep breath and screamed—using every ounce of air in my lungs to do it.

Blade brought the butt end of his gun down on my forehead and wetness ran down my face, blurring my vision and staining the world red.

"Neve!" Twitch called out as he moved closer, panic evident in his voice.

He'd fix this—if anyone knew what to do, it'd be him.

Blade thrust his palm against my face, covering my mouth and nose in an attempt to keep me quiet and I struggled against him, trying to gain a breath. Just as the edges of my vision began to go dark, he removed it and stood up, firing off a shot.

Twitch let out a groan of pain, before firing back. When Blade raised his gun to let off a second shot, I threw my body into his legs. Exhaustion hit me like a freight train almost immediately, but I had to believe it had saved Twitch.

Blade raised his gun again as a bullet whizzed past us, striking a tree a few feet away. "Fuck!"

He tried to drag me further back into the trees, but I fought him with what little I had left, scrambling to get to my men. Another bullet flew by, grazing his ear, and he roared in frustration before taking off into the trees.

I used my forearms to pull myself toward safety. Joker caught sight of me just as I reached the clearing and I collapsed in relief. When I lifted my head up, a scream burst from my mouth. Twitch was lying on his back, the ground stained red beneath him.

No.

Joker was by my side within seconds, pulling me into his arms, even as his eyes scanned the tree-line. He quickly signed, 'How many?' and I managed to hold up one finger before my body began seizing.

My eyes rolled back into my head and then everything went dark.

32

CHARM

I'd done it.

Somehow, against all odds, I had Neve.

When I saw her standing there in a red polka dot dress, that was it for me. Primal instinct had taken over, leaving me with a strong urge to claim her and an even stronger urge to murder any man that looked at her.

I'd held back, even then, waiting for her to come to me willingly. And she had. I'd been given not only her body, but her scars as well, which made me the luckiest son-of-a-bitch alive.

She bore the physical scars, while mine were hidden on my heart—but, she and I? We were the same.

I was finally at peace.

Coming in to find her curled up in bed and lying with her while she read to me from a science textbook—these things had become my new normal. It made it damn near impossible to leave her every morning.

I'd never understood the addict mentality, until Neve. She'd had me hooked from day one, but I hadn't seen it until it was too late. I didn't want to detox—I wanted to fuckin' OD while buried inside of her body; to fade away listening to her soft moans.

Gunner raised his left arm up as he rode ahead of me before bringing it over his head, signaling that he needed us to pull off.

I slid off my bike and walked toward him, teasing, "Why'd we stop? You cold?"

My 'club business' had taken a little longer than planned, so we were late getting back on the road. I patted my pocket, only relaxing once I felt that familiar circular shape. The stop had been well worth it—there wasn't another woman in the world who'd have a ring like hers.

He stared down at his instrument panel, refusing to meet my stare. "Got a problem, Prez. We need to turn around."

My smile faded. "What happened?"

He gripped his handlebars before raising his head up to meet mine. "It's Neve."

Panic wrapped itself around my chest like a vice, squeezing until it was hard to take a breath.

I didn't need any other details. I hopped back on my bike and immediately began scanning the traffic on the highway, looking for an opening to turn around.

Gunner pulled up next to me and I asked a question I didn't know if I wanted the answer to. "Is she hurt?"

He nodded and I exhaled slowly. She was perfect when I left her sleeping this morning—she was going to call me the minute Twitch and Joker showed back up.

"After getting tied up last night, Doc went back to the clubhouse. It was a goddamn massacre, Charm. He told Joker to get her to town— Twitch and Axel—"

This time, I didn't wait for traffic. Without any regard for my own safety, I kicked up gravel getting on the highway and back toward Kasselhessen.

I'm coming, baby.

Hang on.

33

NEVE

*M*y eyes fluttered open and I came to as my body jerked to the side. We were no longer outside the lodge, but in a vehicle. A vehicle that was moving very quickly, judging by the way I was being jolted across the seat. Joker kept his eyes on the road, sneaking glances over at me every few seconds.

I wanted to know where Twitch was, but I couldn't find the words in the heavy fog that had settled over my entire body. The radio played nothing but intermittent static in the background, as if the music was gasping for air.

It took me a minute to realize that the sound was coming from me.

Joker brushed moisture off of his cheeks and shook me to stay awake. I stared up at him in confusion. *Bikers didn't cry, did they?*

The light bounced in and out of the truck as it broke through the trees and I watched it, mesmerized by the colors. It didn't matter how many times I saw it; the sunrises and sunsets were always different. The colors were similar, but slightly varied in shade.

I'd broken my arm when I was eight, attempting a back handspring on the trampoline with my next-door neighbor. The doctors had to put me under to reset my radius, and I remembered lying on the table and being told to count backward from one hundred as they administered the anesthesia.

That was how I felt now—disconnected and drowsy.

I'd never had blow affect me like that before. I'd also never had my face forced into a pile of it. *What had Clint said it was laced with?*

I lost my train of thought; still seeing the colors of the sunset as they burned through my eyelids. Joker shook me again, harder this time, and my eyes reluctantly opened to stare through the passenger window.

Joker was going to fix everything. He was going to get me help—perhaps I was finally going to meet that elusive mountain doctor. If I stared hard enough, I could just make out the edge of his cabin back in the trees. Charm would find Blade and this whole thing would be something we laughed over during dinner tonight.

The vehicle shook again and my body collided with the stick shift before hitting the seat back. A vehicle was really nothing more than a coffin made of metal and glass.

People who live in glass coffins shouldn't throw stones.

I smiled at the thought just before my body began convulsing again.

I awoke beside the back wheel of the truck, just as the last rays of daylight began to fade away. I slowly eased myself into a sitting position and found that I felt much better. Maybe I'd vomited all the drugs up. I tentatively touched my forehead, but it was smooth and dry. Joker must've gotten the bleeding stopped. I knew he'd come through.

"Joker?" I called out, as I used the wheel well to stand up. I could hear his heavy breathing near the front of the truck as I cautiously approached him.

The poor guy was probably traumatized—it had to have brought up memories of Rae for him. He was on his hands and knees on the asphalt, huffing and puffing.

"Joker? I'm feeling better. I'm so sorry I scared you." I reached out a hand to touch his shoulder, but it passed through and I stared at it in confusion before stepping around him.

As I did, my other hand came up to my mouth in a gasp. *It couldn't be.* Wetness hit my cheeks as I shook my head from side to side. Joker wasn't on his hands and knees in shock. He was on his hands and knees doing CPR. *On me.*

There was absolutely no scientific explanation for this—no reason that I should be having an out-of-body experience.

Tears fell from his own face and onto the body that once belonged to me. My face was ashen—cheek bruised and swollen. A stream of dried blood ran from my hairline down to my nose, while white powder clung to my cheek. Joker somehow managed to avoid touching it as he puffed air into my lungs. The eyes that had wanted to remain closed were now wide open, yet unseeing. He continued doing chest compressions and mouth-to-mouth, even as the red and blue lights lit up the highway.

A police officer jumped out and immediately radioed for help, before taking over for Joker when it became apparent that the biker was tiring. An ambulance arrived within minutes and they lifted me off the asphalt.

I couldn't feel any of it.

I pinched my arm, but my body had gone numb. I feared that this was a nightmare that I wasn't going to wake up from. Before I could make the choice of whether or not to stay behind with Joker, I was pulled into the ambulance with my body.

The paramedics slapped tape pads onto my chest as the robotic voice of the defibrillator filled the small cabin. *"Shock advised. Please stand clear."*

This was going to snap me out of this state. I hovered near the back of the ambulance, wringing my hands. My body gave a small jolt, but nothing happened.

"We've got a pulse," one called to the other.

It didn't make sense to me—*if I had a pulse, then why was I here and my body there?*

We arrived at the hospital in Kasselhessen and they rushed me through the sliding doors, but I fought to stay back—to make sure Joker was okay.

He arrived and tried to follow after them, but was stopped by the nurses. "Sir, you'll have to stay out here. Can you tell us what happened?"

He began signing, *'She's been hurt—I don't know if she took something.'* He stopped and his shoulders shook with silent sobs.

"Was she in a car accident?"

He shook his head, clearly growing frustrated by the fact that no one knew what he was trying to communicate.

The nurse gave up her questioning and wrapped an arm around his shoulders before leading him to a private room. Within minutes, another person arrived to translate for him. He signed everything he knew, which was sadly not much. He hadn't seen Blade—the only people who had were all dead. They assured him that they were doing everything they could to save me and left him alone again.

Where was Twitch?

I wanted to believe that he was okay—I needed him to tell the others who was responsible for this. *Why would Joker have left him behind?*

The door to the small waiting area flew open and Rooster burst in, wide-eyed and panting. "Gunner told us—is she okay, J?"

He shook his head and lowered it back down to his hands.

Rooster sank down into the chair closest to him. "The guys are right behind me—what the hell happened?"

"Blade happened. He drugged me and—" My voice broke off in a sob, although neither man appeared to hear me.

"It fucking sucks, doesn't it?"

I jerked my head to the side and saw Axel sitting in a chair a few feet away from Joker and Twitch. "Oh my god, Axel. You're okay!" I ran over and embraced him.

He laughed. "Yeah, about that. Spoiler alert—I don't make it."

The smile faded on my lips. "But, you're here," I protested.

"Neve, I am here, but I'm the only one who can hear and see you. What do you think that means?"

"I think it's a dream. Just some extremely vivid and realistic dream, right? I've heard of this happening in times of extreme stress. I'm probably in a coma—that's it. My brain has imagined this entire situation as a way of coping with my trauma."

He shook his head and replied, "I don't think so."

I swallowed against the lump in my throat. "But they got a pulse. They found a pulse on me! How can you be stuck here if you're dead?"

He looked around. "Well, maybe it's a waiting room—get it? Because we're stuck in an actual waiting room."

"That can't be it—dead people don't have a pulse! Maybe I'm just having a psychotic break brought on by the overdose." It sounded crazy, even to me, but if it meant I wasn't dead—well, I would've believed in just about anything at this point.

He chuckled to himself. "Alright, let's go with that. I was never much of a hippie or new-age guy, but I bet we could rustle up some healing crystals down in the gift shop and give 'em a whirl."

Rooster paced the room, speaking tersely into his cell phone, while Joker stared a hole through the door. Maybe Axel was right—any minute now, a doctor would come in and tell them that I didn't make it. The thought was too painful to dwell on—I needed a distraction.

"How'd you know that something was wrong?"

He leaned back and where I expected the chair to squeak, there was silence. "I've had a bad feeling about Blade for a while now—obviously, I couldn't voice that to Charm, seeing as to how I was just some lowly prospect. After the shit he pulled with you at the clubhouse that day, I kept an eye on him and, when the alarms were tripped at the storage building, I told Charm I'd handle it. I expected to see cops swarming the place, but there was nothing. I thought about it and realized that the alarms provided the perfect diversion, leaving you completely alone. I was too late though."

I mulled over his words. He'd actively gone after the leader of another MC for me. "Why'd you do it?"

He laughed heartily. "Why'd I do it? Neve, you've singlehandedly turned this club around. Everything you touch becomes something else—something better. I didn't get it at first; thought you were just another club whore wannabe. It wasn't until Twitch mistakenly referred to you as Rae that it clicked though. I always had a soft spot for that girl—she was a fucking mess, but there was just something about her.

"I realized you must be pretty damn special if every member of Charm's group was willing to vouch for you. When the guys said he was claiming you—well, that just made everything concrete. I respect the hell out of Charm and he's not a man to fuck with."

My chest tightened at the mention of his name and I wondered if they'd told him. *If I ever woke up again, would he believe that I didn't willingly use?*

The door opened and the men's heads popped up expectantly as Blade calmly walked in. He was wearing a beanie over his hair, probably trying to cover up where Joker grazed him with the bullet. Axel and I were on our feet instantly. We shouldn't have worried—he wasn't able to see us either.

"I came as soon as I heard," he exclaimed.

Rooster furrowed his brow. "And how the fuck did you hear about it? Where have you been? You were supposed to be following us down to the Springs."

I watched as his throat twitched slightly from nervousness. He'd waltzed into a pit of cobras, pretending to be a snake charmer, and I prayed that they'd see right through him and his lies. Unfortunately, he recovered before the others noticed. "Axel...I overheard him mention Neve and the plans he had for her. I tried to hang back and follow him, but I was too late. One of the others directed me here. Is she gonna make it?"

Axel growled and lunged for Blade, falling right through him and onto the linoleum floor. "Motherfucker," he screamed. He got right back up and began throwing punches, all of which easily passed through Blade's body.

It was at that point that the doctor walked in and looked around at the motley crew scattered throughout the waiting room. Axel gripped my shoulder in his hand and I held my breath, awaiting my fate.

"I understand you're here with the female patient..." He trailed off, waiting for someone to give him my name.

Rooster stopped pacing. "Neve. Neve Ryan."

That was most certainly not my last name.

The doctor nodded. "And you are?"

Rooster pointed at Joker, conveniently leaving Blade out. "We're her brothers. Her husband should be here in the next five—"

The door flew open and Charm burst in, his eyes wild. "Where is she?"

Rooster cleared his throat. "As I was just saying, here is her husband."

Charm grabbed the doctor by his forearms and began shaking him furiously. "I need to know if she's alright! She has to be okay!"

The doctor took a step back, clearly terrified of the hulking biker. "If you'll just have a seat, Mr. Ryan. We've got Mrs. Ryan in ICU. Her lab work showed high amounts of cocaine and fentanyl in her system. Based on the lack of any visible puncture wounds, it's my belief that the drugs were inhaled.

"We noted some facial injuries and a couple of cracked ribs as well, but nothing that will require immediate treatment. We were able to get her heart back into a regular rhythm, but she isn't breathing on her own, so she's on a ventilator for now. We've got her mildly sedated in order to monitor the amount of oxygen she's receiving and she'll be weaned off periodically to try and get her to start breathing on her own."

Charm fell into one of the plastic chairs near Joker with a loud exhale. "She'd gotten clean—it doesn't make sense. Where'd she get the drugs?"

Blade stepped up to the doctor. "What happens if she doesn't start breathing on her own?"

That'd work out just peachy for him, wouldn't it?

The doctor looked back at Charm. "In the event she doesn't respond to being off the vent, then she's kept on it indefinitely until you make the decision to take her off."

Charm sprang up out the chair to confront the doctor once again. "What does that mean? What the fuck are you sayin'?"

Rooster rubbed his hands back and forth across his eyes before answering, "It means we'd have to make a decision to keep her alive with a machine, or let her go."

Joker dropped his head back down and his shoulders shook with sobs, while Blade looked relieved at the prospect of me never waking up.

And me?

I tried to process what that would mean—to be stuck in a realm somewhere between life and death. To watch the people I loved most grieve for me, day in and day out.

Charm pounded a fist against the wall above the doctor's head. "That can't happen. You do whatever you can to save her!"

The doctor nodded shakily. "We are, I promise you. Mrs. Ryan did have Narcan in her system—whoever had the foresight to give her that may have saved her life."

Too bad the asshole who gave it to me only did it to get information before finishing me off for good.

The men looked over at Joker, but he shook his head. Charm cleared his throat. "If you didn't give her the Narcan, then who did?"

Yes.

I silently pleaded for them to put the pieces together, but it was a rhetorical question. They'd have no way of knowing where to even begin to look.

After assuring the bikers that he would bring them up to see me soon, the doctor excused himself. The room was so quiet that each tick of the second hand from the clock on the wall was magnified.

Maybe the doctor was used to treating the bikers—he hadn't even questioned them about my injuries.

Wasn't that policy?

Shouldn't there have been cops swarming the place by now?

"I can't believe she went back to using," Blade noted, and Rooster was out of his chair and on him in a second.

He pinned him up against the wall, holding him in place by the throat. "Look, Dick Tracy. Do us all a favor and get the fuck out. You didn't know shit about Neve. *Don't.* You *don't* know shit about her. Way I see it, we got bodies back at the clubhouse that tell a much different story. And last time I checked, your ass was missing from our little caravan down south."

He was already speaking about me in past tense; that didn't bode well for me coming out of this.

"Rooster," Charm's voice was monotone, as if it didn't matter to him whether Blade lived or died.

Rooster let go of his neck and cut-off before taking a step back. "Fuck this. I need a drink."

The door rattled as it slammed shut behind him and Blade soon made the excuse of checking on his club before leaving Charm and Joker alone. I looked around and realized that, at some point during the drama, Axel had disappeared.

He'd gone over and left me behind. I didn't even get to say good-bye. Didn't he have unfinished business? *Weren't spirits supposed to stay behind until it was resolved?*

"What'd I miss?"

I jumped and clutched my chest. "Axel, what the hell? I thought you'd crossed over!"

He smirked. "Nah, apparently, I get to see everyone's reaction to me dying. Not gonna lie—seeing Amber break down was the cherry on top of the fuckin' sundae. She's regretting not moving in with me now."

I shook my head. "You're happy that she's distraught over your death? That's sick. I adore Amber."

He pulled me into a side hug. "Ah, Neve. Think of it as getting to witness karma in action. I asked her to move in; she suddenly had to rethink our entire relationship."

I frowned. Amber hadn't mentioned any of that to me. She and Axel had been high school sweethearts; ending things now made no sense. In all honesty, nothing in my life was making sense at the moment.

He continued, "Now, what's going on with the lying douchebag murderer? Did Charm kill him yet?"

I shook my head and watched as Joker typed feverishly on his phone. A moment later, Charm's phone dinged. He pulled it from his pocket and read it over before nodding.

"One? You're sure?"

Joker nodded and held up one finger.

"I can't be certain, but I think that Joker just told Charm that there's still someone out there who knows what really happened to me. Now, we wait and see how long it takes for the trail to lead back to Blade."

Axel stretched his arms over his head and looked around the room. "Well, what better place to wait than a waiting—"

I held my hand up. "Stop. That's never going to be funny."

He rolled his eyes and sarcastically replied, "Get trapped with Neve in the afterlife, I said. It'll be fun, I said."

34

CHARM

"Here we are, Mr. Ryan. See? She's just sleeping." The nurse patted me on the arm before stepping out and sliding the door shut behind her, leaving us alone.

All the walls were made of glass and as I looked over at her, I couldn't help but think that it looked as if she was lying in a glass coffin.

It was Rae all over again, but Neve looked so much worse. Various tubes and wires ran from her body to a machine that was breathing for her. Her cheek was so swollen that it almost engulfed the lower part of her eye and the forehead that I had kissed more times than I could count was an angry shade of red. The nurse told me that they suspected she'd OD'ed and then fallen down the stairs, but the dead bodies back at the clubhouse made me think something else had gone down.

Something I was absolutely going to get to the bottom of.

"Christ." I managed to croak as I moved around the bed, trying to get closer to her. "What the fuck happened, honey?" I lightly brushed the hair back off of her face with my hand before dropping to my knees on the linoleum floor. I would've given anything to have her sit up in bed and begin spouting off stupid facts.

Hell, I would've even settled for a 'that's what she said' joke.

I found a chair in the corner and pulled it over to the bed with a loud scrape. I'd hoped the noise would jolt her awake, but she didn't even move. She was just there; completely blank. I gently took her hand in mine and was struck by the realization of how small she was compared to me.

She'd needed a protector and I hadn't been there.

I cleared my throat. She needed to hear that I was strong and not falling apart. "They said I should talk to you—because people in comas can still hear what's going on around them." My voice cracked and I rubbed at my eyes. "Well, I need you to hear me, honey. I need you to wake up and tell me what happened. Tell me who did this to you so I can fuckin' end them."

I brushed away the rogue tears on my cheeks and pressed a soft kiss to the back of her hand. "I know we ain't talked about this, but when Rae—passed, I swore I'd find out who supplied her. It was damn near impossible to do though—I just kept hitting dead ends. Then, I overheard Luck talking on the phone one day. And I realized that he knew who killed Rae—he knew and he was fuckin' apologizing to the bastard for it. Something about receiving the message and pulling out of this asshole's territory.

"Rae was collateral for shit he got into and, as much as I wanted to interrupt his conversation by emptying my gun into his body, I knew the club would side with him. So, I took my time—I started at the bottom and watched it ripple into full-blown lawlessness. By the time I was done, there wasn't a single brother that didn't see Luck for what he truly was—a monster who'd fuckin' sacrifice his family to get what he wanted."

I paused and stared down at our hands joined together. I'd written some of it down, but I'd never been able to fully express what had happened back then. Seeing her like this left me with an over-whelming urge to confess it all. I tucked my lip between my teeth as I went to war with the demons in my mind all over again. For her. So she'd know the kind of man I was.

"Once I knew the club was on my side, I put my old man in the ground. I made sure he knew, as he knelt before me, that all of it was for Rae. He never would say who killed her though—said he'd tell me when we met in Hell. I did what I could by pulling the club out of everything—said we'd focus solely on the fact that SSMC owned half of Kasselhessen. We'd go straight and get by just fine, I thought.

"Well, lo and behold, I didn't know shit. Members began defecting to other chapters and clubs, while I was still trying to get the fucking club back into the black. It turned out that I was one unlucky son-of-a-bitch. So, we got back into runnin' semi-autos—it kept us under the radar of every fuckin' alphabet agency around. The money we made got pooled between the businesses we owned and everybody got rich."

Thinking about it almost made me smile. Wet behind the ears didn't even begin to cover it—I guess I always thought that if I got rid of the whores and drugs, we'd automatically turn into a respectable club. Luck had been right when he told me the town relied upon us.

I'd scratched their back, and in return, they were always willing to keep an eye on Neve. That was just it—she'd go into town, but never once had she done anything that led me to believe she was going to relapse. Amber kept her busy, but even on the days when she was alone, Neve seemed more interested in just getting to know the town's history.

Back then, I told myself it meant nothing, but it was impossible not to see that she'd been falling in love with the town while I was falling in love with her.

I couldn't believe that she'd just throw away her sobriety—not after everything we'd been through. I never wanted the position of Prez, but I'd use that power to find out who put her here. No matter the cost.

I sniffed and rubbed at my eyes again. As much as I didn't want to believe it, I was pouring my heart out to a woman who may have already gone on. "I told you that because I'm not a good man, Neve. I ain't ever gonna be on the right side of the law—I've killed and as soon as I find out who did this to you, I'll do it again. There's so much blood on my hands that they ain't ever fully clean, and if the feds ever catch on, we're looking at a mile-long list of charges. The thing is, I've loved two women in my life—you and Rae; and I don't fuckin' deserve you. I'm an outlaw and I don't think I could make up for the shit I've done in a million lifetimes, but I want to keep you here all the same.

"Baby, I'd gladly go through nine circles of Hell to get you back—even if it meant taking your place. I'd petition every god around to retrieve you from the underworld. See, I ain't ever been good at running a club. Then you come along, and suddenly everything starts to go my way. You're my lucky charm, honey and I'm keeping you forever."

I let out a quiet sob, but held my fist to my mouth until it passed. Now, more than ever, she needed me to fight for her.

The door slid open and Gunner walked in, sucking air between his teeth when his eyes landed on her. "Fuck—give me a name and it's done, Prez."

I pressed another kiss to the back of her hand and stood up. "I need you to stay with her for me—don't let her out of your sight. Joker says that Neve was able to tell him there was one more before—before she—" I clenched my jaw to rein in my emotions.

Gunner reached out and gripped my shoulder tightly. "I got this—nobody is coming against her with us here. I swear it."

I wanted to thank him; to tell him that I trusted him with not only my life, but hers as well. Instead, I mashed my lips together and settled for a nod. Content that she was safe for the time being, I left Gunner sitting in the chair by her side and headed out into the hallway.

I just needed a minute.

I found a door marked stairs and slipped inside, sinking down onto one of the cold concrete steps with a guttural roar. My sobs echoed off the walls, each one reopening my chest a little more. I hadn't cried like this since I lost Rae. Any moment now, my heart was going to break free and fall onto the floor.

I'd already buried my sister. If Neve didn't pull through, I doubted that I'd make it much longer. The door opened behind me and I worked to compose myself.

"Charm?" Blade closed the door and I let out a heavy sigh. I wasn't in the mood to deal with anyone's shit right now. I had this uncontrollable desire to stand up and take my grief out on his face.

"The fuck do you want, Blade?" I bit out, refusing to turn around.

He took another step closer and I fought the urge to launch myself at him, knowing it was an unwarranted attack on a fellow club member. I needed his club and the numbers; pissing him off now would destroy everything we'd worked toward.

"I was going to volunteer to sit with Neve if you wanted to head back to the clubhouse. I know you've got a shitload of work to be done."

I instantly shook my head. I trusted Neve with only seven other men and despite the oath he pledged to my MC, I didn't want him near her. "Work? I'm stayin' here. Doc's runnin' things back home and, as soon as he gets shit squared away, he'll be up here too. Now, you wanna tell me how you ended up at my clubhouse right after it happened? You were supposed to be with me."

Blade had a great poker face; it was impossible to tell what he was thinking. "I overheard Axel mention something about Neve a few nights ago on the phone to someone—"

I'd already heard about that from Rooster, but it didn't settle with me. Axel was someone I'd known most of my life; even before he became a prospect, I never would've pegged him as the violent type. And what had been done to my girl most definitely spoke of violence.

"And you never thought about reaching out to me about that shit? I never would've left her had I been made aware that someone was after her. And Axel? He's been with her from day one. Why now? Why wouldn't he have made his move months ago?" My voice remained calm, but my hands remained clenched at my sides, as if I was expecting a fight to break out at any second.

"What the fuck was I supposed to say to you? Huh? That Axel might've been planning something to do with your bitch or he could've simply been noting how great her tits looked in the dress she wore at the gathering—"

I had him pinned up against the wall before the sentence was even finished. "You talk about her like that again and any alliance we have is fuckin' done. You hear me, motherfucker?"

My words came out in a growl as rage pushed me past the point of rationality, begging me to end him right here in this stairwell.

Blade nodded before shrugging out of my grip. "I got it, but you'd better remember who showed up in your time of need, asshole. Not any other MC, but mine. And right now, I'm your best chance at finding the guy who did this to your Ol' Lady."

I fell back into the cinderblock wall and leaned over, clutching my thighs. *Why was I so hellbent on taking this out on him?* He was right—if his club hadn't shown up, the Scarred Savages and Kasselhessen would've been sunk. "I get it, Blade. Your club's been good about showing up when we need them."

He shook my hand and offered to head back to the clubhouse to see if there were any updates. Maybe he and his club could dredge up something we'd missed.

35

NEVE

I followed after Charm only to leave when he and Blade shook hands. I couldn't stomach the sight of the man I loved, making friends with the man who'd destroyed everything.

I was sitting and staring aimlessly through the window in my hospital room when Axel came back.

He'd popped up when I was in the stairwell, scaring the crap out of me with, *"So, I just tried to get us some snacks out of the vending machine, but it didn't work. My hand went right in, but the damn snacks didn't come back out. What'd I miss?"* He'd whispered the words and I'd patted him absently on the arm before replying, *"Can you give us a minute? Isn't there someone you could go haunt for a little while?"*

He'd shrugged. *"I guess I could see Amber again."*

I hadn't broken eye contact with Charm as I answered, *"Yeah, go do that."*

When he reappeared, Joker and PD were dozing in the small chairs. Rooster hadn't made an appearance since he went for a drink. As I had no concept of time, it was hard to speculate how long ago that was.

"Hey..." He came over and sat down in the small window seat next to me. In this weird limbo between life and death that we found ourselves in, space wasn't really a concern.

"Hey." Since witnessing Charm and Blade in the stairwell, I'd been trying to find a way to come back and had even gone as far as laying down on my body in the hopes it would reconnect with whatever it was I'd become.

Obviously, it hadn't worked.

"Somethin' happen with her?" He gestured toward the bed and I shook my head. "No, but Blade's pushing to sit with me...alone. There has to be a way to let the guys know that he's the one they're looking for. How'd your latest round of haunting go?"

He sighed and rested his forehead against the glass. "Amber's pregnant. This whole time I thought she was blowing me off because we aren't the same people we were in high school and it was because she didn't know how to tell me that she was carrying my kid. Did you know?"

I shook my head and pulled him in closer, resting my chin against his shoulder. "No. I didn't even know you'd asked her to move in. I'm so sorry." Blade had already taken so much—and stealing the life of a man who was not only my friend, but a soon-to-be father, only made me despise him even more.

"How long do you think we'll be stuck here?"

His question surprised me and I paused to look beyond the window toward the stars. "I don't know—maybe until Blade is stopped?"

He nodded. "That's what I've been thinking too. We need to find a way to wake you up. Have you tried poking your body?"

"I've poked, prodded, and tickled—nothing. I just don't know what else to do."

Axel stood up. "I'm going to see if I can get back to the clubhouse. Maybe someone there finally figured out what happened to you. Do you think any of the guys saw Blade that day?"

I thought of Twitch and my eyes filled with tears. "Well, I know Joker didn't and Twitch—I don't think he made it."

Axel looked around the room. "Then why hasn't his ass joined us in purgatory?"

I had been trapped inside this hospital for one hundred years. It was only a slight exaggeration; I'd been comatose for what felt like an exceptionally long time, making my prognosis bleak.

With the exception of Doc and Twitch, all of the bikers had taken turns sitting with me. And even when he wasn't in my room, Charm was always nearby, on his phone or pacing.

Axel had disappeared on me again, but by this point, I was growing used to it. He'd be talking to me one minute and gone the next. I just hoped that he was finding a way to stop Blade. I'd tried leaving the hospital, but had only gotten as far as the lobby. There appeared to be some barrier preventing me from going any further. I was still tethered to my body, even if it didn't feel like it.

So, I sat with the guys and waited for a miracle, tensing up anytime Blade appeared. It felt like I'd been in a coma for far too long, yet the doctors had yet to try and wean me off the vent.

"I'm gonna grab some food," Rooster announced, as he pulled his long body from the chair and stretched. Once he'd recovered from his bender, he'd shown back up and refused to leave my side. He questioned everyone who came in, demanding credentials and explanations like he worked for the CIA.

Charm's head popped up almost immediately, as if he'd been woken from a deep sleep. "Okay. I'll just stay with her—you heard anything from Doc?"

Rooster checked his phone. "I got nothin'. I'll check in with him though when I get downstairs, there's better cell service—Gunner and the crew are still out, right?"

"Yeah, they should be back in a few hours. Once they get up here, we'll know more. See if we can't put some motherfuckers in the ground."

The door opened before Rooster could reach it and Blade slipped in. "Hey, any changes?"

Rooster eyed him skeptically before shoulder checking him on the way out.

Blade turned back to Charm. "What the fuck is wrong with him—he on his period or some shit like that?"

Something strange happened in that moment. Just as Charm began to answer, there was a high-pitched buzzing sound that drowned everything else out. I could see his body tense up as his mouth moved, but I couldn't hear anything they were saying.

The two continued talking and then Charm's shoulders relaxed again. He began nodding and stood up, causing my pulse to skyrocket.

Was he leaving me?

Didn't he know what would happen?

Charm reached into his vest and pulled a sprig of greenery out, placing it in my hand. He leaned in and whispered something in my ear, but it was drowned out by the roaring in my ears.

As I moved closer, I realized what he'd left me with.

Mistletoe.

I reached out to grab him just as I caught movement near the edge of the bed. The fingers on my right hand were twitching.

That had to be a good sign. My body was in sync with—well, whatever I was. I pointed directly at Blade and my body mimicked the movement. I could show him who did this, if only he would look at me again.

Axel reappeared, looking completely out of sorts. He began gesturing wildly at me and shouting, but I couldn't hear a word of it. He also didn't look the same as before; it was like looking at a mirage.

When Charm put his hand on the door, it only confirmed what he'd agreed to. He was going to let Blade sit with me—the man who was responsible for not only the deaths of my parents, but my friends as well. He had taken the people I loved from me, and now he was going to do the same to Charm.

First, his sister.

Then, his girlfriend.

He'd get away with it too. The bastard was sneaky and Charm would forever think that I willingly threw away everything I'd built at the clubhouse with them—all for a high.

Tears cascaded down my cheeks and I roared in anguish. How could I fight something when I was medically sedated? *How could I defend myself against this monster when the only person who could help me was walking out the door?*

My body was wracked with sobs and, as if to punish me further, time seemed to slow. I could hear each click of the track as the sliding door opened.

"You can't leave me here with him, Charm. He did this to me! He's responsible for it all!"

The door stopped and he turned around, staring in my direction as if he could see me.

"Don't leave...please." My voice was softer, but whatever hold I'd had on him was broken.

He tucked his lower lip between his teeth and turned back toward the door, stepping out and sliding it shut behind him. The final click was like a prison cell door locking.

Sentencing me to death.

Axel made a move to reach for me, but I managed to slip past him and out into the hallway. I caught the back of Charm's head as he walked away from me.

"Kane!" I screamed his real name until my throat was raw, yet he never once looked back. His phone rang from his pocket, but the buzzing drowned out his voice, leaving me with moving lips and overwhelming dread that this was all going to end soon.

I was going to die before I got a chance to tell him that I loved him.

"Neve...let's go." Axel held my arm in a death grip, but I fought him, trying to get back to Charm. I wouldn't let myself dwell on the fact that I could hear his voice again.

Only the dead had voices...

I weakened and Axel easily moved me back toward my hospital room. It was over. I was nothing more than a star that had run out of hydrogen. I could feel it—the walls were closing in on me and it was only a matter of time before I burned up.

As Axel dragged me back into the room to face my killer, I thought about what happened to stars when they died. A star without hydrogen would contract in on itself, yet burn hotter. The upper layers of the star would then expand, even as the rest collapsed— leaving a red giant in its place.

Helium inside the star would fuse with carbon. Once the helium was demolished, the star would cool down into a white dwarf and then finally, a red dwarf.

Blade stared down at me before moving over to the door and looking out. Satisfied that no one was coming, he pulled the curtain closed and turned back toward the hospital bed.

The death of a normal star didn't cause a huge disruption in the solar system. It burned up and things went back to business as usual. In the case of a larger star, however; things were a little more compli-cated. A large star had more mass. More mass meant the star still had enough carbon after the helium was consumed to fuse with a heavy element, like iron. Once the core turned to iron, the star would no longer burn. The gravity within would force it to collapse in on itself before exploding into a supernova. The remaining core was even capable of becoming a black hole.

Blade pulled a syringe from his pocket and said something indis-cernible before laughing to himself. The reality was that I'd been nothing more than an average-sized star in my life. Well, up until I met my bikers.

Axel had been wrong when he said I'd changed them. It was the other way around. They'd transformed me into something bigger and better.

If this was it, then I was going to have to implode with enough force to take this asshole biker down to the depths of Hell with me.

Axel shoved me from behind and I fell onto the bed. I turned around to protest, but he continued to hold me down—even lying on top of my body to keep me there.

"Fight, Goddammit! Wake up and fight him, Neve! It's the only way!" A single tear ran down his face, but his grip didn't falter.

Another set of hands held me down and I looked up in shock. It was her. She looked just as she had in that picture in Charm's room.

Rae.

"Wake up!" She shouted.

"Neve—open your eyes, sweet girl. You need to fight!" My mother's voice had me straining to find her. She stood near the foot of the bed, her hand on Axel's shoulder. My father stood near her, his eyes bright with unshed tears.

Axel nodded at them and then smiled back at me. "You were always worth saving, Neve. Don't forget that."

My mother and father stepped forward and each pressed a soft kiss to the top of my head before the room dimmed and their faces shifted out of focus. Pain hit me and I closed my eyes as everything spun out of control.

When I reopened them, I was on the back of Charm's bike—the sunlight bathing my face in yellow warmth before dipping back behind the trees, like a game of hide and seek. I gripped his body tightly as we moved around the curves in the road. Neither one of us wore helmets, so our hair was at the mercy of the wind. He kept one hand on the handle while the other moved down to cover my own.

When I blinked, we were suddenly at the cliffs and I stepped up to the edge and jumped, without fear this time. The icy cold water took my breath away, but none of it mattered when I saw his face as I surfaced. Then, I was sitting on the ledge, watching the sunrise with all of them—we were crammed onto the small rock, but we were happy.

We'd been happy, hadn't we?

Like family.

My mind kept taking me somewhere different; forcing me to relive every memory of my life. I went back to lying on the forest floor, to feeling Blade sink the knife into my side. Like my parent's old VCR, I was being rewound on high speed. I traveled through my past; watching in horror as my childhood home burned to the ground with my parents inside. When I saw myself use for the first time, I prayed that death would come swiftly.

Things began to slow and then I saw my mom in a hospital bed, her hair drenched in sweat, but with a huge smile on her face. There was a newborn cradled in her arms—*me*.

"What do you think, little miss? You think Neve would suit you?"

I stared up at her with wide eyes and she laughed. The sound was like a warm blanket, fresh out of the dryer, being wrapped around my shoulders. It was a sound that I'd missed terribly.

"I know it's silly—being named after snow when we live in a place where it never happens, but it just seems right for you," She placed her thumb in my tiny hand and I held on tightly. Her lower lip trembled when she spoke. "I love you, darling girl. And I would give my dying breath to keep you safe. Unconditionally—even if you turn out to be a bratty teenager." She smiled through her tears and brought me up to her chest in a tight embrace.

I blinked through my own flood and then I was back in my hospital room. Everyone else was gone—it was just me.

And Blade.

The rumble of bikes sounded in the distance, like thunder announcing an impending storm. I didn't know how she'd done it, but I was certain that my mom had kept her promise and somehow brought me back from the brink of death.

I lifted my arm and realized it was attached to my body again—the mistletoe clenched tightly in my hand. I was also painfully aware of the tubing that ran down my throat and I began clawing at it desperately, while silently gagging. My mouth was frozen open, but nothing would come out. I continued gagging until tears ran down my cheeks, certain that my face was turning purple from my body's efforts to free the tube.

Blade noticed the movement and froze with his body over mine. "Holy shit," he gasped before jumping back.

Everything still had a surreal feel to it, no doubt residual effects of the sedation. The tubing was taped down on both of my cheeks and it didn't matter how hard I pulled, everything remained where it was.

Panic set in when I realized that I couldn't swallow and memories of being drugged came back to me. Alarms began going off on the monitor as my heart beat wildly in my chest.

Blade used his body weight to lean across me again and I reluctantly gave up on my efforts to pull the tube free as I scratched and clawed at his face.

With a strength I didn't know I possessed, I dug my thumb into the corner of Blade's eye as he grabbed my IV line. "Stop fighting me," he hissed. "It's over."

The curtain flew back and my bikers burst into the room with their guns drawn, just as Blade pressed the tip of the syringe into the line. They had Blade on the floor and away from me by the time the nurses swarmed in.

The next few minutes passed in a blur. Charm wrestled Blade up and turned him over to Gunner before grabbing my hand. He didn't say a word, but I nodded anyway, my eyes tearing from both the vent and the look of devastation on his face. Horror and guilt blended into one seamless expression as he squeezed my hand desperately while doctors and nurses frantically moved around us.

I saw the war in his eyes—he was torn between his need to stay with me and his desire to wipe Blade from the face of the earth. I gave another small nod and looked to the door.

Once he was certain that I was going to be okay on my own and after many reassurances from the medical staff that he was just in the way, he pressed a rough kiss against my forehead and took off after the other bikers. Joker and Guardrail stayed behind, with the former signing faster than I could read.

I shakily held up my hand as if I was going to do a 'peace' sign, before crossing my middle finger over my index finger.

R.

Then I made a fist, keeping my thumb pressed against my index finger.

A.

Finally, I rested all but my pinky finger on top of my thumb.

E.

Joker's eyes widened and he looked back toward the door, questioningly.

I nodded as much as I could with everything I was hooked up to and he patted my foot through the blankets before taking off after them.

I stared up at the bright fluorescent lights above my head as they worked on me, tears steadily coursing down my cheeks. The tube protruding from my mouth rose and fell rhythmically.

Guardrail stayed by my side, his calloused hands brushing my hair back. "We got you, Neve. You're gonna be okay, doll. Just a few more minutes and you'll be breathing on your own again."

He grabbed one of my hands and clasped it tightly in his as the nurse suctioned my mouth. I gagged again when they began suctioning the tube, but Guardrail continued to talk in that quiet voice of his, calming me down.

"One more and they're gonna get this shit out of you so you can breathe. You can be strong for just a few more minutes, can't you?"

I nodded and squeezed my eyes shut, trying to block out everything but the sound of his voice.

"There we go, doll. Just relax. I'm not going anywhere. You feel my hand? If it hurts too much, squeeze my hand—hell, break the damned thing off if it makes you feel better."

I held his hand in a death grip and gagged in silence as the nurse continued suctioning me. "You're a real fighter, Mrs. Ryan. I can definitely say in all my years of nursing, I've never seen anyone wean themselves off of the vent while sedated."

Guardrail placed his other hand against my forehead, preventing me from arching up as I gagged. "That's because our girl's a badass." He said the words with pride as they suctioned me one last time.

The tube came up and out with a small gurgle and I began coughing almost immediately; my lungs working to expel any remnants from being on the vent.

"We're going to give you a little bit of oxygen to keep your levels nice and even. You can relax." The nurse secured the tubing around my nose while Guardrail kept his death grip on me.

I knew Charm was dealing with Blade, but I suddenly wished that I hadn't sent him away. I glanced down at the mistletoe, still in my palm.

What had he said when he placed it in my hands?

It wasn't possible, yet I knew it wasn't just some dream conjured up by a brain deprived of oxygen.

There was still so much that needed to be said—so many questions that still needed to be answered, but without Charm, I was going to have to put the pieces together on my own.

36

NEVE

I swallowed and winced from the pain. I had somehow ended up back where I started—injured and feeling as if I'd gargled with sharp stones. I was told that I'd been out for two days and, if it hadn't hurt to talk, I would've told her that it felt much longer than that.

It had seemed closer to an eternity.

Guardrail's phone had gone off not long after and he pressed a quick kiss to my cheek before leaving me with the nurses. They didn't waste any time in moving me to a regular room. I think they'd probably had enough excitement to last a lifetime thanks to me.

Movement near the cracked door caught my eye and I saw a bouquet of flowers, moving up and down in someone's hand— the person appeared to be having an animated conversation with the wall.

The door came open suddenly and I jumped, wincing at the pain in my side. Twitch gave me a small smile before holding out a bouquet of yellow daisies.

"Hey, kid."

My lower lip trembled violently and my eyes filled. *He was alive.* I tried to speak, but my throat was raw, so I settled for a small wave instead.

His arm was bandaged and in a sling, but he was still breathing. I held out my arms and he placed the flowers on the bedside table before embracing me with his good arm.

"Jesus Christ, kid. I didn't think you were coming back from that—"

I cleared my throat and whispered, "How? Blade shot you." Gone was my soft, lilting voice; I now sounded positively demonic.

He dug into his pocket and pulled out a circular disc. Upon closer inspection, I realized that it was the medallion I'd given him. "That little token you gave me saved my damn life. The bullet should've hit my heart—instead, it hit right in the middle, where it says, 'Miracles Happen.' Now, tell me I'm not the luckiest son-of-a-bitch alive because of you."

I pointed to his shoulder. "But your arm's all bandaged up."

He nodded. "Well, the fucker did manage to graze my shoulder with the second shot, but all in all, I'm fine. I was more worried about you."

He needed to hear the truth—however twisted it was.

I cleared my throat several times and in a brittle voice, I managed to get out, "I have so much to say..."

Twitch brought his free hand up to my mouth. "Shhhh...don't force it."

I shook my head. "Please. I need to tell you what happened. I didn't relapse—this," I gestured to myself, "was done to me."

He nodded and then shifted me over in the bed before climbing in next to me. "Okay."

I looked over at him. "Okay—that's it?"

He nodded again. "I believe you, kid. You don't owe me shit. Blade did this and Charm will handle that motherfucker. I showed up here because I wanna hold you—I've spent the last forty-eight hours afraid I wouldn't get to again—scared that my last memory of you would be hearing your screams for help."

He pulled me in next to his body, his nose nestled in my hair, breathing me in. I'd expected to have to beg and plead for them to believe me. I let out a quiet sob and he tilted my face up to meet his. "What's wrong, kid?"

I sniffed. "Twitch—what he did to Rae…my parents and the fire. I never got the chance to say goodbye to them. How did Charm and the others know to come back?"

Twitch's eyebrows furrowed. "I've been retracing everything since that day—I heard his voice and it stuck. I was sitting at the clubhouse, talking to Doc, when it came to me. Like it'd been spoken out of thin air—*Blade*. I called Charm immediately and he told me that he'd just left you alone with him. I thought I was going to have a heart attack waiting to hear if you were okay.

"He said a minute more and you'd have been gone too—just like Rae. Blade already took so much from us—there wasn't a chance in hell we were giving you up too." Twitch rubbed at his eyes wearily and focused on the ceiling above my head. *It had to have been Axel.* His plan of getting into the clubhouse had been successful.

He looked down at me again. "Did you say your parents? Blade was responsible for the fire?"

I nodded. He might not have started the fire himself, but he set everything in motion. If Clint hadn't had a change of heart at the last second, I would've died with them.

He clicked his tongue against his teeth. "I'll be passing that information along to Charm."

"Twitch, where is he?" It was the only question I could ask. The others still lurked silently below the surface.

Does he blame me for all of this?

Is he going to throw me out of the club?

Will he believe me as easily as you did?

He cleared his throat and looked back toward the door. "He's taking care of some club business, so he sent me."

I folded the corner of the hospital sheet over in my hand. "I see."

He stopped me with his hand on mine. "Do you know what he—what we all risked by bringing you here? Do you know the doctors and nurses that have been paid off to keep the club off the radar? We all put our necks on the line, kid. And we'd do it again in a heartbeat to keep you safe."

My throat tightened and I rubbed at it before replying, "I didn't look at it that way—"

He laughed easily. "You think it's common for a hospital to look the other way when a man tries to kill a patient? Charm and the guys hauled Blade's ass out of here and not one person even batted a fucking eyelash. You showed up beat all to hell and the nurses are trying to get your doctor to release you back to us."

I nodded along with him. "So, where am I going?"

He narrowed his eyes at me. "Where the hell do you think you're going? Home, kid. Where you belong."

"Back to Boulder?"

Twitch leaned closer to me, studying my eyes. "Do you have a fucking concussion? Did they check you for that? Course you're not going back to Boulder—you're going back to the clubhouse. We're your family, Neve."

Voices carried in from the hallway— *"Just said he was going to the bank..."*

"That make any fucking sense to you?"

"Not a damn bit, but I'm following orders."

Bank? I assumed he was dealing with Blade.

I looked at Twitch. "Who's out there?"

He whistled and the door opened immediately, revealing Rooster and Doc.

"Sup, Twitch? Our girl giving you problems already?" Rooster drawled as he sat down on the small couch near the window, placing a brown paper bag on the floor beside him.

I shook my head as Doc checked me over. "What are you guys doing here?"

It took Doc a second to respond as he studied the bruises on my face. "Guarding your room and somebody here thought you'd die if you had to eat the food from the cafeteria, so we snuck some in."

Rooster held up the bag. "Pearl's famous chicken noodle soup—she said you'd be up and shoppin' in no time with some of this in ya."

"Pearl? As in *Pearl's Treasures?*"

Twitch nodded. "The very same. She brought a casserole over to the clubhouse as soon as she heard—she and a few others got the place put back together."

I pressed my lips together in a thin line and Rooster, sensing I was uncomfortable, chimed in. "Wanda had us all come to the café for breakfast and lunch. I'm afraid we were all about to starve to death without you, Darlin'. Now, eat up, because word at the nurse's station is that they're kicking your pretty little ass out."

37

CHARM

"You're sure?"

Twitch sighed and looked over my shoulder. "Yeah. She confirmed it. Thought you were gonna wait for me."

I glanced down at my bloodstained hands and clothes. "Uh, yeah; I was. He got a little mouthy. How's my girl?"

"She's asking about you, Charm. She wakes up and you immediately leave. How do you think she's doing?"

I knew what he thought—what they all probably thought—that my need for revenge was stronger than my need for her. Nothing was further from the truth. This was about so much more than putting Blade to ground; it was about finding out why he'd come after her in the first place.

I had two bodies on my property—one was a guy I'd known since we were kids and the other had an expired driver's license that identified him as Clint Scott. When I pulled that string, it led me to a list of priors. I also found a news article about a house fire in California—a fire in which Jim and Stacy White perished, but their daughter, Neve, was pulled to safety. And who should've pulled her out, but the same guy that was now lying dead out behind my clubhouse.

I struggled to find a connection between Blade and Clint, outside of drugs, but kept hitting dead ends. Just as I was ready to call it a bust, Blade decided to speak up; confirming what I'd already started to suspect—she had something they wanted. I opened and closed my right hand, noting my split knuckles with a smile.

Unlike the two of them, I'd known exactly where to find what they'd been looking for.

I crossed my arms over my chest and looked to Twitch and Gunner. "We'll finish it together."

Blade came to and lifted his head up, looking around as if he had no idea where he was. Blood ran from his scalp down to his chin and he began struggling against his bindings when he saw me. "Charm...I can explain."

I grabbed what I needed from the shelf on the wall behind me and took immense pleasure in watching his eyes widen as I lit up my cigarette with it. I took a couple of puffs before asking, "You familiar with blowtorches, Blade?"

Gunner pulled a length of chain down from the ceiling and, with only a little resistance, he and Twitch strung him up.

"Charm," Blade panted. "We could fund the town for years with what she has. She'll tell you where she's hiding it. She trusts you."

I clenched my jaw, while Twitch gave Blade my answer in the form of his fists. "Let's see how good of a dancer you are, Blade."

A quick death was beneath him.

38

NEVE

"Here, I got you." Doc offered me his arm and helped me out of the backseat of the truck. The very same truck Joker had used to get me to the hospital.

We'd only taken a few steps when I looked up and saw the spot where Axel had taken his last breath. The ground was still red. A small cry escaped my lips and my legs gave out.

"Easy, Neve." Doc kept a tight grip on me and directed me toward the house. The minute we crossed the threshold, memories from the assault came flooding back and I fought back a sob as I looked at the coffee table and relived Blade slamming my face into it. Even though the floor was now clean, I could still see white powder mixed with blood near the doorway.

This house had been my sanctuary—*how could I stay if it was now full of nightmares?*

"Doc," I called out a warning before my vision swam and everything went dark.

When I came to, I was lying on a bed in a dark room. Charm's room, to be exact, yet he was still nowhere to be found. I'd worried that it would come to this. It was only a matter of time before he looked at me and saw his sister.

I'd seen his sister, hadn't I?

My biggest dilemma was in trying to sort fact from fiction—there was no rational explanation for why I'd been able to see Axel. This wasn't *The Sixth Sense*. If I was in a coma, then I shouldn't have been able to walk the halls of the hospital—which meant that what I'd seen was nothing more than a drug-induced hallucination.

But, Charm had been there—I had the mistletoe to prove it.

The bedroom door opened, but I stayed as still as possible on the bed, suddenly afraid of what was to come. I heard the lock turn as the door closed, but the lights remained off. Charm rounded the corner and jumped back when he saw me.

"Jesus Christ, Neve. What are you doing here?"

I pushed myself up into a sitting position against the headboard, clutching my sore ribs. "I'm sorry—I woke up in here. I can go back to my room. Sorry—"

With an aching throat and on the verge of tears, I forced my legs over the side of the bed and stood up with a groan. Charm reached me in two strides. "Stop. What'd I tell you about apologizing for everything? I thought you were still in the hospital. Nobody told me otherwise."

I tried to step around him to leave, but he held me by the shoulders, forcing me to look up at him. That was when I noticed that he was covered in blood.

"Oh my god—you're bleeding!" I tried unsuccessfully to pull his cut-off away from his body, but he stopped me.

"Neve, stop—it ain't my blood."

My hands dropped back down by my sides. "Oh...right. All that blood—it really brings out the color of your eyes."

Charm cocked his head to the side and chuckled. "I swear to god, honey. You say the strangest things when you're nervous."

"So, Blade—he's dead?"

He nodded and took a step back. "He's gone. You wanna tell me what happened to you?"

I sat back down on the bed with a sigh. Here it was—he was either going to believe me or I was going to end up sleeping in the forest again. He leaned against the wall and gestured for me to start talking.

"I didn't relapse—I swear to you."

He nodded, but his jaw remained set in a hard line, so I elaborated. "Blade showed up at the house—I thought that Twitch and Joker had gotten back early. Turns out, Blade had broken in and I'm not going to lie to you, seeing the coke laid out on the coffee table like a Christmas present was tempting. I couldn't do it though. I saw your face—I saw all of your faces."

A lone tear trailed down my cheek, but Charm kept his focus on a spot somewhere above my head. "How'd the drugs get into your system?"

He didn't believe me.

I took a deep breath. "Blade said he was there on business— said you were going to meet with him. I told him to leave because the deal was off. He hit me and the next thing I knew, I was on the floor with him on top of me." I squeezed my eyes shut as the images assaulted me.

Charm knelt near my feet and gripped my knees. "Jesus, I shouldn't have pushed you. You don't owe me an explanation."

I shook my head and forced myself to finish. "I—I tried to fight him off, but he was so much stronger. He pushed me onto the coffee table and I tried not to, but I inhaled some of the drugs."

The whole thing sounded unbelievable. People didn't get forced into using drugs; that was just some lie we were all told growing up.

Charm's eyes focused on mine and his grip tightened on my legs; a clear indication that he was still listening and waiting for me to continue.

Axel had claimed that fentanyl was highly potent and Doc backed it up, saying that what I didn't inhale had most likely been absorbed through my skin—something that sounded fishy, at best.

"I knew something was off within a few seconds. It was like trying to breathe through a straw and then my throat went numb. Axel or Clint created a diversion long enough to get me out of the house. Blade killed Axel first…and then Clint. They died trying to help me."

Charm looked down at me. "Clint wasn't involved? Are you sure?"

I nodded. "Blade was responsible for all of it. Clint got in too deep with him and—" I mashed my lips together as salty tears ran down my face.

Charm cupped my chin in his blood-stained hand and wiped away my tears with his thumb. "It's okay, honey. You're safe now."

My entire body shook, but I kept talking. "The fire. It was to get my parent's money. He was the one who stabbed me; I didn't put it together until he showed up at the clubhouse. He thought he'd get me high and I'd give up the money. Clint thought that the drugs were for Blade and cut the coke with fentanyl." I couldn't finish—couldn't tell him that it was the same drug that had been used against his sister.

He immediately reached for me, pulling me up against his chest. "I'm sorry, honey. God, to think that I almost lost you…"

I focused on the warmth of his large hands framing my face and not on the fact that the knuckles of his right hand were split wide open before whispering, "I have a confession to make. I've needed to say it for a while now, but haven't known how. You have a right to know though."

His body tensed and he rocked back on his heels, letting me go. "Okay."

I traced the stitching on the comforter. "I found your journal my first week here. I didn't mean to pry, but I wanted to know more about you."

His brows furrowed, but I kept going. "That book became an addiction for me and I read it every chance I got. Initially, it was just to see what kind of person you were, but I quickly became invested in everyone's lives. The things you overcame and the things you did for Rae and Joker—it speaks volumes about your character. The night of the gathering, Doc told me that I'd made you different.

"I didn't believe him until I found the other journal, but by then it didn't matter. You see, the thing is—I'd already fallen in love with your kindness when I read about Bones. I'd fallen in love with your character when you gave up on your dreams to stay and protect your sister. You did everything in your power to set things right so that no one else would ever know loss like you had. Reading what you wrote in your journal about me was just the final link in the chain—I'd fallen in love with you as a man long before that. I just needed a push in the right direction."

There was so much left that needed to be said and I was quickly growing tired, but I managed with a gravelly whisper, "I couldn't have left—was never even given a choice in the matter. It was always meant to be you. Every awful event I went through led me to the woods by the clubhouse and I—I love you, Kane. I realize you may not feel the same any—"

He moved his thumb until it covered my lips, silencing me. "Look around you, baby. Do I look like a man who would risk everything for just anyone?"

I shook my head, but he kept his thumb where it was and continued. "Fuck no. I love you. You're stuck with me—you're gonna marry me...carry my babies..."

I swallowed hard and talked around his hand. "You wanna marry me?" It came out in a hoarse squeak.

He nodded impatiently, as if we'd already covered the topic hundreds of times. "And knock you up—that way everyone sees you're mine too." He dropped his hand inside the pocket of his pants and pulled out a small ring. It was a simple, hand forged silver band with a small ruby in the center. The corner of his mouth turned up in a slight smile. "Reminded me of your lips the night of the gathering."

I stared at it in wonder and complete shock, while waiting for him to drop to one knee and ask me 'the question.'

He cocked his head to the side. "What? You don't like it?"

I smiled. "No, I love it. I was just waiting on you to do this properly." I glanced down toward the wood floor and he sighed.

"You're shittin' me, right?"

I shook my head. "If you want an answer, you have to ask me a question."

That cocky grin reappeared. "And what makes you think I'm askin', honey? I claimed you."

My own smile widened. "If you want me to wear that pretty little ring on my finger, you'll ask me like a damn gentleman, Kane."

He bit down on his lower lip before dropping to one knee beside the bed. "Alright then—baby, will you marry me? I can't promise you that it'll be easy, but I'll keep you safe. I'll give you my name and a family within the club. You'll never want for anything." The moonlight streaming in through the window made his eyes look suspiciously shiny.

I nodded happily. "Yes, Kane. I'll marry you."

He leaned in and pressed his lips to mine before slipping the ring onto my finger. "That official enough for ya, boss?"

I lightly bit the inside of my cheek to keep from laughing. It hurt too much for that. "It's a start, Kane. It's a start."

He kissed me fiercely before stepping back to strip out of his cutoff and t-shirt.

"What are you doing?"

He paused with his hands on his jeans and looked up at me. "What does it look like I'm doin', honey? I'm getting out of these bloody clothes and then I'm gonna shower. After that, I'm gonna sink into you until the only memories you have are of me and you forget the hell you went through."

My mouth went drier than the Sahara and my tongue tangled in knots. It took me several tries before I could form a coherent sentence. "Don't shower."

It was his turn to look shocked. "Like this?"

I nodded slowly. "Just like that."

He cocked his head to the side and gave another lopsided smile. "Damn, honey. Come here."

I walked over to where he stood, fighting the urge to leap into his arms. My ribs, however, applauded my decision to move slowly. "You need something, Prez?"

He pulled on the drawstring of my sweatpants, forcing me closer to his body as he worked them down my legs. "Just you."

Charm managed to gently lift the hem of my t-shirt until it was over my head. His eyes narrowed almost immediately and he let out a low growl before flipping the light switch on in the bathroom.

"Is it bad?" I asked as he began checking me over, finally stepping around him and moving over to the mirror to assess the damage. Dark streaks ran down my side and if I looked closely enough, I was sure I would've been able to see the outline from Blade's boots. My face hadn't fared much better—I was a canvas of black, blue, and purple.

"Jesus," Charm stood behind me, his head resting gently on top of mine. "I'd kill him all over again if I could, baby. What he did to you —" His voice cut off in a rough sob and I reached down for his hands, knowing that this was a side of him only I would ever see.

It felt like an honor had been bestowed upon me. He was vulnerable with me and knowing that somehow made the details over the last few days irrelevant. It didn't matter if the entire thing had been a drug-induced hallucination, his love was real. Of that I was certain.

I broke the tension the only way I knew how, by getting him to laugh. "I'm back to looking like a mangy dog again, don't you think?"

Charm didn't laugh...didn't even crack a smile. His arms encircled my waist and he lifted me up onto the bathroom counter, my legs straddling his body. "Should've never said that to you—I'm not a good man. I ain't ever gonna be on the right side of the law, Neve. I've killed a lot of people, the most recent being Blade; and I know I don't fuckin' deserve you—doesn't mean I'm willing to stand back and let a better man claim you though.

"I'm a selfish prick and a million lifetimes wouldn't be enough to make up for all the shit I've done. Knowing that, I wanna keep you all the same—I can't do this without you."

He scrubbed the blood from his hands under steaming water as I watched in confusion. His words had triggered a strange sense of déjà vu, and then it hit me—he'd said almost the exact same thing when I was in a coma. Before I could pepper him with the questions racing through my brain, his mouth came down hard on mine.

He held my face in his rough hands and gently pressed a kiss to the cut on my forehead. Under the bright lights, he used his hands and mouth to apologize for everything that had happened to me.

I brought his face back up to mine and his tongue trailed lightly across my jaw, igniting a fire in my blood. My fingers traced along his tattoos, slowly working my way down to his belt.

I took my time unfastening it and toyed with him by dipping my fingers beneath the waistband of his jeans, stopping just as I brushed against his hard length. Growing impatient with my attempts at seduction, Charm let out another low growl before dragging his jeans and boxers down over his hips.

His fingers moved up and down my slit and I found that watching him with the lights on only turned me on further. His middle finger circled my clit before sliding into me.

My mouth fell open and a moan slipped out as he slowly pumped in and out of me. Taking my whimpers as a contest, he added a second finger, curling them along my front wall. "Oh god..." I breathed out as I wrapped his long hair up in my hands, keeping him in place.

He grinned before sucking one of my nipples into his mouth, somehow managing to maintain his rhythm while doing it.

This time, it was me who grew frustrated. I was close, but needed more. I pushed his hand away and reached for him.

He raised his head up with a smirk. "What do you need?"

"You," I groaned. "Please."

I sucked in a breath as he sank into me inch by inch, until my only thought was of his name—*Kane.* I moaned it repeatedly and held him in with my hips as he lovingly pieced me back together, my skin taking on the blood that coated his—each of us sharing the burden of the sins he'd committed in my honor. My nails dug into his shoulders as I fell apart, but he kept thrusting.

Charm panted in my ear, "You keep squeezing me like that, honey, and I'm not gonna last."

I bit down on my lip and tightened around him again.

"Always challengin' me," he said, before crushing his mouth up against mine, muffling my screams as he filled me.

It wouldn't have mattered if I'd been given a choice to stay or not —we were like two halves—each in need of the other to feel whole.

39

NEVE

Strong arms slipped beneath my lower back and behind my knees, lifting me up off the mattress. I groaned in protest and got a throaty chuckle in response.

"I know it's early, baby. We need to talk."

Those four words were enough to jolt me fully awake. "Talk?" I rasped. "Did we not already do that?"

In fact, I'd been hoping to sleep most of the day to make up for all the 'talking' we'd done last night. My brain was mush and I longed to stay buried underneath the covers until it had recovered.

He carried me downstairs, stopping to grab a blanket on his way out the back door. "Need to tell you somethin'."

I tried to sit up in his arms, briefly throwing him off balance. The cold early morning air hit my face and nearly took my breath away. "Couldn't you just tell me in bed, where it's warm?"

Charm shook his head. "Nope, wouldn't be the same." He led me onto the patio where he had a fire burning in the outdoor fireplace. He wrapped the blanket around my shoulders and settled me on his lap.

The sky began to lighten and I had a flashback to being in the truck with streaks of sunlight beaming through the trees onto my face. "Kane?"

He rubbed my shoulders through the blanket. "Yeah?"

I leaned into his chest. "Um, last night in the bathroom, those things you said...had you said them before?"

His grip tightened around me. "What do you mean? You think I'd say shit like that to anyone else?"

Either this would make perfect sense to him, or he'd think that the coke and fentanyl had done a number on my brain.

I took a deep breath. "No, it's just—god, this is gonna sound crazy —I heard you. When I was in that coma, I could see and hear everything. In the waiting room, you told the doctor to do whatever he could to save me—"

Charm interrupted. "Neve, I did say that, but it's somethin' anyone would've said given the situation. Maybe you dreamed it—"

I shook my head impatiently. "No, you wanted to know who gave me the Narcan—it was Blade, by the way. You—you—" I was getting frantic to prove that I hadn't imagined what had happened. "You talked to me about Luck...told me I was your lucky charm. You gave me mistletoe and..." I trailed off, unsure of what else to say.

Charm let out a low whistle. "Jesus, honey..."

My cheeks flushed as I stuttered, "I—I know it sounds insane; maybe it was just some crazy hallucination—"

He tightened his hold on my shoulder, turning me around to face him. "You didn't dream it—I've heard of coma patients being able to hear people around them talking, but nothing like this. It's true then— you said my name the morning I left you with Blade, didn't you?"

I nodded. "You heard me?"

He brought his hand up, running his thumb over my cheek, while seemingly lost in thought. "Clear as fuckin' day. I could've sworn you were standing right behind me."

"What did you say—before you left?"

Charm suddenly looked uncomfortable. "It—uh—I just said that I loved you."

I laughed and poked his side. "You did not. Tell me!"

"You're not gonna drop it, are you?" I shook my head and he sighed. "I gave you the mistletoe and said that I would petition every god necessary to resurrect you."

"Is that why you brought me out here? To declare your undying love for me?" I laughed easily, but his face turned solemn.

Clearing his throat, he lowered his hands down to clasp mine. "I found the money, Neve."

I couldn't help it; I laughed again at the sheer madness of it. "Oh, okay. Good to know. That'll really clear up everyone trying to kill me for it now, won't it?"

His expression never changed. "I'm serious, baby. Blade was close, but he was a fuckin' moron."

I narrowed my eyes at him and shifted closer to the fire as the sun hit the horizon; chasing away the darkness and bathing everything in light. "I don't understand—how did you find the money if I didn't even know it existed?"

The corner of his mouth turned up in a smile and I couldn't help myself; I leaned forward and pressed my lips to it.

It widened even further. "You told me that after your parents died, you tried to OD and when that didn't work, you snorted yourself into oblivion. I figured your parents had to have known that you might relapse. They would've wanted to ensure that you didn't blow through the money, right?"

My mouth dropped open. "Oh my god—they put it in a trust!"

He nodded. "Bingo. Your parents left you everything, but they also knew you were an addict. So, they had everything put into a trust— real estate, bank accounts, stocks, and bonds."

I shook my head. "I don't understand how you figured it out, when Blade and Clint couldn't."

Charm laughed and pulled me into a hug. "Because they were fuckin' idiots, like I said. They were so damn convinced that your parents would've left you everything, free and clear, that they never looked anywhere else. Me? I ain't ever had any kids, but my sister was an addict and I know that I'd never leave her money without some qualifiers in place."

I was still crushed up against his chest, so my words were muffled. "The trust has stipulations that must be met, I'm guessing?"

He pulled a piece of paper from his pocket and read from it. "Beneficiary must be a college graduate. Funds have been set aside for tuition and living costs."

They'd known I was strung out, yet they had faith that I would come back from it. The only way I was ever going to graduate was if I sobered up. I'd had the money the entire time—and it wouldn't have mattered who they killed, Blade and Clint would've never gotten a dime of it.

"It still doesn't matter—I never finished college."

Charm moved me away and stood up to pace. "Yeah, that's why I wanted to talk to you. I told myself that I'd make all the money you'd ever need—that there was no point in telling you about the inheritance. I can't do it though. You gotta go back and finish school. Live your dream and make your parents proud."

He trailed off, leaving the birds to sing their early morning songs in peace. I wasn't entirely familiar with normal relationships, but I was fairly certain that guys didn't propose right before a break up, *did they?*

I hugged my knees to my chest to stop them from shaking. "So, you want me to leave?"

Charm looked out over the landscape and ran his hands through his hair in frustration. "Fuck no. I want you to stay here—but it's not about me. I may be an asshole, but I couldn't live with myself if I kept you from fulfilling their dying wish."

Tears fell from my eyes onto the fleece blanket. Each drop connecting with the last until the tops of my knees were damp. "You asked me to marry you..."

His jaw tightened as he nodded, still looking away from me. "Yeah, honey, but I can't force you to stay here. This isn't a life for you. You deserve to finish school and then do whatever you want with your millions. See the world—"

His voice cut off suddenly as he continued to look beyond the wilderness and to a life that didn't include me in it.

I slid off the chair and wrapped my arms around him, resting my face against his back. "That sounds nice," His body tensed beneath me. "But I want to be with my family. You're my family, Kane. My home is here with you and I wouldn't give that up for all the money in the world."

His hands dropped down to cover mine. "You wanna stay here? What about the trust fund?"

I smiled to myself. "I'll enroll in online classes—if I need to drive to Boulder a couple of days a week, I can. I think my biggest concern right now is making an honest man out of you though."

His back vibrated beneath my cheek as he laughed. "You could have the entire world, but you wanna stay here and marry me?"

I stepped around him until we were face to face. "Meh, why waste hours sitting on a plane when I can see the world on the back of your bike?"

40

NEVE

Six Months Later...

"Now, hold still, dear. I've almost got it." Pearl knelt on the thick carpet behind me, straight pins sticking out of her mouth haphazardly.

I took another look in the mirror and resisted the urge to twirl around. It was unlike anything I'd ever seen before. The ivory wedding gown was sleeveless with a straight neckline that hit just above my collarbone. It tapered in at the waist with a small satin belt and then flared out into an A-line skirt that hit just below my knees. It was classic and modest—exactly what I'd been looking for.

Once Pearl found out that I was engaged to Charm, she'd insisted on finding me the perfect dress. We looked everywhere, and I'd almost given up and decided to get married in all leather, when she pulled her own gown out of storage. The first time I'd tried it on, she and I both knew that it was the one.

The bruises and cuts that marred my skin had faded away, along with the nightmares of my past. I'd slipped happily back into my role as 'clubhouse caretaker,' with the exception that I was now a college student again.

I'd had enough credits from some courses I took in high school to be considered a second semester freshman and, if I worked hard, I would be eligible to graduate in two short years. That included taking summer classes too, but it was definitely within the realm of possibility.

They still argued with me over wanting to cook and clean, but these bikers had saved my life—in more ways than one. They'd pulled me from a life of addiction and given me purpose. The least I could do was take care of the place we called home.

I found Amber not long after I got out of the hospital and verified that she was indeed pregnant with Axel's baby—further proof that my odd experience in the hospital had been more than a dream.

Gunner had insisted that she have a place at the clubhouse —*Gunner, of all people.* I hadn't complained; not only did I have help with housekeeping, but I now had my best friend under the same roof as well.

When Ali showed up, the three of us were unstoppable. Oh yes, PD had given up the act and fully committed to the bubbly yoga instructor.

And Charm?

Well, it turned out that the menacing biker was a complete softie when it came to me. I got a side of him that no one else did and I would never take it for granted.

"You know, you're about the same size that I was when I married, so I didn't have to take in much at all. I'd always wanted to have kids, especially a daughter, but it just wasn't meant to be.

"Jerry was in the mining industry, like almost everyone else around here was. The price of oil dropped in the '80s and suddenly almost everyone we knew was out of a job." She paused as she made some adjustments to my dress.

I watched her dark hair as she worked. "What happened?"

She looked up and met my eyes in the mirror. "Well, for better or worse, the Scarred Savages showed up. Luck was building an army and he took on any man who wanted in. Jerry was hesitant to join, but we were desperate—"

I interrupted. "Sorry—your husband was part of the MC? How has this not come up before now?"

She laughed as she placed another stitch, before pulling the bottom of her shirt up to reveal a small tattoo on her lower stomach. It was a skull with flames coming out of it—the same as the MC logo.

She pointed to it and smiled. "It didn't always have this many wrinkles in it. Back then, Luck ran things much differently. He ruled over Kasselhessen like a tyrant; the town was prosperous, but people were terrified of him."

I cleared my throat when she got quiet. "Um, Pearl? Did you know Charm when he was a kid?"

He'd mentioned wanting Miss Pearl to take Bones in; he had to have been referring to her. I knew that he was young when Luck moved them up to Colorado, and as much as he'd deny it, someone somewhere had nurtured his compassionate side.

Pearl's entire face lit up. "Oh, yes. Kane and Raegan were like the grandchildren that Jerry and I never had. That boy would've done anything for her. Women," she paused and rolled her eyes, "or 'bitches', as we were called back then, weren't welcome at the clubhouse. I offered to keep the kids when the club held church.

"So, the kids were with me a lot. They didn't know much about having a mother and I didn't know much about having kids, but we made the best of it. It killed me to watch Raegan fall into drugs, and her daddy just let it happen. Never said a word." Her voice shook as she spoke, indicating the anger she still held toward Luck.

I knew how the rest of this story went. By the time Rae got hooked on heroin, Jerry had gotten sick with cancer. Pearl was trying to run a business and care for her husband. She felt like things might've turned out differently had she been there for Rae.

Her voice startled me from my thoughts. "Jerry died within weeks of that poor girl. Once he heard the news, he just lost his will to fight anymore. I took comfort in the thought that at least she'd have someone to look after her up there."

I nodded. Luck seemed to have no use for club members who were dying and the families who were left behind. Once Jerry was gone,

Pearl had struggled to continue running the boutique without the club's support.

Charm admitted to me that once he took over, his first order of business had been getting Pearl back to where she never had to worry about money again. It made me smile now, knowing that he'd done it because he saw her as the mother he never had.

He'd taken a run-down mining town and made it prosperous, while instilling a sense of family in the townspeople—something his father had never been able to achieve. Everything he'd accomplished was a testament to the love that this woman had for him as a boy.

"There. I think that about does it. Let me know what you think." Pearl sat back and began sticking the straight pins back into the pincushion near her feet.

I did a slow twirl in the mirror. The dress fit me like a glove. She'd even sewn a small patch onto the back of the dress to match Charm's.

"I love it." I twirled again.

She gave me a wide smile. "Well, in that case, we'd better get over to Sandra's for hair and makeup. Can't have you running late for your big day."

―――――――

"Damn, Darlin'. You look absolutely perfect." Rooster rested his arm against the door frame.

I self-consciously tucked a strand of hair behind my ear before remembering that Amber said it was meant to 'fall in loose waves' around my face, so I quickly untucked it.

"Thanks, Rooster. Are there a lot of people out there?"

He must've heard the slight panic in my voice because he replied lazily, "Only one who matters is waiting down by the alter. He sent me to make sure you didn't try and make a run for it."

Joker stepped around from behind him and stopped short once he saw me. He ran a hand over his face in awe.

Beautiful.

I blinked away the tears that formed and smiled softly. "I'm a little nervous, guys."

Guardrail and Twitch shoved their way through the crowd. "That's why we're here," they exclaimed simultaneously.

Twitch cocked his brow and continued. "I know you don't have family, kid. That's why I'm here—gonna walk you down the aisle.

Doc's laugh came from somewhere near the back. "Fat chance of that, Twitch. That's why I'm here—I found her in the forest that day; it should be me."

The men began bickering amongst themselves and I took a moment to finish fastening the opal earrings that Pearl had lent me. They were the same ones she'd worn when she married Jerry— *"Something borrowed,"* she'd said as she dropped them into my hand before she and Amber slipped out to join the others in the church sanctuary.

Yeah, I was getting married in a church. The Lutheran church downtown was by far the largest building that Kasselhessen had to offer. I'd been shocked when Charm suggested it. I'd expected a small ceremony at the clubhouse, but from the sounds of it, the entire town had turned out to watch him take his vows.

Vows.

Cold sweat broke out on my forehead.

I was really doing it—I was marrying the leader of a biker gang. In a million years, I never would've imagined this. Surprisingly, it was better than anything I could've planned for myself.

I had the love of a great man and it came with seven built-in brothers to boot. Seven brothers who were still arguing over who was going to walk me down the aisle.

"I was the biggest asshole to her. It should be me that walks her," Gunner deadpanned before everyone cracked up.

I was laughing so hard that I had to fan my eyes to keep my makeup from running. "Okay, here's how this is gonna go—you're all going to walk me down the aisle. I don't even know how to make this work—"

Gunner clapped his hands together. "I got it. PD, Twitch— hallway now. Let's make this happen."

I stared after them in puzzlement until Doc spoke. "He thinks that because they're former Marines they're the only ones qualified to organize this." He raised his voice. "Never mind that I was a fucking field medic in the Army!"

Laughter sounded from out in the hall and PD responded with, "Army? Never heard of her."

Doc spoke through a clenched jaw. "Fucking Marines, thinking they're the only branch of the military."

The other guys found the whole thing hilarious, but I cleared my throat uncomfortably. "Um, I don't think you're supposed to curse inside a church—you'll go straight to Hell."

Joker's eyes widened and I amended, "Not you, J. You're perfect." He relaxed again on the small settee in the corner.

Within a few minutes, the men came back into the room and Gunner spoke. "Okay, Neve, we've got it all worked out—we're gonna line up. I'll act as Convoy Commander, obviously, and PD will be Assistant Convoy Commander. I'll lead and then the rest will either flank you or bring up the rear. Sound good?"

I tried to push my lips together, but it was no use. Once I started laughing, it was almost impossible to stop. "That's what she said," I managed to wheeze out.

Gunner sighed, "Goddammit, Neve," before fighting a smile himself.

Rooster groaned and put his head in his hands. "It's bad enough you got Charm sayin' that shit all the time now, Darlin'. Is it really necessary?"

I grinned. "My wedding—my rules. Don't you guys know anything about being bridesmaids?"

Guardrail shook his head. "I didn't sign up to be a goddamn bridesmaid."

I sighed, "Fine—bride *escort*. Are we ready to go yet?"

Gunner whipped out his cell phone. "We're just waiting on the coordinator and then our mission begins."

I didn't think it was possible, but *someone* was definitely taking this wedding business more seriously than I was. I checked my makeup again in the mirror—*Where There's Smoke, There's Fire* was the perfect choice for today. Pearl's friends at the beauty shop did my makeup in such a way that the red complimented the ivory in the dress, instead of taking away from it. And Amber had ensured that my hair looked elegant, but not overdone.

I caught Joker waving at me from the corner of my eye and he began signing frantically. PD gave us both a puzzled look. "What's wrong with him?"

I replied, "Well, he's worried that I don't have *something old, something new, something borrowed, or something blue.* I'm wearing Pearl's wedding gown, so that's my something old—and I borrowed her earrings. My shoes are new, so really I'm only missing something blue."

PD jumped up. "I got it—be right back."

I fidgeted with the belt on my dress and traced circles in the carpet with my shoe while we waited. He burst back in and held up a baby blue handkerchief.

The guys chuckled when I wrinkled up my nose. "PD, no offense, but I am not carrying your used handkerchief even if it's supposed to bring me fifty years of good luck."

He shook his head. "No, it's brand new. I bought it back before you helped me. It's just been sitting in the saddle bag on my bike. Ask Ali, she'll tell you."

I nodded. "Okay, if you swear it's never been used, then it looks like I'm set." He took my bouquet, courtesy of Deb over at *Main St. Flowers,* and wrapped the handkerchief around the base.

A knock at the door from the church coordinator sent the men scattering to their prearranged positions. I took one last look in the mirror and a deep breath before following after them.

The music started, something acoustic, yet vaguely familiar to me. Twitch joined me in the small vestibule, nodding approvingly at the music selection. "Pearl Jam—good choice."

I laughed when I realized that he was absolutely right—we were listening to an instrumental version of 'Just Breathe.' Pearl Jam had been playing in Clint's truck the night I ran for my life. It had seemed like I'd reached my lowest point then, but the close of that chapter had led me straight to Charm. It was fitting that another one of their songs would play as I started a new one as his wife.

Twitch patted my arm. "You nervous, kid?"

I nodded. "A little, but he's it for me. I've known it for a while now—it's just time to make it official."

The doors opened and there he was—in all his leather glory. *Kane.* I should've known he wouldn't be in a tux since the other guys weren't. He looked like an actor rehearsing his lines, the worry lines on his face a clear indicator that he was afraid of messing them up.

True to Gunner's word, each man was positioned at a specific point leading down to where my groom stood nervously. The minute his eyes met mine though, a grin broke out on his face and he visibly relaxed. Everyone rose and turned toward me expectantly.

Twitch led me a few steps down the aisle before turning me over to Guardrail. He then slipped into position behind us. Guardrail squeezed my arm before handing me off to Joker. Each biker brought me closer to Charm like a proud father, before slipping back into their more familiar role as bodyguard.

By the time I reached the front of the church, I had a line of men trailing behind me. Gunner took my hand last and we walked the remaining steps before he placed it in Charm's. I found that his palm was sweaty, much like mine had been when he held my hand for the first time out on the ledge.

The officiant began, but I was only halfheartedly listening. My entire focus was on the man in front of me. My voice cracked several times as I recited my vows, but his firm grip on my hands helped me get through it.

He never once broke eye contact as he recited his. My biker, who had killed men with his bare hands, looked about as ferocious as a bunny rabbit standing in front of me.

We exchanged rings—Pearl had known someone who forged metal, so I was able to find a ring for him that was similar to mine, yet still completely unique. We stood, smiling at each other like a couple of fools as the officiant concluded, "By the power vested in me by the state of Colorado, I now pronounce you husband and wife. You may now kiss the bride."

He dipped me backward before pressing his mouth to mine. The church erupted in cheers and raucous catcalls from the bikers, along with a discreet throat clearing from the officiant before the music kicked on.

I swayed slightly as he brought me back to my feet, but he kept me in his arms, ensuring that I remained upright. We began walking toward the back of the church, with people stepping out into the aisle to offer their congratulations and words of wisdom. About halfway down, Charm groaned in frustration and swung me up and over his shoulder.

I giggled as he began moving faster toward the exit, even as throngs of people kept approaching us. He took a couple of steps forward before roaring, "Fuck off—she's mine now!"

And that was how I knew that, while I may not have lived a fairy tale life, I had most certainly found my Prince Charming in the foul-mouthed biker carrying me out of the church.

EPILOGUE

NEVE

Two Years Later

Sweat beaded on my brow before dripping into my eyes, stinging them, and I found that I didn't even have the strength to reach up to wipe it away.

I closed my eyes with a groan when a cool washcloth touched my forehead. "You doing okay, honey?"

I panted heavily. "Does it look like I'm okay, sweetheart?"

Charm patted my back awkwardly. "You got this, Neve. Just—uh—just keep on doing what you're doing."

I winced as another wave of pain washed over me and cried out. It was like my body was breaking apart from the inside out. Once the contraction subsided, I forced out between clenched teeth. "I should've been graduating summa cum laude right now. Instead—" I let out an anguished howl. "I'm in friggin' labor. You promised me that this baby would stay in until I graduated—you gave...me... your...word."

Charm looked like he was fighting a small smile until I gripped the front of his shirt and yanked him down next to me. His eyes widened.

"Babies do what they want to do, honey—including showing up two weeks early."

I let out a small sob and released him. "I wanted to walk across the stage...I haven't packed my bag for the hospital...the book said I should've done it already. I'm already failing at being a mother."

Something settled on top of my head and I looked up with a sniffle. Rooster stepped back and grinned. "It's perfect, Darlin'—really brings out your eyes."

I looked past him to the mirror hanging on the wall opposite my bed. I didn't want to think about why there would be a mirror there. *Who in their right mind would want to see that?*

Rooster had placed my graduation cap on my head—my black graduation cap. I exhaled slowly. "My eyes are blue, jackass."

He shook his head. "Nuh-uh. Right now, they're black, like a cave. Speaking of, is your pain getting worse? Are you leaking fluid? We're supposed to note the color of the fluid—not sure why—maybe pink for girl and blue for boy? Anywho—"

Guardrail chimed in. "I think we need to boil some water—maybe cut up some sheets. What if we put a knife under the bed? My mama said it would cut her pain in half."

Another contraction hit and I moaned. "Charm—if you love me at all, you will get them the hell out of here," I paused as the vice around my abdomen tightened before ordering, in a voice that sounded nothing like mine, "NOW!"

He reluctantly left my side and stood up. "Outside—go!"

I cried out and he immediately came back over to me, his eyes narrowed with concern. Maybe I should've taken the nurse's advice and gotten the epidural.

He re-wet the washcloth and held it to my forehead as I panted like a madwoman. "I'm gonna call a nurse—you shouldn't have to feel like this."

I shook my head and he glared at me. "Dammit, honey. Ain't no one gonna give you a shiny medal for going through this without pain meds."

The band around my belly tightened, taking my breath away. I attempted to sit up, kicking the blankets off my legs because I just knew that I would feel better if I could sit up and push for a second. Charm gripped my hand and helped me into a sitting position. I leaned forward and grabbed the backs of my knees, letting my body take over. He was right; I was going to get the damn epidural and sleep until this baby decided to show up

"How're we doing in he—Okay, let me just grab your doctor," The nurse quickly said before trying to slip back out.

Charm stopped her. "She's in a lot of pain. Can we get that epidural now?"

She shook her head and said with a laugh. "Honey, I can see the top of that baby's head; we're past the point of medication. And unless you want me to deliver, then I better grab Dr. James."

I made the mistake of glancing toward the mirror and could definitely see a head of dark hair peeking out at me. Charm's eyes followed mine and then he went into full-blown panic mode.

"Jesus—I can pay you. Name the amount—just help her...please." He pleaded.

She began explaining why they couldn't administer anything and I zoned out, envisioning myself unzipping my skin and running from the room. I was not having any more children. Charm would just have to deal.

"Baby, look at me."

I looked up into his amber eyes as he stroked the side of my face with his thumb. "I want you to think about the ledge—just imagine sitting and watching the sun come up. Nobody else is awake; it's just the two of us. Do you see it?"

I nodded before bearing down into a push again.

The doctor and several more nurses rushed in and began prepping the room, but he kept talking, keeping me calm.

"The sky begins to lighten to purple and then pink."

I held onto the sound of his voice and pushed through the pain, imagining myself curled up outside in his arms.

"Neve, we need you to push on the next contraction. Give us

everything you've got," Dr. James sat down on a small stool near the foot of the bed.

Charm had one hand wrapped around my shoulder and his other tightly clenched in mine.

"Kane—I'm scared."

He kissed my temple. "Not my girl—you got this. Where are we right now?"

The contraction was like a band wrapping around the top of my stomach and forcing its way down into my pelvis. I ground my teeth together and pushed, but it felt as if the poor baby's shoulders were hung.

What if they couldn't get him or her out?

"Baby, focus. Where are we?"

I took a deep breath. "On the ledge. Just us."

Dr. James looked up at me. "This is it, Neve. One big push."

I held my breath and gave it my all, feeling a sense of emptiness the minute my body gave the baby up. It was quiet—the only sound in the room came from the suction the nurse was using.

Just as I began to panic, the baby started wailing. "It's a boy!" Dr. James exclaimed as he clipped the cord and handed him off to a nurse.

With a relieved sigh, I fell back against the pillow. Tears fell onto my face, but I couldn't distinguish which ones were mine and which ones belonged to my husband.

"What about Clarence?" Twitch offered.

I shook my head. "Clarence? What does he look like—an eighty-year-old man?"

Rooster peered down to the bundle in my arms. "Well...he's got dark hair, but he seems kind of wrinkly. He could pass for seventy easily, but I think eighty is pushing it."

I stuck my tongue out. "For your information, he has a name—Axel Kane Ryan."

Gunner nodded approvingly. "Amber will love that. She said to tell you that she'll be up here later—Shiloh needed a nap."

It seemed only fitting that a man whose name had meant 'father of peace' would have a daughter whose name meant 'tranquil.' I didn't know when it happened exactly—maybe when he asked her to move in with us; but somewhere along the way, Amber and Gunner had gotten together.

Grumpy had found love.

He was by her side when she gave birth to Shiloh and hadn't wasted any time adopting her either.

I caught PD's eye and winked before mouthing, *'you're next.'*

The color drained from his face as he mumbled, "She told you already?"

I shook my head with a grin. I hadn't known a thing, but it appeared our biker family was going to be getting even bigger in the coming year.

The hospital door opened and Charm slipped in, carrying bags. "Amber packed your bag and the diaper bag—said this was everything you should need. I also snuck out and got you some dinner too."

Axel opened his eyes and blinked several times, obviously awakened by the sound of his daddy's voice. I patted a spot next to me and he set everything down before joining me.

The men were sprawled lazily across the furniture in the room and my heart felt as if it could burst. I was surrounded by my family—after losing my parents, I didn't think I'd be able to say that ever again.

I thought I was running for my life when I was in those woods; and in a way, I was—just not the life I expected. I was running for my future. Every step led me closer to them—men who would sacrifice their own lives for mine, without hesitation. Men who would prove that family isn't always blood—it's the people who keep showing up.

When you least deserve it.

When you're at your absolute worst.

I nestled into Charm's body and smiled. I knew that we would be able to overcome any obstacle that life threw at us. And there wasn't a single doubt in my mind that we would live happily ever after.

The End

In need of another fairytale fix? Are you a fan of *The Little Mermaid*? Then read on for a sneak peek of Through The Water, coming 2/2020.

Not ready to leave the biker world behind? Keep reading for a sneak peek of *Deserter*, book one of the Silent Phoenix MC series.

Want to be the first to know when my books go on sale? Follow me on BookBub!

For new release alerts, follow me on Amazon!

AUTHOR NOTES

In case you may have missed it, this was a modern day take on the tale of *Little Snow White* by the Grimm Brothers. I added some of the *Disney* elements in as the seven men weren't named in the original version.

I liked the idea of a princess who wasn't perfect. Too often, these women are portrayed as being ethereal and it's hard to relate. I needed a heroine who'd made some poor decisions, but still had enough fight in her to turn it around.

As always, my research led me to some unexpected twists and turns in the plot. Fentanyl is indeed a very real drug that, when mixed with other drugs, can quickly prove fatal. It's so potent (fifty times that of heroin) that you can overdose even if it just comes in contact with your skin.

With it being a fairy tale, I added in the fantasy element in terms of what Neve witnesses once she's in a coma. This wasn't too far off though from what addicts have claimed to have experienced after an overdose.

I hadn't planned on incorporating Norse mythology into this book, despite my love of all things Thor, but the mistletoe storyline just worked its way in. Interestingly enough, after I'd added in that aspect, I discovered that the most accurate account of Baldr comes from Jacob Grimm—one half of the Grimm brothers.

The Fairest series will continue with modern day interpretations of old favorites and each book will be a complete standalone.

ALSO BY SHANNON MYERS

From This Day Forward Duet

(David & Elizabeth's Story)

From This Day Forward

Forsaking All Others

Standalone Novels

(Travis & Katya's Story)

You Save Me

Operation Series

(Dakota & Zane's Story)

Operation Fit-ish

(Kate and Nate's Story)

Operation Annulment

Silent Phoenix MC Series

(Grey & Celia's Story)

Deserter (Book One)

Protector (Book Two)

(Mike & Lauren's Story)

Renegade (Book Three)

Traitor (Book Four)

(Full Cast)

Savior (Book Five)

ABOUT THE AUTHOR

Shannon is a born and raised Texan. She grew up inventing clever stories, usually to get herself out of trouble. Her mother was not amused. In junior high, she began writing fractured fairy tales from the villain's point of view and that was the moment she knew that she was going to use her powers for evil instead of good.

In 2003, she moved to Denver and met the love of her life. After some relentless stalking and a few well-timed sarcastic remarks, the man eventually gave in to her charms and wifed her so hard. They welcomed a son in 2007 that they named after their favorite Marvel superhero, Spiderman.

Sick of seeing beautiful mountains through their window every day, the three escaped back to the desolate landscape of the west Texas desert in 2009. She welcomed her second son not long after and soon realized that being surrounded by three men was nothing at all like she'd imagined in her fantasies.

After an unplanned surgery in 2014 and a long pity party, she decided to pen a novel about the worst thing that could happen to a person in order to cheer herself up. She's twisted like that. Thus, From This Day Forward was born and the rest, as they say, is history. Not only does Shannon enjoy stalking people, she also has a fondness for being stalked.

Find her online at: http://shannonshaemyers.com
Or in her reader group, The Forsaken: https://www.facebook.com/groups/630229377127363/

www.ingramcontent.com/pod-product-compliance
Lightning Source LLC
Chambersburg PA
CBHW060948030726
47503CB00003B/786